VAMPIRES IN THE LEMON GROVE

Karen Russell, a native of Miami, has been featured in the *New Yorker*'s debut fiction issue, was chosen as one of Granta's Best Young American Novelists in 2007, and was most recently named one of *New Yorker* magazine's '20 Under 40'. Her first story collection, *St Lucy's Home for Girls Raised by Wolves*, was longlisted for the *Guardian* first book award. Her novel, *Swamplandia!*, was longlisted for the 2011 Orange Prize and shortlisted for the 2012 Pulitzer Prize.

KAREN RUSSELL

Vampires in the Lemon Grove

VINTAGE BOOKS
London

Published by Vintage 2014

2 4 6 8 10 9 7 5 3 1

Selected stories in this work were previously published in the following:
"Vampires in the Lemon Grove" in *Zoetrope: All Story* (2007) and
subsequently in *The Best American Short Stories* (2008) and *Making
Literature Matter, 5th Edition* (2011); "The Barn at the End of Our Term"
in *Granta* (Spring 2007); "The Seagull Army Descends on Strong Beach" in
Tin House (Fall 2009) and subsequently in *The Best American Short Stories*
(2010); "Dougbert Shackleton's Rules for Antarctic Tailgating" in *Tin House*
(Spring 2010); "The Graveless Doll of Eric Mutis" in *Conjunctions* (Fall
2010); "Proving Up" was published as "The Hox River Window" in *Zoetrope:
All Story* (Fall 2011); "Reeling for the Empire" in *Tin House* (Winter 2012);
and 'The New Veterans" in *Granta* (Winter 2013).

First published in Great Britain in 2013 by
Chatto & Windus

Vintage
Random House, 20 Vauxhall Bridge Road,
London SW1V 2SA

www.vintage-books.co.uk

Addresses for companies within The Random House Group Limited
can be found at: www.randomhouse.co.uk/offices.htm

The Random House Group Limited Reg. No. 954009

A CIP catalogue record for this book is available from the British Library

ISBN 9780099578963

The Random House Group Limited supports The Forest Stewardship
Council® (FSC®), the leading international forest-certification organisation.
Our books carrying the FSC label are printed on FSC®-certified paper.
FSC is the only forest-certification scheme supported by the leading
environmental organisations, including Greenpeace. Our
paper procurement policy can be found at
www.randomhouse.co.uk/environment

Printed and bound in Great Britain by Clays Ltd, St Ives plc

For J.T.

CONTENTS

Vampires in the
Lemon Grove

Vampires in the Lemon Grove

In October, the men and women of Sorrento harvest the *primo-fiore*, or "first flowering fruit," the most succulent lemons; in March, the yellow *bianchetti* ripen, followed in June by the green *verdelli*. In every season you can find me sitting at my bench, watching them fall. Only one or two lemons tumble from the branches each hour, but I've been sitting here so long their falls seem contiguous, close as raindrops. My wife has no patience for this sort of meditation. "Jesus Christ, Clyde," she says. "You need a hobby."

Most people mistake me for a small, kindly Italian grandfather, a *nonno*. I have an old *nonno*'s coloring, the dark walnut stain peculiar to southern Italians, a tan that won't fade until I die (which I never will). I wear a neat periwinkle shirt, a canvas sunhat, black suspenders that sag at my chest. My loafers are battered but always polished. The few visitors to the lemon grove who notice me smile blankly into my raisin face and catch the whiff of some sort of tragedy; they whisper that I am a widower, or an old man who has survived his children. They never guess that I am a vampire.

Santa Francesca's Lemon Grove, where I spend my days and nights, was part of a Jesuit convent in the 1800s. Today it's privately owned by the Alberti family, the prices are excessive, and the locals know to buy their lemons elsewhere. In summers a teenage girl named Fila mans a wooden stall at the back of the grove. She's painfully thin, with heavy black bangs. I can tell by the careful way she saves the best lemons for me, slyly kicking them under my bench, that she knows I am a monster. Sometimes she'll smile vacantly in my direction, but she never gives me any trouble. And because of her benevolent indifference to me, I feel a swell of love for the girl.

Fila makes the lemonade and monitors the hot dog machine, watching the meat rotate on wire spigots. I'm fascinated by this machine. The Italian name for it translates as "carousel of beef." Who would have guessed at such a device two hundred years ago? Back then we were all preoccupied with visions of apocalypse; Santa Francesca, the foundress of this very grove, gouged out her eyes while dictating premonitions of fire. What a shame, I often think, that she foresaw only the end times, never hot dogs.

A sign posted just outside the grove reads:

CIGERETTE PIE

HEAT DOGS

GRANITE DRINKS

Santa Francesca's Limonata—

THE MOST REFRISHING DRANK ON THE PLENET!!

Every day, tourists from Wales and Germany and America are ferried over from cruise ships to the base of these cliffs. They ride the funicular up here to visit the grove, to eat "heat dogs" with speckly brown mustard and sip lemon ices. They snap photographs of the Alberti brothers, Benny and Luciano, teenage twins who cling to the trees' wooden supports and make a grudging show of harvesting lemons, who spear each other with trowels and refer to the tourist women as "vaginas" in Italian slang. "*Buona sera,* vaginas!" they cry from the trees. I think the tourists are getting stupider. None of them speak Italian anymore, and these new women seem deaf to aggression. Often I fantasize about flashing my fangs at the brothers, just to keep them in line.

As I said, the tourists usually ignore me; perhaps it's the dominoes. A few years back, I bought a battered red set from Benny, a prop piece, and this makes me invisible, sufficiently banal to be hidden in plain sight. I have no real interest in the game; I mostly stack the pieces into little houses and corrals.

At sunset, the tourists all around begin to shout. "Look! Up there!" It's time for the path of *I Pipistrelli Impazziti*—the descent of the bats.

They flow from cliffs that glow like pale chalk, expelled from caves in the seeming billions. Their drop is steep and vertical, a black hail. Sometimes a change in weather sucks a bat beyond the lemon trees and into the turquoise sea. It's three hundred feet to the lemon grove, six hundred feet to the churning foam of the Tyrrhenian. At the precipice, they soar upward and crash around the green tops of the trees.

"Oh!" the tourists shriek, delighted, ducking their heads.

Up close, the bats' spread wings are alien membranes—fragile, like something internal flipped out. The waning sun washes their bodies a dusky red. They have wrinkled black faces, these bats, tiny, like gargoyles or angry grandfathers. They have teeth like mine.

Tonight, one of the tourists, a Texan lady with a big strawberry red updo, has successfully captured a bat in her hair, simultaneously crying real tears and howling: "TAKE THE GODDAMN PICTURE, Sarah!"

I stare ahead at a fixed point above the trees and light a cigarette. My bent spine goes rigid. Mortal terror always trips some old wire that leaves me sad and irritable. It will be whole minutes now before everybody stops screaming.

THE MOON IS a muted shade of orange. Twin disks of light burn in the sky and the sea. I scan the darker indents in the skyline, the cloudless spots that I know to be caves. I check my watch again. It's eight o'clock, and all the bats have disappeared into the interior branches. Where is Magreb? My fangs are throbbing, but I won't start without her.

I once pictured time as a black magnifying glass and myself as a microscopic flightless insect trapped in that circle of night. But then Magreb came along, and eternity ceased to frighten me. Suddenly each moment followed its antecedent in a neat chain, moments we filled with each other.

I watch a single bat falling from the cliffs, dropping like a stone: headfirst, motionless, dizzying to witness.

Pull up.

I close my eyes. I press my palms flat against the picnic table and tense the muscles of my neck.

Pull UP. I tense until my temples pulse, until little black-and-red stars flutter behind my eyelids.

"You can look now."

Magreb is sitting on the bench, blinking her bright pumpkin eyes. "You weren't even *watching*. If you saw me coming down, you'd know you have nothing to worry about." I try to smile at her and find I can't. My own eyes feel like ice cubes.

"It's stupid to go so fast." I don't look at her. "That easterly could knock you over the rocks."

"Don't be ridiculous. I'm an excellent flier."

She's right. Magreb can shape-shift midair, much more smoothly than I ever could. Even back in the 1850s, when I used to transmute into a bat two, three times a night, my metamorphosis was a shy, halting process.

"Look!" she says, triumphant, mocking. "You're still trembling!"

I look down at my hands, angry to realize it's true.

Magreb roots through the tall, black blades of grass. "It's late, Clyde; where's my lemon?"

I pluck a soft, round lemon from the grass, a summer moon, and hand it to her. The *verdelli* I have chosen is perfect, flawless. She looks at it with distaste and makes a big show of brushing off a marching ribbon of ants.

"A toast!" I say.

"A toast," Magreb replies, with the rote enthusiasm of a Christian saying grace. We lift the lemons and swing them to our faces. We plunge our fangs, piercing the skin, and emit a long, united hiss: *"Aaah!"*

OVER THE YEARS, Magreb and I have tried everything—fangs in apples, fangs in rubber balls. We have lived everywhere: Tunis, Laos, Cincinnati, Salamanca. We spent our honeymoon hopping continents, hunting liquid chimeras: mint tea in Fez, coconut slurries in Oahu, jet-black coffee in Bogotá, jackal's milk in Dakar, Cherry Coke floats in rural Alabama, a thousand beverages purported to have magical quenching properties. We went thirsty in every region of the globe before finding our oasis here, in the blue boot of Italy, at this dead nun's lemonade stand. It's only these lemons that give us any relief.

When we first landed in Sorrento I was skeptical. The pitcher of lemonade we ordered looked cloudy and adulterated. Sugar clumped at the bottom. I took a gulp, and a whole small lemon lodged in my mouth; there is no word sufficiently lovely for the first taste, the first feeling of my fangs in that lemon. It was bracingly sour, with a delicate hint of ocean salt. After an initial prickling—a

sort of chemical effervescence along my gums—a soothing blankness traveled from the tip of each fang to my fevered brain. These
lemons are a vampire's analgesic. If you have been thirsty for a long
time, if you have been suffering, then the absence of those two
feelings—however brief—becomes a kind of heaven. I breathed
deeply through my nostrils. My throbbing fangs were still.

By daybreak, the numbness had begun to wear off. The lemons relieve our thirst without ending it, like a drink we can hold
in our mouths but never swallow. Eventually the original hunger
returns. I have tried to be very good, very correct and conscien-
tious about not confusing this original hunger with the thing I
feel for Magreb.

I CAN'T JOKE about my early years on the blood, can't even
think about them without guilt and acidic embarrassment. Unlike
Magreb, who has never had a sip of the stuff, I listened to the village gossips and believed every rumor, internalized every report
of corrupted bodies and boiled blood. Vampires were the favorite
undead of the Enlightenment, and as a young boy I aped the diction
and mannerisms I read about in books: Vlad the Impaler, Count
Heinrich the Despoiler, Goethe's bloodsucking bride of Corinth.
I eavesdropped on the terrified prayers of an old woman in a cemetery, begging God to protect her from . . . me. I felt a dislocation
then, a spreading numbness, as if I were invisible or already dead.
After that, I did only what the stories suggested, beginning with
that old woman's blood. I slept in coffins, in black cedar boxes,
and woke every night with a fierce headache. I was famished,
perennially dizzy. I had unspeakable dreams about the sun.

In practice I was no suave viscount, just a teenager in a red
velvet cape, awkward and voracious. I wanted to touch the edges
of my life—the same instinct, I think, that inspires young mortals
to flip tractors and enlist in foreign wars. One night I skulked into

a late Mass with some vague plan to defeat eternity. At the back of the nave, I tossed my mousy curls, rolled my eyes heavenward, and then plunged my entire arm into the bronze pail of holy water. Death would be painful, probably, but I didn't care about pain. I wanted to overturn my sentence. It was working; I could feel the burn beginning to spread. Actually, it was more like an itch, but I was sure the burning would start any second. I slid into a pew, snug in my misery, and waited for my body to turn to ash.

By sunrise, I'd developed a rash between my eyebrows, a little late-flowering acne, but was otherwise fine, and I understood I truly was immortal. At that moment I yielded all discrimination; I bit anyone kind or slow enough to let me get close: men, women, even some older boys and girls. The littlest children I left alone, very proud at the time of this one scruple. I'd read stories about Hungarian *vampirs* who drank the blood of orphan girls, and mentioned this to Magreb early on, hoping to impress her with my decency. *Not children!* she wept.

She wept for a day and a half.

Our first date was in Cementerio de Colón, if I can call a chance meeting between headstones a date. I had been stalking her, following her swishing hips as she took a shortcut through the cemetery grass. She wore her hair in a low, snaky braid that was coming unraveled. When I was near enough to touch her trailing ribbon she whipped around. "Are you following me?" she asked, annoyed, not scared. She regarded my face with the contempt of a woman confronting the town drunk. "Oh," she said, "your teeth . . ."

And then she grinned. Magreb was the first and only other vampire I'd ever met. We bared our fangs over a tombstone and recognized each other. There is a loneliness that must be particular to monsters, I think, the feeling that each is the only child of a species. And now that loneliness was over.

Our first date lasted all night. Magreb's talk seemed to lunge forward like a train without a conductor; I suspect even she didn't know what she was saying. I certainly wasn't paying attention, staring dopily at her fangs, and then I heard her ask: "So, when did you figure out that the blood does nothing?"

At the time of this conversation, I was edging on 130. I had never gone a day since early childhood without drinking several pints of blood. *The blood does nothing?* My forehead burned and burned.

"Didn't you think it suspicious that you had a heartbeat?" she asked me. "That you had a reflection in water?"

When I didn't answer, Magreb went on, "Every time I saw my own face in a mirror, I knew I wasn't any of those ridiculous things, a bloodsucker, a *sanguina*. You know?"

"Sure," I said, nodding. For me, mirrors had the opposite effect: I saw a mouth ringed in black blood. I saw the pale son of the villagers' fears.

THOSE INITIAL DAYS with Magreb nearly undid me. At first my euphoria was sharp and blinding, all my thoughts spooling into a single blue thread of relief—*The blood does nothing! I don't have to drink the blood!*—but when that subsided, I found I had nothing left. If we didn't have to drink the blood, then what on earth were these fangs for?

Sometimes I think she preferred me then: I was like her own child, raw and amazed. We smashed my coffin with an ax and spent the night at a hotel. I lay there wide-eyed in the big bed, my heart thudding like a fish tail against the floor of a boat.

"You're really sure?" I whispered to her. "I don't have to sleep in a coffin? I don't have to sleep through the day?" She had already drifted off.

A few months later, she suggested a picnic.

"But the sun."

Magreb shook her head. "You poor thing, believing all that garbage."

By this time we'd found a dirt cellar in which to live in Western Australia, where the sun burned through the clouds like dining lace. That sun ate lakes, rising out of dead volcanoes at dawn, triple the size of a harvest moon and skull-white, a grass-scorcher. Go ahead, try to walk into that sun when you've been told your bones are tinder.

I stared at the warped planks of the trapdoor above us, the copper ladder that led rung by rung to the bright world beyond. Time fell away from me and I was a child again, afraid, afraid. Magreb rested her hand on the small of my back. "You can do it," she said, nudging me gently. I took a deep breath and hunched my shoulders, my scalp grazing the cellar door, my hair soaked through with sweat. I focused my thoughts to still the tremors, lest my fangs slice the inside of my mouth, and turned my face away from Magreb.

"Go on."

I pushed up and felt the wood give way. Light exploded through the cellar. My pupils shrank to dots.

Outside, the whole world was on fire. Mute explosions rocked the scrubby forest, motes of light burning like silent rockets. The sun fell through the eucalyptus and Australian pines in bright red bars. I pulled myself out onto my belly, balled up in the soil, and screamed for mercy until I'd exhausted myself. Then I opened one watery eye and took a long look around. The sun wasn't fatal! It was just uncomfortable, making my eyes itch and water and inducing a sneezing attack.

After that, and for the whole of our next thirty years together, I watched the auroral colors and waited to feel anything but terror. Fingers of light spread across the gray sea toward me, and I couldn't see these colors as beautiful. The sky I lived under was a hideous, lethal mix of orange and pink, a physical deformity. By the 1950s we were living in a Cincinnati suburb; and as the day's first light hit the kitchen windows, I'd press my face against the linoleum and gibber my terror into the cracks.

"Sooo," Magreb would say, "I can tell you're not a morning person." Then she'd sit on the porch swing and rock with me, patting my hand.

"What's wrong, Clyde?"

I shook my head. This was a new sadness, difficult to express. My bloodlust was undiminished but now the blood wouldn't fix it.

"It never fixed it," Magreb reminded me, and I wished she would please stop talking.

That cluster of years was a very confusing period. Mostly I felt grateful, aboveground feelings. I was in love. For a vampire, my life was very normal. Instead of stalking prostitutes, I went on long bicycle rides with Magreb. We visited botanical gardens and rowed in boats. In a short time, my face had gone from lithium white to the color of milky coffee. Yet sometimes, especially at high noon, I'd study Magreb's face with a hot, illogical hatred, each pore opening up to swallow me. *You've ruined my life,* I'd think. To correct for her power over my mind I tried to fanta-size about mortal women, their wild eyes and bare swan necks; I couldn't do it, not anymore—an eternity of vague female smiles eclipsed by Magreb's tiny razor fangs. Two gray tabs against her lower lip.

But like I said, I was mostly happy. I was making a kind of progress.

One night, children wearing necklaces of garlic bulbs arrived giggling at our door. It was Halloween; they were vampire hunt-ers. The smell of garlic blasted through the mail slot, along with their voices: "Trick or treat!" In the old days, I would have cow-ered from these children. I would have run downstairs to barri-cade myself in my coffin. But that night, I pulled on an undershirt and opened the door. I stood in a square of green light in my boxer shorts hefting a bag of Tootsie Pops, a small victory over the old fear.

"Mister, you okay?"

I blinked down at a little blond child and then saw that my two hands were shaking violently, soundlessly, like old friends wishing not to burden me with their troubles. I dropped the candies into the children's bags, thinking: *You small mortals don't realize the power of your stories.*

WE WERE DOWNING strawberry velvet cocktails on the Seine when something inside me changed. Thirty years. Eleven thousand dawns. That's how long it took for me to believe the sun wouldn't kill me.

"Want to go see a museum or something? We're in Paris, after all."

"Okay."

We walked over a busy pedestrian bridge in a flood of light, and my heart was in my throat. Without any discussion, I understood that Magreb was my wife.

Because I love her, my hunger pangs have gradually mellowed into a comfortable despair. Sometimes I think of us as two holes cleaved together, two twin hungers. Our bellies growl at each other like companionable dogs. I love the sound, assuring me we're equals in our thirst. We bump our fangs and feel like we're coming up against the same hard truth.

Human marriages amuse me: the brevity of the commitment and all the ceremony that surrounds it, the calla lilies, the veiled mother-in-laws like lilac spiders, the tears and earnest toasts. Till death do us part! Easy. These mortal couples need only keep each other in sight for fifty, sixty years.

Often I wonder to what extent a mortal's love grows from the bedrock of his or her foreknowledge of death, love coiling like a green stem out of that blankness in a way I'll never quite understand. And lately I've been having a terrible thought: *Our love affair will end before the world does.*

One day, without any preamble, Magreb flew up to the caves. She called over her furry, muscled shoulder that she just wanted to sleep for a while.

"What? Wait! What's wrong?"

I'd caught her mid-shift, halfway between a wife and a bat.

"Don't be so sensitive, Clyde! I'm just tired of this century, so very tired, maybe it's the heat? I think I need a little rest . . ."

I assumed this was an experiment, like my cape, an old habit to which she was returning, and from the clumsy, ambivalent way she crashed around on the wind I understood I was supposed to follow her. Well, too bad. Magreb likes to say she freed me, disabused me of the old stories, but I gave up more than I intended: I can't shudder myself out of this old man's body. I can't fly anymore.

FILA AND I are alone. I press my dry lips together and shove dominoes around the table; they buckle like the cars of a tiny train.

"More lemonade, *nonno*?" She smiles. She leans from her waist and boldly touches my right fang, a thin string of hanging drool. "Looks like you're thirsty."

"Please," I gesture at the bench. "Have a seat."

Fila is seventeen now and has known about me for some time. She's toying with the idea of telling her boss, weighing the sentence within her like a bullet in a gun: *There is a vampire in our grove.*

"You don't believe me, Signore Alberti?" she'll say, before taking him by the wrist and leading him to this bench, and I'll choose that moment to rise up and bite him in his hog-thick neck. "Right through his stupid tie!" she says with a grin.

But this is just idle fantasy, she assures me. Fila is content to let me alone. "You remind me of my *nonno,*" she says approvingly, "you look very Italian."

In fact, she wants to help me hide here. It gives her a warm feeling to do so, like helping her own fierce *nonno* do up the small buttons of his trousers, now too intricate a maneuver for his palsied hands. She worries about me, too. And she should: lately I've gotten sloppy, incontinent about my secrets. I've stopped polishing my shoes; I let the tip of one fang hang over my pink lip. "You must be more careful," she reprimands. "There are tourists *everywhere.*"

I study her neck as she says this, her head rolling with the natural expressiveness of a girl. She checks to see if I am watching her collarbone, and I let her see that I am. I feel like a threat again.

LAST NIGHT I went on a rampage. On my seventh lemon I found with a sort of drowsy despair that I couldn't stop. I crawled around on all fours looking for the last *bianchettis* in the dewy grass: soft with rot, mildewed, sun-shriveled, blackened. Lemon skin bulging with tiny cellophane-green worms. Dirt smells, rain smells, all swirled through with the tart sting of decay.

In the morning, Magreb steps around the wreckage and doesn't say a word.

"I came up with a new name," I say, hoping to distract her. "*Brandolino.* What do you think?"

I have spent the last several years trying to choose an Italian name, and every day that I remain Clyde feels like a defeat. Our names are relics of the places we've been. "Clyde" is a souvenir from the California Gold Rush. I was callow and blood-crazed back then, and I saw my echo in the freckly youths panning along the Sacramento River. I used the name as a kind of bait.

"Clyde" sounded innocuous, like someone a boy might get a malt beer with or follow into the woods.

Magreb chose her name in the Atlas Mountains for its etymology, the root word *ghuroob,* which means "to set" or "to be hidden." "That's what we're looking for," she tells me. "The setting place. Some final answer." She won't change her name until we find it.

She takes a lemon from her mouth, slides it down the length of her fangs, and places its shriveled core on the picnic table. When she finally speaks, her voice is so low the words are almost unintelligible.

"The lemons aren't working, Clyde."

But the lemons have never worked. At best, they give us eight hours of peace. We aren't talking about the lemons.

"How long?"

"Longer than I've let on. I'm sorry."

"Well, maybe it's this crop. Those Alberti boys haven't been fertilizing properly, maybe the *primofiore* will turn out better."

Magreb fixes me with one fish-bright eye. "Clyde, I think it's time for us to go."

Wind blows the leaves apart. Lemons wink like a firmament of yellow stars, slowly ripening, and I can see the other, truer night behind them.

"Go where?" Our marriage, as I conceive it, is a commitment to starve together.

"We've been resting here for decades. I think it's time . . . what is that thing?"

I have been preparing a present for Magreb, for our anniversary, a "cave" of scavenged materials—newspaper and bottle glass and wooden beams from the lemon tree supports—so that she can sleep down here with me. I've smashed dozens of bottles of fruity beer to make stalactites. Looking at it now, though, I see the cave is very small. It looks like an umbrella mauled by a dog.

"That thing?" I say. "That's nothing. I think it's part of the hot dog machine."

"Jesus. Did it catch on fire?"

"Yes. The girl threw it out yesterday."

"Clyde." Magreb shakes her head. "We never meant to stay here forever, did we? That was never the plan."

"I didn't know we had a plan," I snap. "What if we've outlived our food supply? What if there's nothing left for us to find?"

"You don't really believe that."

"Why can't you just be grateful? Why can't you be happy and admit defeat? Look at what we've found here!" I grab a lemon and wave it in her face.

"Good night, Clyde."

I watch my wife fly up into the watery dawn, and again I feel the awful tension. In the flats of my feet, in my knobbed spine. Love has infected me with a muscular superstition that one body can do the work of another.

I consider taking the funicular, the ultimate degradation—worse than the dominoes, worse than an eternity of sucking cut lemons. All day I watch the cars ascend, and I'm reminded of those American fools who accompany their wives to the beach but refuse to wear bathing suits. I've seen them by the harbor, sulking in their trousers, panting through menthol cigarettes and pacing the dock while the women sea-bathe. They pretend they don't mind when sweat darkens the armpits of their suits. When their wives swim out and leave them. When their wives are just a splash in the distance.

Tickets for the funicular are twenty lire. I sit at the bench and count as the cars go by.

THAT EVENING, I take Magreb on a date. I haven't left the lemon grove in upward of two years, and blood roars in my ears as I stand and clutch at her like an old man. We're going to the Thursday night show at an antique theater in a castle in the center of town. I want her to see that I'm happy to travel with her, so long as our destination is within walking distance.

A teenage usher in a vintage red jacket with puffed sleeves escorts us to our seats, his biceps manacled in clouds, threads loosening from the badge on his chest. I am jealous of the name there: GUGLIELMO.

The movie's title is already scrolling across the black screen: SOMETHING CLANDESTINE IS HAPPENING IN THE CORN!

Magreb snorts. "That's a pretty lousy name for a horror movie. It sounds like a student film."

"Here's your ticket," I say. "I didn't make the title up."

It's a vampire movie set in the Dust Bowl. Magreb expects a comedy, but the Dracula actor fills me with the sadness of an old photo album. An Okie has unwittingly fallen in love with the monster, whom she's mistaken for a rich European creditor eager to pay off the mortgage on her family's farm.

"That Okie," says Magreb, "is an idiot."

I turn my head miserably and there's Fila, sitting two rows in front of us with a greasy young man. Benny Alberti. Her white neck is bent to the left, Benny's lips affixed to it as she impassively sips a soda.

"Poor thing," Magreb whispers, indicating the pigtailed actress. "She thinks he's going to save her."

Dracula shows his fangs, and the Okie flees through a cornfield. Cornstalks smack her face. "Help!" she screams to a sky full of crows. "He's not actually from Europe!"

There is no music, only the girl's breath and the *fwap-fwap-fwap* of the off-screen fan blades. Dracula's mouth hangs wide as a sewer grate. His cape is curiously still.

The movie picture is frozen. The *fwap*ping is emanating from the projection booth; it rises to a grinding *r-r-r*, followed by lyrical

Italian cussing and silence and finally a tidal sigh. Magreb shifts in her seat.

"Let's wait," I say, seized with empathy for these two still figures on the screen, mutely pleading for repair. "They'll fix it."

People begin to file out of the theater, first in twos and threes and then in droves. "I'm tired, Clyde."

"Don't you want to know what happens?" My voice is more frantic than I intend.

"I already know what happens."

"Don't you leave now, Magreb. I'm telling you, they're going to fix it. If you leave now, that's it for us, I'll never . . ."

Her voice is beautiful, like gravel underfoot: "I'm going to the caves."

I'M ALONE in the theater. When I turn to exit, the picture is still frozen, the Okie's blue dress floating over windless corn, Dracula's mouth a hole in his white greasepaint.

Outside I see Fila standing in a clot of her friends, lit by the marquee. These kids wear too much makeup and clothes that move like colored oils. They all look rained on. I scowl at them and they scowl back, and then Fila crosses to me.

"Hey, you," she says, grinning, breathless, so very close to my face. "Are you stalking somebody?"

My throat tightens.

"Guys!" Her eyes gleam. "Guys, come over and meet the *vampire*."

But the kids are gone.

"Well! Some friends," she says, then winks. "Leaving me alone, defenseless . . ."

"You want the old vampire to bite you, eh?" I hiss. "You want a story for your friends?"

Fila laughs. Her horror is a round, genuine thing, bouncing in both her black eyes. She smells like hard water and glycerin. The hum of her young life all around me makes it difficult to think. A bat filters my thoughts, opens its trembling lampshade wings.

Magreb. She'll want to hear about this. How ridiculous, at my age, to find myself down this alley with a young girl: Fila powdering her neck, doing her hair up with little temptress pins, yanking me behind this Dumpster. "Can you imagine"—Magreb will laugh—"a teenager goading you to attack her! You're still a menace, Clyde."

I stare vacantly at a pale mole above the girl's collarbone. *Magreb,* I think again, and I smile, and the smile feels like a muzzle stretched taut against my teeth. It seems my hand has tightened on the girl's wrist, and I realize with surprise, as if from a great distance, that she is twisting away.

"Hey, *nonno,* come on now, what are you—"

THE GIRL'S HEAD lolls against my shoulder like a sleepy child's, then swings forward in a rag-doll circle. The starlight is white mercury compared to her blotted-out eyes. There's a dark stain on my periwinkle shirt, and one suspender has snapped. I sit Fila's body against the alley wall, watch it dim and stiffen. Spidery graffiti weaves over the brick behind her, and I scan for some answer contained there: GIOVANNA & FABIANO. VAFFANCULO! VAI IN CULO.

A scabby-furred creature, our only witness, arches its orange back against the Dumpster. If not for the lock I would ease the girl inside. I would climb in with her and let the red stench fill my nostrils, let the flies crawl into the red corners of my eyes. I am a monster again.

I ransack Fila's pockets and find the key to the funicular office, careful not to look at her face. Then I'm walking, running for the lemon grove. I jimmy my way into the control room and turn the silver key, relieved to hear the engine roar to life. Locked, locked, every funicular car is locked, but then I find one with thick tape in *X*s over a busted door. I dash after it and pull myself onto the cushion, quickly, because the cars are already moving. Even now, after what I've done, I am still unable to fly, still imprisoned in my wretched *nonno*'s body, reduced to using the mortals' machinery to carry me up to find my wife. The box jounces and trembles. The chain pulls me into the heavens link by link.

My lips are soon chapped; I stare through a crack in the glass window. The box swings wildly in the wind. The sky is a deep blue vacuum. I can still smell the girl in the folds of my clothes.

THE CAVE SYSTEM at the top of the cliffs is vaster than I expected; and with their grandfather faces tucked away, the bats are anonymous as stones.

I walk beneath a chandelier of furry bodies, heartbeats wrapped in wings the color of rose petals or corn silk. Breath ripples through each of them, a tiny life in its translucent envelope.

"Magreb?"

Is she up here?

Has she left me?

(I will never find another vampire.)

I double back to the moonlit entrance that leads to the open air of the cliffs, the funicular cars. When I find Magreb, I'll beg her to tell me what she dreams up here. I'll tell her my waking dreams in the lemon grove: The mortal men and women floating serenely by in balloons freighted with the ballast of their deaths. Millions of balloons ride over a wide ocean, lives darkening the sky. Death is a dense powder cinched inside tiny sandbags, and in the dream I am given to understand that instead of a sandbag I have Magreb.

I make the bats' descent in a cable car with no wings to spread, knocked around by the wind with a force that feels personal. I struggle to hold the door shut and look for the green speck of our grove.

The box is plunging now, far too quickly. It swings wide, and the igneous surface of the mountain fills the left window. The tufa shines like water, like a black, heat-bubbled river. For a dizzying instant I expect the rock to seep through the glass.

Each swing takes me higher than the last, a grinding pendulum that approaches a full revolution around the cable. I'm on my hands and knees on the car floor, seasick in the high air, pressing my face against the floor grate. I can see stars or boats burning there, and also a ribbon of white, a widening fissure. Air gushes through the cracks in the glass box. With a lurch of surprise, I realize that I could die.

WHAT DOES MAGREB SEE, if she is watching? Is she waking from a nightmare to see the line snap, the glass box plummet? From her inverted vantage, dangling from the roof of the cave, does the car seem to be sucked upward, rushing not toward the sea but into another sort of sky? To a black mouth open and foaming with stars?

I like to picture my wife like this: Magreb shuts her thin eyelids tighter. She digs her claws into the rock. Little clouds of dust plume around her toes as she swings upside down. She feels something growing inside her, a dreadful suspicion. It is solid, this new thing, it is the opposite of hunger. She's emerging from a dream of distant thunder, rumbling and loose. Something has happened tonight that she thought impossible. In the morning, she will want to tell me about it.

Reeling for the Empire

Several of us claim to have been the daughters of samurai, but
of course there is no way for anyone to verify that now. It's a
relief, in its way, the new anonymity. We come here tall and
thin, noblewomen from Yamaguchi, graceful as calligraphy; short
and poor, Hida girls with bloody feet, crow-voiced and vulgar;
entrusted to the Model Mill by our teary mothers; rented out
by our destitute uncles—but within a day or two the drink the
Recruitment Agent gave us begins to take effect. And the more
our *kaiko*-bodies begin to resemble one another, the more frantically each factory girl works to reinvent her past. One of the
consequences of our captivity here in Nowhere Mill, and of the
darkness that pools on the factory floor, and of the polar fur that
covers our faces, blanking us all into sisters, is that anybody can be
anyone she likes in the past. Some of our lies are quite bold: Yuna
says that her great-uncle has a scrap of sailcloth from the Black
Ships. Dai claims that she knelt alongside her samurai father at the
Battle of Shiroyama. Nishi fibs that she once stowed away in the
imperial caboose from Shimbashi Station to Yokohama, and saw
Emperor Meiji eating pink cake. Back in Gifu I had tangly hair

like a donkey's tail, a mouth like a small red bean, but I tell the others that I was very beautiful.

"Where are you from?" they ask me.

"The castle in Gifu, perhaps you know it from the famous woodblocks? My great-grandfather was a warrior."

"Oh! But Kitsune, we thought you said your father was the one who printed the woodblocks? The famous *ukiyo-e* artist, Utagawa Kuniyoshi . . ."

"Yes. He was, yesterday."

I'll put it bluntly: we are all becoming reelers. Some kind of hybrid creature, part *kaiko,* silkworm caterpillar, and part human female. Some of the older workers' faces are already quite covered with a coarse white fur, but my face and thighs stayed smooth for twenty days. In fact I've only just begun to grow the white hair on my belly. During my first nights and days in the silk-reeling factory I was always shaking. I have never been a hysterical person, and so at first I misread these tremors as mere mood; I was in the clutches of a giddy sort of terror, I thought. Then the roiling feeling became solid. It was the thread: a color purling invisibly in my belly. Silk. Yards and yards of thin color would soon be extracted from me by the Machine.

Today, the Agent drops off two new recruits, sisters from the Yamagata Prefecture, a blue village called Sakegawa, which none of us have visited. They are the daughters of a salmon fisherman and their names are Tooka and Etsuyo. They are twelve and nineteen. Tooka has a waist-length braid and baby fat; Etsuyo looks like a forest doe, with her long neck and watchful brown eyes. We step into the light and Etsuyo swallows her scream. Tooka starts wailing—"Who are you? What's happened to you? What is this place?"

Dai crosses the room to them, and despite their terror the Sakegawa sisters are too sleepy and too shocked to recoil from her embrace. They appear to have drunk the tea very recently, because they're quaking on their feet. Etsuyo's eyes cross as if she is about to faint. Dai unrolls two tatami mats in a dark corner, helps them to stretch out. "Sleep a little," she whispers. "Dream."

"Is this the silk-reeling factory?" slurs Tooka, half-conscious on her bedroll.

"Oh, yes," Dai says. Her furry face hovers like a moon above them.

Tooka nods, satisfied, as if willing to dismiss all of her terror to continue believing in the Agent's promises, and shuts her eyes.

Sometimes when the new recruits confide the hopes that brought them to our factory, I have to suppress a bitter laugh. Long before the *kaiko* change turned us into mirror images of one another, we were sisters already, spinning identical dreams in beds thousands of miles apart, fantasizing about gold silks and an "imperial vocation." We envisioned our future dowries, our families' miraculous freedom from debt. We thrilled to the same tales of women working in the grand textile mills, where steel machines from Europe gleamed in the light of the Meiji sunrise. Our world had changed so rapidly in the wake of the Black Ships that the poets could barely keep pace with the scenes outside their own windows. Industry, trade, unstoppable growth: years before the Agent came to find us, our dreams anticipated his promises.

Since my arrival here, my own fantasies have grown as dark as the room. In them I snip a new girl's thread midair, or yank all the silk out of her at once, so that she falls lifelessly forward like a *Bunraku* puppet. I haven't been able to cry since my first night here—but often I feel a water pushing at my skull. "Can the thread migrate to your brain?" I've asked Dai nervously. Silk starts as a liquid. Right now I can feel it traveling below my navel, my thread. Foaming icily along the lining of my stomach. Under the blankets I watch it rise in a hard lump. There are twenty workers sleeping on twelve tatami, two rows of us, our heads ten centimeters apart, our earlobes curled like snails on adjacent leaves, and though we are always hungry, every one of us has a round belly. Most nights I can barely sleep, moaning for dawn and the Machine.

Every aspect of our new lives, from working to sleeping, eating and shitting, bathing when we can get wastewater from the Machine, is conducted in one brick room. The far wall has a single oval window, set high in its center. Too high for us to see much besides scraps of cloud and a woodpecker that is like a celebrity to us, provoking gasps and applause every time he appears. *Kaiko-joko,* we call ourselves. Silkworm-workers. Unlike regular *joko,* we have no foreman or men. We are all alone in the box of this room. Dai says that she's the dormitory supervisor, but that's Dai's game.

We were all brought here by the same man, the factory Recruitment Agent. A representative, endorsed by Emperor Meiji himself, from the new Ministry for the Promotion of Industry.

We were all told slightly different versions of the same story.

Our fathers or guardians signed contracts that varied only slightly in their terms, most promising a five-yen advance for one year of our lives.

The Recruitment Agent travels the countryside to recruit female workers willing to travel far from their home prefectures to a new European-style silk-reeling mill. Presumably, he is out recruiting now. He makes his pitch not to the woman herself but to her father or guardian, or in some few cases, where single women cannot be procured, her husband. I am here on behalf of the nation, he begins. In the spirit of *Shokusan-Kōgyō. Increase production, encourage industry.* We are recruiting only the most skillful and loyal mill workers, he continues. Not just peasant girls—like your offspring, he might say with his silver tongue to men in the Gifu and Mie prefectures—but the well-bred daughters of noblemen. Samurai and aristocrats. City-born governors have begged me to train their daughters on the Western technologies. Last week, the Medical General of the Imperial Army sent his nineteen-year-old twins, by train! Sometimes there is resistance from the father or guardian, especially among the hicks, those stony-faced men from distant centuries who still make bean paste, wade into rice paddies, brew sake using thousand-year-old methods; but the Agent waves all qualms away—Ah, you've heard about x-Mill or y-Factory? No, the French *yatoi* engineers don't drink girls' blood, haha, that is what they call *red wine.* Yes, there *was* a fire at Aichi Factory, a little trouble with tuberculosis in Suwa. But our factory is quite different—it is a national secret. Yes, a place that makes even the French filature in the backwoods of Gunma, with its brick walls and steam engines, look antiquated! This phantom factory he presents to her father or guardian with great cheerfulness and urgency, for he says we have awoken to dawn, the Enlightened Era of the Meiji, and we must all play our role now. Japan's silk is her world export. The Blight in Europe, the pébrine virus, has killed every silkworm, forever halted the Westerners' cocoon production. The demand is as vast as the ocean. This is the moment to seize. Silk-reeling is a sacred vocation—she will be reeling for the empire.

The fathers and guardians nearly always sign the contract. Publicly, the *joko*'s family will share a cup of hot tea with the Agent. They celebrate her new career and the five-yen advance against her legally mortgaged future. Privately, an hour or so later, the Agent will share a special toast with the girl herself.

The Agent improvises his tearooms: an attic in a forest inn or a locked changing room in a bathhouse or, in the case of Iku, an abandoned cowshed.

After sunset, the old blind woman arrives. "The zookeeper," we call her. She hauls our food to the grated door, unbars the lower panel. We pass her that day's skeins of reeled silk, and she pushes two sacks of mulberry leaves through the panel with a long stick. The woman never speaks to us, no matter what questions we shout at her. She simply waits, patiently, for our skeins, and so long as they are acceptable in quality and weight, she slides in our leaves. Tonight she has also slid in a tray of steaming human food for the new recruits. Tooka and Etsuyo get cups of rice and miso soup with floating carrots. Hunks of real ginger are unraveling in the broth, like hair. We all sit on the opposite side of the room and watch them chew with a dewy nostalgia that disgusts me even as I find myself ogling their long white fingers on their chopsticks, the balls of rice. The salt and fat smells of their food make my eyes ache. When we eat the mulberry leaves, we lower our new faces to the floor.

They drink down the soup in silence. "Are we dreaming?" I hear one whisper.

"The tea drugged us!" the younger sister, Tooka, cries at last. Her gaze darts here and there, as if she's hoping to be contradicted. They traveled nine days by riverboat and oxcart, Etsuyo tells us, wearing blindfolds the entire time. So we could be that far north of Yamagata, or west. Or east, the younger sister says. We collect facts from every new *kaiko-joko* and use them to draw thread maps of Japan on the factory floor. But not even Tsuki the Apt can guess our whereabouts.

Nowhere Mill, we call this place.

Dai crosses the room and speaks soothingly to the sisters; then she leads them right to me. Oh, happy day. I glare at her through an unchewed mouthful of leaves.

"Kitsune is quite a veteran now," says smiling Dai, leading the fishy sisters to me, "she will show you around—"

I hate this part. But you have to tell the new ones what's in store for them. Minds have been spoiled by the surprise.

"Will the manager of this factory be coming soon?" Etsuyo asks, in a grave voice. "I think there has been a mistake."

"We don't belong here!" Tooka breathes.

There's nowhere else for you now, I say, staring at the floor. That tea he poured into you back in Sakegawa? The Agent's drink is remaking your insides. Your intestines, your secret organs. Soon your stomachs will bloat. You will manufacture silk in your gut with the same helpless skill that you digest food, exhale. The *kaiko*-change, he calls it. A revolutionary process. Not even Chiyo, who knows sericulture, has ever heard of a tea that turns girls into silkworms. We think the tea may have been created abroad, by French chemists or British engineers. *Yatoi*-tea. Unless it's the Agent's own technology.

I try to smile at them now.

In the cup it was so lovely to look at, wasn't it? An orange hue, like something out of the princess's floating world woodblocks.

Etsuyo is shaking. "But we can't undo it? Surely there's a cure. A way to reverse it, before it's . . . too late."

Before we look like you, she means.

"The only cure is a temporary one, and it comes from the Machine. When your thread begins, you'll understand . . ."

It takes thirteen to fourteen hours for the Machine to empty a *kaiko-joko* of her thread. The relief of being rid of it is indescribable.

These seashore girls know next to nothing about silkworm cultivation. In the mountains of Chichibu, Chiyo tells them, everyone in her village was involved. Seventy families worked together in a web: planting and watering the mulberry trees, raising the *kaiko* eggs to pupa, feeding the silkworm caterpillars. The art of silk production was very, very inefficient, I tell the sisters. Slow and costly. Until us.

I try to weed the pride from my voice, but it's difficult. In spite of everything, I can't help but admire the quantity of silk that we *kaiko-joko* can produce in a single day. The Agent boasts that he has made us the most productive machines in the empire, surpassing even those steel zithers and cast-iron belchers at Tomioka Model Mill.

Eliminated: mechanical famine. Supply problems caused by the cocoons' tiny size and irregular quality.

Eliminated: waste silk.

Eliminated: the cultivation of the *kaiko*. The harvesting of their eggs. The laborious collection and separation of the silk cocoons. We silkworm-girls combine all these processes in the single factory of our bodies. Ceaselessly, even while we dream, we are generating thread. Every droplet of our energy, every moment of our time flows into the silk.

I guide the sisters to the first of the three workbenches. "Here are the basins," I say, "steam heated, quite modern, eh, where we boil the water."

I plunge my left hand under the boiling water for as long as I can bear it. Soon the skin of my fingertips softens and bursts, and fine waggling fibers rise from them. Green thread lifts right out of my veins. With my right hand I pluck up the thread from my left fingertips and wrist.

"See? Easy."

A single strand is too fine to reel. So you have to draw several out, wind six or eight around your finger, rub them together, to get the right denier; when they are thick enough, you feed them to the Machine.

Dai is drawing red thread onto her reeler, watching me approvingly.

"Are we monsters now?" Tooka wants to know.

I give Dai a helpless look; that's a question I won't answer.

Dai considers.

In the end she tells the new reelers about the *juhyou*, the "snow monsters," snow-and-ice-covered trees in Zao Onsen, her home. "The snow monsters"—Dai smiles, brushing her white whiskers—"are very beautiful. Their disguises make them beautiful. But they are still trees, you see, under all that frost."

While the sisters drink in this news, I steer them to the Machine.

The Machine looks like a great steel-and-wood beast with a dozen rotating eyes and steaming mouths—it's twenty meters long and takes up nearly half the room. The central reeler is a huge and ever-spinning *O*, capped with rows of flashing metal teeth. Pulleys swing our damp thread left to right across it, refining it into finished silk. Tooka shivers and says it looks as if the Machine is smiling at us. *Kaiko-joko* sit at the workbenches that face the giant wheel, pulling glowing threads from their own fingers, stretching threads across their reeling frames like zither strings. A stinging music.

No *tebiki* cranks to turn, I show them. Steam power has freed both our hands.

"'Freed,' I suppose, isn't quite the right word, is it?" says Iku drily. Lotus-colored thread is flooding out of her left palm and reeling around her dowel. With her right hand she adjusts the outflow.

Here is the final miracle, I say: our silk comes out of us in colors. There is no longer any need to dye it. There is no other silk like it on the world market, boasts the Agent. If you look at it from the right angle, a pollen seems to rise up and swirl into your eyes. Words can't exaggerate the joy of this effect.

Nobody has ever guessed her own color correctly—Hoshi predicted hers would be peach and it was blue; Nishi thought pink, got hazel. I would have bet my entire five-yen advance that mine would be light gray, like my cat's fur. But then I woke and pushed the swollen webbing of my thumb and a sprig of green came out. On my day zero, in the middle of my terror, I was surprised into a laugh: here was a translucent green I swore I'd never seen before anywhere in nature, and yet I knew it as my own on sight.

"It's as if the surface is charged with our aura," says Hoshi, counting syllables on her knuckles for her next haiku.

About this I don't tease her. I'm no poet, but I'd swear to the silks' strange glow. The sisters seem to agree with me; one looks like she's about to faint.

"Courage, sisters!" sings Hoshi. Hoshi is our haiku laureate. She came from a school for young noblewomen and pretends to have read every book in the world. We all agree that she is generally insufferable.

"Our silks are sold in Paris and America—they are worn by Emperor Meiji himself. The Agent tells me we are the treasures of the realm." Hoshi's white whiskers extend nearly to her ears now. Hoshi's optimism is indefatigable.

"That girl was hairy when she got here," I whisper to the sisters, "if you want to know the truth."

The old blind woman comes again, takes our silks, pushes the leaves in with a stick, and we fall upon them. If you think we *kaiko-joko* leave even one trampled stem behind, you underestimate the deep, death-thwarting taste of the mulberry. Vital green, as if sunlight is zipping up your spinal column.

In other factories, we've heard, there are foremen and managers and whistles to announce and regulate the breaks. Here the clocks and whistles are in our bodies. The thread itself is our boss. There is a fifteen-minute period between the mulberry orgy—"call it *the evening meal,* please, don't be disgusting," Dai pleads, her saliva still gleaming on the floor—and the regeneration of the thread. During this period, we sit in a circle in the center of the room, an equal distance from our bedding and the Machine. Stubbornly we reel backward: Takayama town. Oyaka village. Toku. Kiyo. Nara. Fudai. Sho. Radishes and pickles. Laurel and camphor smells of Shikoku. Father. Mother. Mount Fuji. The Inland Sea.

All Japan is undergoing a transformation—we *kaiko-joko* are not alone in that respect. I watched my grandfather become a share-cropper on his own property. A dependent. He was a young man when the Black Ships came to Edo. He grew foxtail millet and red buckwheat. Half his crop he paid in rent; then two-thirds; finally, after two bad harvests, he owed his entire yield. That year, our capital moved in a ceremonial, and real, procession from Kyoto to Edo, now Tokyo, the world shedding names under the carriage wheels, and the teenage emperor in his palanquin traveling over the mountains like an imperial worm.

In the first decade of the Mejii government, my grandfather was forced into bankruptcy by the land tax. In 1873, he joined the farmer's revolt in Chūbu. Along with hundreds of others of the newly bankrupted and dispossessed from Chūbu, Gifa,

Aichi, he set fire to the creditor's offices where his debts were recorded. After the rebellion failed, he hanged himself in our barn. The gesture was meaningless. The debt still existed, of course.

My father inherited the debts of his father.

There was no dowry for me.

In my twenty-third year, my mother died, and my father turned white, lay flat. Death seeded in him and began to grow tall, like grain, and my brothers carried Father to the Inoba shrine for the mountain cure.

It was at precisely this moment that the Recruitment Agent arrived at our door.

The Agent visited after a thundershower. He had a parasol from London. I had never seen such a handsome person in my life, man or woman. He had blue eyelids, a birth defect, he said, but it had worked out to his extraordinary advantage. He let me sniff at his vial of French cologne. It was as if a rumor had materialized inside the dark interior of our farmhouse. He wore Western dress. He also had—and I found this incredibly appealing—mid-ear sideburns and a mustache.

"My father is sick," I told him. I was alone in the house. "He is in the other room, sleeping."

"Well, let's not disturb him." The Agent smiled and stood to go.

"I can read," I said. For years I'd worked as a servant in the summer retreat of a Kobe family. "I can write my name."

Show me the contract, I begged him.

And he did. I couldn't run away from the factory and I couldn't die, either, explained the Recruitment Agent—and perhaps I looked at him a little dreamily, because I remember that he repeated this injunction in a hard voice, tightening up the grammar: "If you die, your father will pay." He was peering deeply into my face; it was April, and I could see the rain in his mustache. I met his gaze and giggled, embarrassing myself.

"Look at you, blinking like a firefly! Only it's very serious—"

He lunged forward and grabbed playfully at my waist, causing my entire face to darken in what I hoped was a womanly blush. The Agent, perhaps fearful that I was choking on a radish, thumped my back.

"There, there, Kitsune! You will come with me to the model factory? You will reel for the realm, for your emperor? For me, too," he added softly, with a smile.

I nodded, very serious myself now. He let his fingers brush softly against my knuckles as he drew out the contract.

"Let me bring it to Father," I told the Agent. "Stand back. Stay here. His disease is contagious."

The Agent laughed. He said he wasn't used to being bossed by a *joko*. But he waited. Who knows if he believed me?

My father would never have signed the document. He would not have agreed to let me go. He blamed the new government for my grandfather's death. He was suspicious of foreigners. He would have demanded to know, certainly, where the factory was located. But I could work whereas he could not. I saw my father coming home, cured, and finding the five-yen advance. I had never used an ink pen before. In my life as a daughter and a sister, I had never felt so powerful. No woman in Gifu had ever brokered such a deal on her own. KITSUNE TAJIMA, I wrote in the slot for the future worker's name, my heart pounding in my ears. When I returned it, I apologized for my father's unsteady hand.

On our way to the *kaiko*-tea ceremony, I was so excited that I could barely make my questions about the factory intelligible. He took me to a summer guesthouse in the woods behind the Miya River, which he told me was owned by a Takayama merchant family and, at the moment, empty.

Something is wrong, I knew then. This knowledge sounded with such clarity that it seemed almost independent of my body, like a bird calling once over the trees. But I proceeded, following the Agent toward a dim staircase. The first room I glimpsed was elegantly furnished, and I felt my spirits lift again, along with my caution. I counted fourteen steps to the first landing, where he opened the door onto a room that reflected none of the downstairs refinement. There was a table with two stools, a bed; otherwise the room was bare. I was surprised to see a large brown blot on the mattress. One porcelain teapot. One cup. The Agent lifted the tea with an unreadable expression, frowning into the pot; as he poured, I thought I heard a little splash; then he cursed, excused himself, said he needed a fresh ingredient. I heard him continuing up the staircase. I peered into the cup and saw that there was something alive inside it—writhing, dying—a fat white *kaiko*. I shuddered but I didn't fish it out. What sort of tea ceremony was this? Maybe, I thought, the Agent is testing me, to see if I am squeamish, weak. Something bad was coming—the stench of a bad and thickening future was everywhere in that room. The bad thing was right under my nose, crinkling its little legs at me.

I pinched my nostrils shut, just as if I were standing in the mud a heartbeat from jumping into the Miya River. Without so much as consulting the Agent, I squinched my eyes shut and gulped.

The other workers cannot believe I did this willingly. Apparently, one sip of the *kaiko*-tea is so venomous that most bodies go into convulsions. Only through the Agent's intervention were they able to get the tea down. It took his hands around their throats.

I arranged my hands in my lap and sat on the cot. Already I was feeling a little dizzy. I remember smiling with a sweet vacancy at the door when he returned.

"You—drank it."

I nodded proudly.

Then I saw pure amazement pass over his face—I passed the test, I thought happily. Only it wasn't that, quite. He began to laugh.

"No *joko*," he sputtered, "not one of you, ever—" He was rolling his eyes at the room's corners, as if he regretted that the hilarity of this moment was wasted on me. "No girl has ever gulped a pot of it!"

Already the narcolepsy was buzzing through me, like a hive of bees stinging me to sleep. I lay guiltily on the mat—why couldn't I sit up? Now the Agent would think I was worthless for work. I opened my mouth to explain that I was feeling ill but only a smacking sound came out. I held my eyes open for as long as I could stand it.

Even then, I was still dreaming of my prestigious new career as a factory reeler. Under the Meiji government, the hereditary classes had been abolished, and I even let myself imagine that the Agent might marry me, pay off my family's debts. As I watched, the Agent's genteel expression underwent a complete transformation; suddenly it was as blank as a stump. The last thing I saw, before shutting my eyes, was his face.

I slept for two days and woke on a dirty tatami in this factory with Dai applauding me; the green thread had erupted through my palms in my sleep—the metamorphosis unusually accelerated. I was lucky, as Chiyo says. Unlike Tooka and Etsuyo and so many of the others I had no limbo period, no cramps from my guts unwinding, changing; no time at all to meditate on what I was becoming—a secret, a furred and fleshy silk factory.

What would Chiyo think of me, if she knew how much I envy her initiation story? That what befell her—her struggle, her screams—I long for? That I would exchange my memory for Chiyo's in a heartbeat? Surely this must be the final, inarguable proof that I am, indeed, a monster.

Many workers here have a proof of their innocence, some physical trace, on the body: scar tissue, a brave spot. A sign of struggle that is ineradicable. Some girls will push their white fuzz aside to show you: Dai's pocked hands, Mitsuki's rope burns around her neck. Gin has wiggly lines around her mouth, like lightning, where she was scalded by the tea that she spat out.

And me?

There was a moment, at the bottom of the stairwell, and a door that I could easily have opened back into the woods of Gifu. I alone, it seems, out of twenty-two workers, signed my own contract.

"Why did you drink it, Kitsune?"

I shrug.

"I was thirsty," I say.

Roosters begin to crow outside the walls of Nowhere Mill at five a.m. They make a sound like gargled light, very beautiful, which I picture as Dai's red and Gin's orange and Yoshi's pink thread singing on the world's largest reeler. Dawn. I've been lying awake in the dark for hours.

"Kitsune, you never sleep. I hear the way you breathe," Dai says.

"I sleep a little."

"What stops you?" Dai rubs her belly sadly. "Too much thread?"

"Up here." I knock on my head. "I can't stop reliving it: the Agent walking through our fields under his parasol, in the rain . . ."

"You should sleep," says Dai, peering into my eyeball. "Yellowish. You don't look well."

Midmorning, there is a malfunction. Some hitch in the Machine causes my reeler to spin backward, pulling the thread from my fingers so quickly that I am jerked onto my knees; then

I'm dragged along the floor toward the Machine's central wheel like an enormous, flopping fish. The room fills with my howls. With surprising calm, I become aware that my right arm is on the point of being wrenched from its socket. I lift my chin and begin, with a naturalness that belongs entirely to my terror, to swivel my head around and bite blindly at the air; at last I snap the threads with my *kaiko*-jaws and fall sideways. Under my wrist, more thread kinks and scrags. There is a terrible stinging in my hands and my head. I let my eyes close: for some reason I see the space beneath my mother's cedar chest, where the moonlight lay in green splashes on our floor. I used to hide there as a child and sleep so soundly that no one in our one-room house could ever find me. No such luck today: hands latch onto my shoulders. Voices are calling my name—"Kitsune! Are you awake? Are you okay?"

"I'm just clumsy," I laugh nervously. But then I look down at my hand. Short threads extrude from the bruised skin of my knuckles. They are the wrong color. Not my green. Ash.

Suddenly I feel short of breath again.

It gets worse when I look up. The silk that I reeled this morning is bright green. But the more recent thread drying on the bottom of my reeler is black. Black as the sea, as the forest at night, says Hoshi euphemistically. She is too courteous to make the more sinister comparisons.

I swallow a cry. Am I sick? It occurs to me that five or six of these black threads dragged my entire weight. It had felt as though my bones would snap in two before my thread did.

"Oh no!" gasp Tooka and Etsuyo. Not exactly sensitive, these sisters from Sakegawa. "Oh, poor Kitsune! Is that going to happen to us, too?"

"Anything you want to tell us?" Dai prods. "About how you are feeling?"

"I feel about as well as you all look today," I growl.

"I'm not worried," says Dai in a too-friendly way, clapping my shoulder. "Kitsune just needs sleep."

But everybody is staring at the spot midway up the reel where the green silk shades into black.

My next mornings are spent splashing through the hot water basin, looking for fresh fibers. I pull out yards of the greenish-black thread. Soiled silk. Hideous. Useless for kimonos. I sit and reel for my sixteen hours, until the Machine gets the last bit out of me with a shudder.

My thread is green three days out of seven. After that, I'm lucky to get two green outflows in a row. This transformation happens to me alone. None of the other workers report a change in their colors. It must be my own illness then, not *kaiko*-evolution. If we had a foreman here, he would quarantine me. He might destroy me, the way silkworms infected with the blight are burned up in Katamura.

And in Gifu? Perhaps my father has died at the base of Mount Inaba. Or has he made a full recovery, journeyed home with my brothers, and cried out with joyful astonishment to find my five-yen advance? Let it be that, I pray. My afterlife will be whatever he chooses to do with that money.

Today marks the forty-second day since we last saw the Agent. In the past he has reliably surprised us with visits, once or twice per month. Factory inspections, he calls them, scribbling notes about the progress of our transformations, the changes in our weight and shape, the quality of our silk production. He's never stayed away so long before. The thought of the Agent, either coming or not coming, makes me want to retch. Water sloshes in my head. I lie on the mat with my eyes shut tight and watch the orange tea splash into my cup . . .

"I hear you in there, Kitsune. I know what you're doing. You didn't sleep."

Dai's voice. I keep my eyes shut.

"Kitsune, stop thinking about it. You are making yourself sick."

"Dai, I can't."

Today my stomach is so full of thread that I'm not sure I'll be able to stand. I'm afraid that it will all be black. Some of us are now forced to crawl on our hands and knees to the Machine, toppled by our ungainly bellies. I can smell the basins heating. A thick, greasy steam fills the room. I peek up at Dai's face, then let my eyes flutter shut again.

"Smell that?" I say, more nastily than I intend to. "In here we're dead already. At least on the stairwell I can breathe forest air."

"Unwinding one cocoon for an eternity," she snarls. "As if you had only a single memory. Reeling in the wrong direction."

Dai looks ready to slap me. She's angrier than I've ever seen her. Dai is the Big Mother but she's also a samurai's daughter, and sometimes that combination gives rise to a ferocious kind of caring. She's tender with the little ones, but if an older *joko* plummets into a mood or ill health, she'll scream at us until our ears split. Furious, I suppose, at her inability to defend us from ourselves.

"The others also suffered in their pasts," she says. "But we sleep, we get up, we go to work, some crawl forward if there is no other way . . ."

"I'm not like the others," I insist, hating the baleful note in my voice but desperate to make Dai understand this. Is Dai blind to the contrast? Can she not see that the innocent recruits—the ones who were signed over to the Agent by their fathers and their brothers—produce pure colors, in radiant hues? Whereas my thread looks rotten, greeny-black.

"Sleep can't wipe me clean like them. I chose this fate. I can't blame a greedy uncle, a gullible father. I drank the tea of my own free will."

"Your free will," says Dai, so slowly that I'm sure she's about to mock me; then her eyes widen with something like joy. "Ah! So: use that to stop drinking it at night, in your memory. Use your will to stop thinking about the Agent."

Dai is smiling down at me like she's won the argument.

"Oh, yes, very simple!" I laugh angrily. "I'll just stop. Why didn't I think of that? Say, here's one for you, Dai," I snap. "Stop reeling for the Agent at your workbench. Stop making the thread in your gut. Try that, I'm sure you'll feel better."

Then we are shouting at each other, our first true fight; Dai doesn't understand that this memory reassembles itself in me mechanically, just as the thread swells in our new bodies. It's nothing I control. I see the Agent arrive; my hand trembling; the ink lacing my name across the contract. My regret: I know I'll never get to the bottom of it. I'll never escape either place, Nowhere Mill or Gifu. Every night, the cup refills in my mind.

"Go reel for the empire, Dai. Make more silk for him to sell. Go throw the little girls another party! Make believe we're not slaves here."

Dai storms off, and I feel a mean little pleasure.

For two days we don't speak, until I worry that we never will again. But on the second night, Dai finds me. She leans in and whispers that she has accepted my challenge. At first I am so happy to hear her voice that I only laugh, take her hand. "What challenge? What are you talking about?"

"I thought about what you said," she tells me. She talks about her samurai father's last stand, the Satsuma Rebellion. In the countryside, she says, there are peasant armies who protest "the blood tax," refuse to sow new crops. I nod with my eyes shut, watching my grandfather's hat floating through our fields in Gifu.

"And you're right, Kitsune—we have to stop reeling. If we don't, he'll get every year of our futures. He'll get our last breaths. The silk belongs to us, *we* make it. We can use that to bargain with the Agent."

The following morning, Dai announces that she won't move from her mat.

"I'm on strike," she says. "No more reeling."

By the second day, her belly has grown so bloated with thread that we are begging her to work. The mulberry leaves arrive, and she refuses to eat them.

"No more room for that." She smiles.

Dai's face is so swollen that she can't open one eye. She lies with her arms crossed over her chest, her belly heaving.

By the fourth day, I can barely look at her.

"You'll die," I whisper.

She nods resolutely.

"I'm escaping. He might still stop me. But I'll do my best."

We send a note for the Agent with the blind woman. "Please tell him to come."

"Join me," Dai begs us, and our eyes dull and lower, we sway. For five days, Dai doesn't reel. She never eats. Some of us, I'm sure, don't mind the extra fistful of leaves. (A tiny voice I can't gag begins to babble in the background: *If x-many others strike, Kitsune, there will be x-much more food for you . . .*)

Guiltily, I set her portion aside, pushing the leaves into a little triangle. *There,* I think. The flag of Dai's resistance. Something flashes on one—a real silkworm. Inching along in its wet and stupid oblivion. My stomach flips to see all the little holes its hunger has punched into the green leaf.

During our break, I bring Dai my blanket. I try to squeeze

some of the water from the leaf-velvet onto her tongue, which she refuses. She doesn't make a sound, but I hiss—her belly is grotesquely distended and stippled with lumps, like a sow's pregnant with a litter of ten piglets. Her excess thread is packed in knots. Strangling Dai from within. Perhaps the Agent can call on a Western veterinarian, I find myself thinking. Whatever is happening to her seems beyond the ken of Emperor Meiji's own doctors.

"Start reeling again!" I gasp. "Dai, please."

"It looks worse than it is. It's easy enough to stop. You'll see for yourself, I hope."

Her skin has an unhealthy translucence. Her eyes are standing out in her shrunken face, as if every breath costs her. Soon I will be able to see the very thoughts in her skull, the way red thread fans into veiny view under her skin. Dai gives me her bravest smile. "Get some rest, Kitsune. Stop poisoning yourself on the stairwell of Gifu. If I can stop reeling, surely you can, too."

When she dies, all the silk is still stubbornly housed in her belly, "stolen from the factory," as the Agent alleges. "This girl died a thief."

Three days after her death, he finally shows up. He strides over to Dai and touches her belly with a stick. When a few of us grab for his legs, he makes a face and kicks us off.

"Perhaps we can still salvage some of it," he grumbles, rolling her into his sack.

A great sadness settles over our whole group and doesn't lift. What the Agent carried off with Dai was everything we had left:

Chiyo's clouds and mountains, my farmhouse in Gifu, Etsuyo's fiancé. It's clear to us now that we can never leave this room—we can never be away from the Machine for more than five days. Unless we live here, where the Machine can extract the thread from our bodies at speeds no human hand could match, the silk will build and build and kill us in the end. Dai's experiment has taught us that.

You never hear a peep in here about the New Year anymore.

I'm eating, I'm reeling, but I, too, appear to be dying. Thread almost totally black. The denier too uneven for any market. In my mind I talk to Dai about it, and she is very reassuring: "It's going to be fine, Kitsune. Only, please, you have to stop—"

Stop thinking about it. This was Dai's final entreaty to me.

I close my eyes. I watch my hand signing my father's name again. I am at the bottom of a stairwell in Gifu. The first time I made this ascent I felt weightless, but now the wood groans under my feet. Just as a single cocoon contains a thousand yards of silk, I can unreel a thousand miles from my memory of this one misstep.

Still, I'm not convinced that you were right, Dai—that it's such a bad thing, a useless enterprise, to reel and reel out my memory at night. Some part of me, the human part of me, is kept alive by this, I think. Like water flushing a wound, to prevent it from closing. I am a lucky one, like Chiyo says. I made a terrible mistake. In Gifu, in my raggedy clothes, I had an unreckonable power. I didn't know that at the time. But when I return to the stairwell now, I can feel them webbing around me: my choices, their infinite variety, spiraling out of my hands, my invisible thread. Regret is a pilgrimage back to the place where I was free to choose. It's become my sanctuary here in Nowhere Mill. A threshold where I still exist.

One morning, two weeks after Dai's strike, I start talking to Chiyo about her family's cottage business in Chichibu. Chiyo complains about the smells in her dry attic, where they destroy the silkworm larvae in vinegary solutions. Why do they do that? I want to know. I've never heard this part before. Oh, to stop them from undergoing the transformation, Chiyo says. First, the silkworms stop eating. Then they spin their cocoons. Once inside, they molt several times. They grow wings and teeth. If the caterpillars are allowed to evolve, they change into moths. Then these moths bite through the silk and fly off, ruining it for the market.

Teeth and wings, wings and teeth, I keep hearing all day under the whine of the cables.

That night, I try an experiment. I let myself think the black thoughts all evening. Great wheels inside me turn backward at fantastic, groaning velocities. What I focus on is my shadow in the stairwell, falling slantwise behind me, like silk. I see the ink spilling onto the contract, my name bloating monstrously.

And when dawn comes, and I slug my way over to the workbench and plunge my hands into the boiling vat, I see that the experiment was a success. My new threads are stronger and blacker than ever; silk of some nameless variety we have never belly-spun before. I crank them out of my wrist and onto the dowel. There's not a fleck of green left, not a single frayed strand. "Moonless," says Hoshi, shrinking from them. Opaque. Midnight at Nowhere Mill pales in comparison. Looking down into the basin, I feel a wild excitement. I made it that color. So I'm no mere carrier, no diseased *kaiko*—I can channel these dyes from my mind into the tough new fiber. I can change my thread's denier, control its production. Seized by a second inspiration, I begin to unreel at speeds I would have just yesterday thought laughably impossible. Not even Yuna can produce as much thread in an hour. I ignore the whispers that pool around me on the workbench:

"Kitsune's fishing too deep—look at her finger slits!"

"They look like gills." Etsuyo shudders.

"Someone should stop her. She's fishing right down to the bone."

"What is she making?"

"What are you making?"

"What are you going to do with all that, Kitsune?" Tooka asks nervously.

"Oh, who knows? I'll just see what it comes to."

But I *do* know. Without my giving a thought to what step comes next, my hands begin to fly.

The weaving comes so naturally to me that I am barely aware I am doing it, humming as if in a dream. But this weaving is instinctual. What takes effort, what requires a special kind of concentration, is generating the right density of the thread. To do so, I have to keep forging my father's name in my mind, climbing those stairs, watching my mistake unfurl. I have to drink the toxic tea and feel it burn my throat, lie flat on the cot while my organs are remade by the Agent for the factory, thinking only, *Yes, I chose this.* When these memories send the fierce regret spiraling through me, I focus on my heartbeat, my throbbing palms. Fibers stiffen inside my fingers. Grow strong, I direct the thread. Go black. Lengthen. Stick. And then, when I return to the vats, what I've produced is exactly the necessary denier and darkness. I sit at the workbench, at my ordinary station. And I am so happy to discover that I can do all this myself: the silk-generation, the separation, the dyeing, the reeling. Out of the same intuition, I discover that I know how to alter the Machine. "Help me, Tsuki," I say, because I want her to watch what I am doing. I begin to explain, but she is already disassembling my reeler. "I know, Kitsune," she says, "I see what you have in mind." Words seem to be unnecessary now between me and Tsuki—we beam thoughts soundlessly across the room. Perhaps speech will be the next superfluity in Nowhere Mill. Another step we *kaiko*-girls can skip.

Together we adjust the feeder gears, so that the black thread travels in a loop; after getting wrung out and doubled on the Machine's great wheel, it shuttles back to my hands. I add fresh fibers, drape the long skein over my knees. It is going to be as tall as a man, six feet at least.

Many girls continue feeding the Machine as if nothing unusual is happening. Others, like Tsuki, are watching to see what my fingers are doing. For the past several months, every time I've reminisced about the Agent coming to Gifu, bile has risen in my throat. It seems to be composed of every bitterness: grief and rage, the acid regrets. But then, in the middle of my weaving, obeying a queer impulse, I spit some onto my hand. This bile glues my fingers to my fur. Another of nature's wonders. So even the nausea of regret can be converted to use. I grin to Dai in my head. With this dill-colored glue, I am at last able to rub a sealant over my new thread and complete my work.

It takes me ten hours to spin the black cocoon.

The first girls who see it take one look and run back to the tatami.

The second girls are cautiously admiring.

Hoshi waddles over with her bellyful of blue silk and screams.

I am halfway up the southern wall of Nowhere Mill before I realize what I am doing; then I'm parallel to the woodpecker's window. The gluey thread collected on my palms sticks me to the glass. For the first time I can see outside: from this angle, nothing but clouds and sky, a blue eternity. *We will have wings soon,* I think, and ten feet below me I hear Tsuki laugh out loud. Using my thread and the homemade glue, I attach the cocoon to a wooden beam; soon, I am floating in circles over the Machine, suspended by my own line. "Come down!" Hoshi yells, but she's the only one. I secure the cocoon and then I let myself fall, all my weight supported by one thread. Now the cocoon sways over the Machine, a furled black flag, creaking slightly. I think of my grandfather hanging by the thick rope from our barn door.

More black thread spasms down my arms.

"Kitsune, please. You'll make the Agent angry! You shouldn't waste your silk that way—pretty soon they'll stop bringing you the leaves! Don't forget the trade, it's silk for leaves, Kitsune. What happens when he stops feeding us?"

But in the end I convince all of the workers to join me. Instinct obviates the need for a lesson—swiftly the others discover that they, too, can change their thread from within, drawing strength from the colors and seasons of their memories. Before we can begin to weave our cocoons, however, we first agree to work night and day to reel the ordinary silk, doubling our production, stockpiling the surplus skeins. Then we seize control of the machinery of Nowhere Mill. We spend the next six days dismantling and reassembling the Machine, using its gears and reels to speed the production of our own shimmering cocoons. Each dusk, we continue to deliver the regular number of skeins to the zookeeper, to avoid arousing the Agent's suspicions. When we are ready for the next stage of our revolution, only then will we invite him to tour our factory floor.

Silkworm moths develop long ivory wings, says Chiyo, bronzed with ancient designs. Do they have antennae, mouths? I ask her. Can they see? Who knows what the world will look like to us if our strike succeeds? I believe we will emerge from it entirely new creatures. In truth there is no model for what will happen to us next. We'll have to wait and learn what we've become when we get out.

The old blind woman really is blind, we decide. She squints directly at the wrecked and rerouted Machine and waits with her arms extended for one of us to deposit the skeins. Instead, Hoshi pushes a letter through the grate.

"We don't have any silk today."

"Bring this to the Agent."

"Go. Tell. Him."

As usual, the old woman says nothing. The mulberry sacks sit on the wagon. After a moment she claps to show us that her hands are empty, kicks the wagon away. Signals: no silk, no food. Her face is slack. On our side of the grate, I hear girls smacking their jaws, swallowing saliva. Fresh forest smells rise off the sacks. But we won't beg, will we? We won't turn back. Dai lived without food for five days. Our faces press against the grate. Several of our longest whiskers tickle the zookeeper's withered cheeks; at last, a dark cloud passes over her face. She barks with surprise, swats the air. Her wrinkles tighten into a grimace of fear. She backs away from our voices, her fist closed around our invitation to the Agent.

"NO SILK," repeats Tsaiko slowly.

The Agent comes the very next night.

"Hello?"

He raps at our grated door with a stick, but he remains in the threshold. For a moment I am sure that he won't come in.

"They're gone, they're gone," I wail, rocking.

"What!"

The grate slides open and he steps onto the factory floor, into our shadows.

"Yes, they've all escaped, every one of them, all your *kaiko-joko*—"

Now my sisters drop down on their threads. They fall from the ceiling on whistling lines of silk, swinging into the light, and

I feel as though I am dreaming—it is a dreamlike repetition of our initiation, when the Agent dropped the infecting *kaiko* into the orange tea. Watching his eyes widen and his mouth stretch into a scream, I too am shocked. We have no mirrors here in Nowhere Mill, and I've spent the past few months convinced that we were still identifiable as girls, women—no beauty queens, certainly, shaggy and white and misshapen, but at least half human; it's only now, watching the Agent's reaction, that I realize what we've become in his absence. I see us as he must: white faces, with sunken noses that look partially erased. Eyes insect-huge. Spines and elbows incubating lace for wings. My muscles tense, and then I am airborne, launching myself onto the Agent's back—for a second I get a thrilling sense of what true flight will feel like, once we complete our transformation. I alight on his shoulders and hook my legs around him. The Agent grunts beneath my weight, staggers forward.

"These wings of ours are invisible to you," I say directly into the Agent's ear. I clasp my hands around his neck, lean into the whisper. "And in fact you will never see them, since they exist only in our future, where you are dead and we are living, flying."

I then turn the Agent's head so that he can admire our silk. For the past week every worker has used the altered Machine to spin her own cocoon—they hang from the far wall, coral and emerald and blue, ordered by hue, like a rainbow. While the rest of Japan changes outside the walls of Nowhere Mill, we'll hang side by side, hidden against the bricks. Paralyzed inside our silk, but spinning faster and faster. Passing into our next phase. Then, we'll escape. (Inside his cocoon, the Agent will turn blue and suffocate.)

"And look," I say, counting down the wall: twenty-one workers, and twenty-two cocoons. When he sees the black sac, I feel his neck stiffen. "We have spun one for you." I smile down at him. The Agent is stumbling around beneath me, babbling something that I admit I make no great effort to understand. The glue sticks my knees to his shoulders. Several of us busy ourselves with getting the gag in place, and this is accomplished before the Agent can scream once. Gin and Nishi bring down the cast-iron grate behind him.

The slender Agent is heavier than he looks. It takes four of us to stuff him into the socklike cocoon. I smile at the Agent and instruct the others to leave his eyes for last, thinking that he will be very impressed to see our skill at reeling up close. Behind me, even as this attack is under way, the other *kaiko-joko* are climbing into their cocoons. Already there are girls half swallowed by them, winding silk threads over their knees, sealing the outermost layer with glue.

Now our methods regress a bit, get a little old-fashioned. I reel the last of the black cocoon by hand. Several *kaiko-joko* have to hold the Agent steady so that I can orbit him with the thread. I spin around his chin and his cheekbones, his lips. To get over his mustache requires several revolutions. Bits of my white fur drift down and disappear into his nostrils. His eyes are huge and black and void of any recognition. I whisper my name to him, to see if I can jostle my old self loose from his memory: Kitsune Tajima, of Gifu Prefecture.

Nothing.

So then I continue reeling upward, naming the workers of Nowhere Mill all the while: "Nishi. Yoshi. Yuna. Uki. Etsuyo. Gin. Hoshi. Raku. Chiyoko. Mitsuko. Tsaiko. Tooka. Dai.

"Kitsune," I repeat, closing the circle. The last thing I see before shutting his eyes is the reflection of my shining new face.

The Seagull Army Descends
on Strong Beach, 1979

The gulls landed in Athertown on July 11, 1979. Clouds of them,
in numbers unseen since the ornithologists began keeping records
of such things. Scientists all over the country hypothesized about
erratic weather patterns and redirected migratory routes. At first
sullen Nal barely noticed them. Lost in his thoughts, he dribbled
his basketball up the boardwalk, right past the hundreds of gulls
on Strong Beach, gulls grouped so thickly that from a distance
they looked like snowbanks. Their bodies capped the dunes. If
Nal had looked up, he would have seen a thunderhead of seagulls
in the well of the sky, rolling seaward. Instead, he ducked under
the dirty turquoise umbrella of the Beach Grub cart and spent his
last dollar on a hamburger; while he struggled to open a packet
of yellow mustard, one giant gull swooped in and snatched the
patty from its bun with a surgical jerk. Nal took two bites of
bread and lettuce before he realized what had happened. The gull
taunted him, wings akimbo, on the Beach Grub umbrella, glug-

ging down his burger. Nal went on chewing the greasy bread, concluding that this was pretty much par for his recent course.

All summer long, since his mother's termination, Nal had begun to sense that his life had jumped the rails—and then right at his nadir, he'd agreed to an "avant" haircut performed by Cousin Steve. Cousin Steve was participating in a correspondence course with a beauty school in Nevada, America, and to pass his Radical Metamorphosis II course, he decided to dye Nal's head a vivid blue and then razor the front into tentacle-like bangs. "Radical," Nal said drily as Steve removed the foil. Cousin Steve then had to airmail a snapshot of Nal's ravaged head to the United States desert, $17.49 in postage, so that he could get his diploma. In the photograph, Nal looks like he is going stoically to his death in the grip of a small blue octopus.

Samson Wilson, Nal's brother, took his turn in Cousin Steve's improvised barber chair—a wrecked church pew that Steve had carted into his apartment from off the street. Cousin Steve used Samson as a guinea pig for "Creative Clippers." He gave Samson a standard buzz cut to start, but that looked so good that he kept going with the razor. Pretty soon Samson had a gleaming cue ball head. He'd cracked jokes about the biblical significance of this, and Nal had secretly hoped that his brother's power over women would in fact be diminished. But to Nal's dismay, the ladies of Athertown flocked to Samson in greater multitudes than before. Girls trailed him down the boardwalk, clucking stupidly about the new waxy sheen to his head. Samson was seventeen and had what Nal could only describe as a bovine charm: he was hale and beefy, with a big laugh and the deep serenity of a grazing creature. Nal loved him, too, of course—it was impossible not to—but he was baffled by Sam's ease with women, his ease in the world.

That summer Nal was fourteen and looking for excuses to have extreme feelings about himself. He and Samson played a lot of basketball on summer nights and weekends. Nal would replay every second of their games until he was so sick of his own inner sportscaster that he wanted to puke. He actually had puked once—last September he had walked calmly out of the JV try-outs and retched in the frangipani. The voice in his head logged every on-court disaster, every stolen ball and missed shot, the unique fuckups and muscular failures that he had privately termed "Nal-fouls." Samson had been on the varsity team since his fresh-man year, and he wasn't interested in these instant replays—he wanted the game to move forward. Nal and his brother would play for hours, and when he got tired of losing, Nal would stand in the shade of a eucalyptus grove and dribble in place.

"It's just a pickup game, Nal," Samson told him.

"Quit eavesdropping on me!" Nal shouted, running the ball down the blacktop. "I'm talking to myself."

Then he'd take off sprinting down the road, but no matter how punishing the distance he ran—he once dribbled the ball all the way down to the ruined industrial marina at Pier 12, where the sea rippled like melted aluminum—Nal felt he couldn't get away from himself. He sank hoops and it was always Nal sinking them; he missed, and he was Nal missing. He felt incapable of spontaneous action: before he could do anything, a tiny homun-culus had to generate a flowchart in his brain. If p, then q; If z, then back to a. This homunculus could gnaw a pencil down to a nub, deliberating. All day, he could hear the homunculus clacking in his brain like a secretary from a 1940s movie: Nal shouldn't! Nal can't! Nal won't! and then hitting the bell of the carriage return. He pictured the homunculus as a tiny, blankly handsome man in a green sweater, very agreeably going about his task of wringing the life from Nal's life.

He wanted to get to a place where he wasn't thinking about every movement at every second; where he wasn't even really Nal any longer but just weight sinking into feet, feet leaving the pavement, fingers fanning forcelessly through air, the *swish!* of a made basket and the net birthing the ball. He couldn't remember the last time he had acted without reservation on a single desire. Samson seemed to do it all the time. Once, when Nal returned home from his miles-long run with the ball, sweating and furious, they had talked about his aspiration for vacancy—the way he wanted to be empty and free. He'd explained it to Samson in a breathless rush, expecting to be misunderstood.

"Sure," Samson said. "I know what you're talking about."

"You do?"

"From surfing. Oh, it's wild, brother." Why did Samson have to know him so well? "The feeling of being part of the same wave that's lifting you. It's like you're coasting outside of time, outside your own skin."

Nal felt himself redden. Sometimes he wished his brother would simply say, "No, Nal, what the hell do you mean?" Samson had a knack for this kind of insight: he was like a grinning fisherman who could wrench a secret from the depths of your chest and dangle it in front of you, revealing it to be nothing but a common, mud-colored fish.

"You know what else can get you there, Nal, since you're such a shitty athlete?" Samson grinned and cocked his thumb and his pinky, tipped them back. "Boozing. Or smoking. Last night I was out with Vanessa and we were maybe three pitchers in when the feeling happened. All night I was in love with everybody."

So Samson was now dating Vanessa Grigalunas? Nal had been infatuated with her for three years and had been so certain, for so long, that they were meant to be together, he was genuinely confused by this development, as if the iron of his destiny had gone soft and pliant as candle wax. Vanessa was in Nal's grade, a fellow survivor of freshman year. He had sat behind her in Japanese class and it was only in that language—where he was a novice and felt he had license to stammer like a fool—that he could talk to her. "K-k-k," he'd say. Vanessa would smile politely as he revved his stubborn syllable engine, until he was finally able to sputter out a "Konnichiwa."

Nal had never breathed a word about his love for Vanessa to anyone. And then in early June, out of the clear blue, Samson began raving about her. "Vanessa Grigalunas? But . . . why her?" Nal asked, thinking of all the hundreds of reasons that he'd by now collected. It didn't seem possible that the desire to date Vanessa could have co-evolved in Samson. Vanessa wasn't his type at all; Samson usually dated beach floozies, twentysome-things with hair like dry spaghetti, these women he'd put up with because they bought him liquor and pot, who sat on his lap in Gerlando's, Athertown's only cloth-napkin restaurant, and cawed laughter. Vanessa's hair shone like a lake. Vanessa read books and moved through the world as if she were afraid that her footsteps might wake it.

"I can't stop thinking about her," Samson grinned, running a paw over his bald head. "It's crazy, like I caught a Vanessa bug or something."

Nal nodded miserably—now he couldn't stop thinking about the two of them together. He sketched out interview questions in his black composition notebook that he hoped to one day ask her:

1. What is it that you like about my brother? List three things (not physical).

2. What made you want to sleep with my brother? What was your thought in the actual moment when you decided? Was it a conscious choice, like, Yes, I will do this! or was it more like collapsing onto a sofa?

3. Under what circumstances can you imagine sleeping with me? Global apocalypse? National pandemic? Strep throat shuts down the high school? What if we were to do it immediately after I'd received a lethal bite from a rattlesnake so you could feel confident that I would die soon and tell no one? Can

you just quantify for me, in terms of beer, what it would take?

It made Nal sadder still that even Vanessa's mom, Mrs. Grigalunas—a woman who had no sons of her own and who treated all teenage boys like smaller versions of her husband—even kindly, delusional Mrs. Grigalunas recognized Nal as a deterrent to love. One Saturday night Samson informed him that the *three* of them would be going on a date to Strong Beach together; they needed Nal's presence to reassure Mrs. Grigalunas that nothing dangerous or fun would happen.

"Yes, you two can go to the beach," she told Vanessa, "but bring that Nal along with you. He's such a nice boy."

WHAT WERE all these seagulls doing out flying at night? They were kelp gulls, big ones. Nal was shocked to see how many of the birds now occupied Strong Beach. Where'd they all come from? He turned to point out the seagull invasion to Vanessa and Samson, but they were strolling hand in hand over a tall dune, oblivious to both Nal and the gulls' wheeling shadows. Nal hoped the flock would leave soon. He was trying to finish a poem. White globs of gull shit kept falling from the sky, a cascade that Nal found inimical to his writing process. The poem that Nal was working on had nothing to do with his feelings—poetry, he'd decided, was to honor remote and immortal subjects, like the moon. "Lambent Planet, Madre Moon" was the working title of this one, and he'd already jotted down three sestets. *Green nuclei of fireflies,* Nal wrote. *The red commas of two fires.* A putrid, stinky blob fell from above and put out his word. "Shoo, you shit balloons!" he yelled as the gulls rained on.

There were no fireflies on the beach that night, but there were plenty of spider fleas, their abdomens pulsing with low-grade toxins. The air was tangy and cold. Between two lumps of sand about a hundred yards behind him, Vanessa and Nal's brother, Samson, were . . . Nal couldn't stand to think about it. In five minutes' time they had given up on keeping their activities a secret from him, or anybody. Vanessa's low moan was rising behind him, rich and feral and nothing like her classroom whisper.

Nal felt a little sick.

What on earth was the moon like? he wondered, squinting. What did the moon most resemble to him? Nal wiped at his dry eyes and dug into the paper. One of the seagulls had settled on an auburn coil of seaweed a few feet away from his bare foot. He tried to ignore it, but the gull was making a big production out of eviscerating a cigarette. It drew out red flakes of tobacco with its pincerlike bill and ate them. Perfect, Nal thought. Here I am trying to eulogize Mother Nature and this is the scene she presents me with.

Behind him, Samson growled Vanessa's name. Don't look back, you asshole! he thought. Good advice, from Orpheus to Lot. But Nal couldn't help himself. He lacked the power to look away, but he never worked up the annihilating courage to look directly at them either; instead, he angled his body and let his eyes slide to the left. This was like taking dainty sips of poison. Samson's broad back had almost completely covered Vanessa—only her legs were visible over the dune, her pink feet twitching as if she were impatient for sleep. "Oh!" said Vanessa, over and over again. "Oh!" She sounded happy, astonished.

Nal was a virgin. He kicked at a wet clump of sand until it exploded. He went on a rampage, doing whirling karate kicks into a settlement of abandoned sand castles along the beach for a full minute before he paused, panting, to recover himself. The tide rushed icy fingers of water up the beach and covered Nal's foot.

"Ahh!" Nal cried into one of the troughs of silence between

Samson and Vanessa's moans. He had wandered to the water's edge, six or seven dunes away from them. His own voice was drowned out by the ocean. The salt water sleuthed out cuts on his legs that he had forgotten about or failed to feel until now, and he almost enjoyed the burning. He looked around for something else to kick, but only one turret remained on the beach, a bucket-shaped stump in the middle of damp heaps. The giant seagull was standing beside it. Up close the gull seemed as large as a house cat. Its white face was luminous, its wings ink-dipped; its beak was fixed in that perennial shit-eating grin of all shearwaters and frigate birds.

"What are you grinning at?" Nal muttered. As if in response, the gull spread its wings and opened its shadow over the miniature ruins of the castle—too huge, Nal thought, and vaguely humanoid in shape—and then it flew off, laboring heavily against the wind. In the soft moonlight this created the disturbing illusion that the bird had hitched itself to Nal's shadow and was pulling his darkness from him.

NAL WASN'T SUPPOSED to be in town that summer. He had been accepted to LMASS, the Lake Marion Achievement Summer Seminars: a six-week precollege program for the top three percent of the country's high school students. It was a big deal—seniors who completed all four summers of the program were automatically admitted to Lake Marion College with a full scholarship package. "Cream Rises" was the camp's motto; their mascot was an oblong custard-looking thing, the spumy top layer of which Nal guessed was meant to represent the gifted. In March a yellow T-shirt with this logo had arrived in the mail, bundled in with his acceptance letter. Nal tried to imagine a hundred kids wearing the same shirt in the Lake Marion dormitories, kids with overbites and cowlicks and shy, squint-eyed ambitions—LMASS!

he thought, a kind of heaven. Had he worn the shirt with the custard-thing to his own school, it would have been a request for a punch in the mouth.

But then one day his mom came home from work and said she was being scapegoated by the Paradise Nursing Facility for what management was calling "a distressing oversight." Her superiors recommended that she not return to work. But for almost two weeks Nal's mother would set her alarm for five o'clock, suit up, take the number 14 bus to Paradise. Only after she was officially terminated did she file for unemployment, and so far as Nal could tell this was the last real action she had taken; she'd been on their couch for three months now and counting. Gradually she began to lose her old habits, as if these, too, were a uniform that she could slip out of: she stopped cooking entirely, slept at odd hours, mummied herself in blankets in front of their TV. What was she waiting for? There was something maddening about her posture—the way she sat there with one ear cocked sideways as if listening for a break in the weather. Nal had been forced to forfeit his deposit at Lake Marion and interview for a job behind the register at Penny's Grocery. He took a pen to the Help Wanted ads and papered their fridge with them. This was back in April, when he'd still believed his mom might find another job in time to pay the Lake Marion fee.

"Mom, just look at these, okay?" he'd shout above the surf roar of their TV. "I circled the good ones in green." She'd explain again without looking over that the whole town was against her. Nobody was going to hire Claire Wilson *now*. All these changes came about as the result of a single failed mainstay. The windows at Paradise were supposed to be fitted with a stop screw, to prevent what the Paradise manual euphemistically referred to as "elopement." Jailbreak was another word for this, suicide, accidental defenestration—as Nal's mom put it, many of the residents were forty-eight cards to a deck and couldn't be trusted with their own lives. With the stop screws in place, no window opened more than six inches. But as it happened, a stop screw was missing from a sixth-floor window—one of the hundred-plus windows in Paradise—an oversight that was discovered when a ninety-two-year-old resident shoved it open to have a smoke. A visitor found the old woman leaning halfway out the window and drew her back inside the frame. The visitor described the "near fatal incident" to Nal's mother while the "victim" plucked ash from her tongue. According to Nal's mom, the Paradise administrators came to the sudden agreement that it had always been Claire Wilson's responsibility to check the window locks. She came home that night babbling insincere threats: "They try to pin this on me, boys, you watch, I will quit in a heartbeat." But then the resident's daughter wrote a series of histrionic letters to the newspaper, and the sleepy Athertown news station decided to do an "exposé" of Paradise, modeled on the American networks, complete with a square-jawed black actress to play the role of Nal's mother.

Only Nal had watched the dramatization through to its ending. They'd staged a simulation of a six-story fall using a flour sack dummy, the sack splitting open on the gates and spilling flour everywhere, powdering the inscrutable faces of the stone angels in the garden below. Lawsuits were filed, and, in the ensuing din of threats and accusations, Nal's mother was let go.

Nal had expected his mom to react to this with a froth and vengeance that at least matched his own, perhaps even file a legal action. But she returned home from her final day at work exhausted. Her superiors had bullied her into a defeated sort of gratitude: "They said it was my job, who knows? I'm not perfect. I'm just glad they caught the problem when they did," she kept saying.

"Quit talking like that!" Nal moaned. "It wasn't your fault,

Mom. You've been brainwashed by these people. Don't be such a pushover."

"A pushover!" she said. "Who's pushing me over? I know it wasn't my fault, Nal. I can't be grateful that nobody got killed?" She described the "averted tragedy" in the canned language of the Paradise directors: the chance of one of her charges flailing backward out the window and onto the gate's tiny spears. In her dreams the victim wasn't a flour sack dummy but a body with no face, impaled on the spikes.

"That's your body, Ma!" Nal cried. "That's you!" But she didn't see it that way.

"Let's just be thankful nobody was hurt," she mumbled.

Nal didn't want his mom to relinquish her first fury. "How can you say that? They fired you, Mom! Now everything's . . . off course."

His mom stroked a blue curl of Nal's hair and gave him a tired smile. "Ooh, we're off course, right. I forgot. And what course was that?"

Nal picked up more shifts at the grocery store. He ran eggs and pork tenderloins down the register, the scanner catching his knuckles in a web of red light. Time felt heavy inside Penny's. *Beep!* he whimpered along with the machine, swiping a tin of tomatoes. *Beep!* Sometimes he could still feel the progress of his lost future inside him, the summer at Lake Marion piping like a vacant bubble through his blood.

"Mom, can I still go away to college, though?" he asked her one Sunday, when they were sitting in the aquarium light of the TV. He'd felt the bubble swell to an unbearable pressure in his lungs. "Sure," she said, not looking over from the TV. Her eyes were like Samson's, bright splashes of blue in an oak-stained face. "You can do whatever you want."

When the bubble in him would burst, Nal would try to start

a fight. He shouted that what she called his "choices" about college and LMASS and Penny's Grocery were her consequences, a
domino run of misfortune. He told her that he wouldn't be able
to go to college if she didn't find another job, that it was lying to
pretend he could.

"I heard you guys going at it," Samson said later in the kitchen,
clapping mayonnaise onto two slices of bread. "Give Mom a
break, kid. I think she's sick."

But Nal didn't think that his mom had contracted any particular illness—he was terrified that she was more generally dying,
or disintegrating, letting her white roots grow out and fusing her
spine to their couch. She was still sitting in front of the TV with
the shades drawn when he got off his shift at six thirty.

Nal wrote a poem about how his mother had become the
sea hum inside the conch shell of their living room. He thought
it must be the best poem he'd ever written because he tried to
recite it to his bathroom reflection and his throat shut, and his
eyes stung so badly he could barely see his own face. She was
sitting out there now, watching TV reruns and muttering under
her breath. Samson was out drinking that night with Vanessa.
Nal gave his mother the poem to read and found it under a dirty
mug, accumulating rings, when he came back to check on her
that Friday.

Nal got a second job housesitting for his high school science teacher, Mr. McGowen, who was going to Lake Marion to
teach an advanced chemistry course. Now Nal spent his nights
in the shell of Mr. McGowen's house. Each week Mr. McGowen
sent him a check for fifty-six dollars, and his mom lived on this
income plus the occasional contribution from Samson, wads of
cash that Sam had almost certainly borrowed from someone else.
"It helps," she said, "it's such a help," and whenever she said this
Nal felt his guts twist. Mr. McGowen's two-room rental house
was making slow progress down the cliffs; another hurricane

would finish it. The move there hadn't mattered in any of the ways that Nal had hoped it would. Samson had buffaloed him into giving him a spare key, and now Nal would wake up to find his brother standing in the umbilical hallway between the two rooms at odd hours:

SUNDAY: "How you living, Nal? Living easy? Easy living? You get paid yet this week? I need you to do me a solid, brotherman . . ." He was already peeling the bills out of Nal's wallet.
MONDAY: "Cable's out. I want to watch the game tonight, so I'll probably just crash here . . ."
TUESDAY: "You're out of toilet paper again. I fucking swear, I'm going to get a rash from coming over here! Some deadly fucking disease . . ."
WEDNESDAY: "Shit, kid, you need to get to the store. Your fridge is just desolate. What have you been eating?"

For three days, Nal hadn't ingested anything besides black coffee and a pint of freezer-burned ice cream. Weight was tumbling from his body. Nal was living on liquid hatred now.

"Hey, Nal," said Samson, barging through the door. "Listen, Vanessa and I were sort of hoping we could spend the night here? She lied and told Mrs. Griga-looney that she's crashing at a friend's spot. Cool? Although you should really pick up before she gets here, this place is gross."

"Cool," Nal said, his blue hair igniting in the flashing light of the TV. "I just did laundry. Fresh sheets for you guys." Nal left Samson to root around the empty fridge and fished clean sheets out of Mr. McGowen's dryer. He made the twin bed with hospital corners, pushed his sneakers and sweaty V-necks under the frame, filled two glasses at the sink faucet and set them on the nightstand. He lit Mr. McGowen's orange emergency candles to provide a romantic accent. Nal knew this was not the most excellent strategy to woo Vanessa—making the bed so that she could sleep with his brother—but he was getting a sick pleasure from this seduction by proxy. The bedroom was freezing, Nal realized, and he reached over to shut the window—then screamed and leapt a full foot back.

A giant seagull was strutting along Nal's sill, a bouquet of eelgrass dangling from its beak. Its crown feathers waggled at Nal like tiny fingers. He felt a drip of fear. "What are you doing here?" He had to flick at the webbing of its slate feet before it moved and he could shut the window. The gull cocked its head and bored into Nal with its bright eyes; it was still looking at him as he backed out of the room.

"Hey," Vanessa greeted him shyly in the kitchen. "So this is McGowen's place." She was wearing thin silver bracelets up her arm and had blown out her hair. She had circled her eyes in lime and magenta powder; to Nal it looked as if she'd allowed a bag of candy to melt on her face. He thought she looked much prettier in school.

"Do you guys want chips or anything?" he asked stupidly, looking from Samson to Vanessa. "Soda? I have chips."

Vanessa kept her eyes on the nubby carpet. "Soda sounds good."

"He's just leaving," Samson said. He squeezed Nal's shoulder as he spun him toward the door. "Thank you," he said, leaning in so close that Nal could smell the spearmint and vodka mix on his breath, "thank you *so much*"—which somehow made everything worse.

"NAL DRIVES THE LANE! Nal brings the ball upcourt with seconds to play!" Nal whispered, dribbling his ball well past midnight. He dribbled up and down the main street that led to Strong Beach, and kept spooking himself with his own image in the dark storefront windows. "Nal has the ball . . ." He continued down to the public courts. "Jesus! Not you again!" A giant seagull had perched on the backboard and was staring opaquely forward. "Get out of here!" Nal threw the ball until the backboard juddered, but the bird remained. Maybe it's sick, Nal thought. Maybe it has some kind of neurological damage. He tucked the ball under his arm and walked farther down Strong Beach. The seagull flew over his head and disappeared into a dark thicket of pines, the beginnings of the National Reserve forest that lined Strong Beach. Nal was surprised to find himself jogging after it, following the bird into those shadows.

"Gull?" he called after it, his sneakers sinking into the dark leaves.

He found it settled on a low pine branch. The giant seagull had a sheriff's build—distended barrel chest, spindly legs splayed into star-shaped feet. Nal had a sudden presentiment: "Are you my conscience?" he asked, reaching out to stroke the vane of one feather. The gull blatted at Nal and began digging around the underside of one wing with its beak like a tiny man sniffing his armpits. Okay, not my conscience, then, Nal decided. But maybe some kind of omen? Something was dangling from its lower beak—another cigarette, Nal thought at first, then realized it was a square of glossy paper. As he watched, the gull lifted off the branch and soared directly into one of the trees. In the moonlight, Nal saw a hollow there about the size of his basketball: gulls kept disappearing into this hole. Dozens of them were flying around the moon-bright leaves—they moved with the organized frenzy of bees or bats. How deep was the hollow? he wondered. Was this normal nocturnal activity for this kind of gull? The birds flew in absolute silence. Their wingtips sailed as softly as paintbrushes across the night sky; every so often single birds descended from this cloud. Each gull flapped into the hollow and didn't reemerge for whole minutes.

Nal chucked his basketball at the hollow to see if it would disappear, go winking into another dimension, like objects did in that terrible TV movie he secretly loved, *Magellan Maps the Black Hole*. The basketball bounced back and caught Nal hard against his jaw. He winced and shot a look up and down Strong Beach to make sure that nobody had seen. The hollow was almost a foot above Nal's head, and when he pushed up to peek inside it he saw nothing: just the pulpy reddish guts of the tree. No seagulls, and no passage through that he could divine. There was a nest in the tree hollow, though, a dark wet cup of vegetation. The bottom of the nest was lined with paper scraps—a few were tickets, Nal saw, not stubs or fragments but whole squares, some legible: Mary Gloster's train tickets to Florence, a hologram stamp for a Thai *Lotus Blossom* day cruise, a roll of carnival-red ADMIT ONEs. Nal riffled through the top layer. Mary Gloster's tickets, he noticed, were dated two years in the future. He saw a square edge with the letters WIL beneath a wreath of blackened moss and tugged at it. My ticket, Nal thought wonderingly. WILSON. How did the gulls get this? It was his pass for the rising sophomore class's summer trip to Whitsunday Island, a glowing ember of volcanic rock that was just visible from the Athertown marina. He was shocked to find it here; his mother hadn't been able to pay the fee back in April, and Nal's name had been removed from the list of participants. The trip was tomorrow.

Nal was at the marina by 8:00 a.m. He was sitting on a barrel when his teacher arrived, and he watched as she tore open a sealed envelope and distributed the tickets one by one to each of his classmates. He waited until all the other students had disappeared onto the ferry to approach her.

"Nal Wilson? Oh dear. I wasn't aware that you were coming . . ." She gave him a tight smile and shook out the empty manila envelope, as if trying to convince him that his presence here was a slightly embarrassing mistake.

" 'S okay, I have my ticket here." Nal waved the orange ticket, which was shot through with tiny perforations from where the gull's beak had stabbed it. He lined up on the waffled copper of the ferry ramp. The boat captain stamped his ticket REDEEMED, and Nal felt that he had won a small but significant battle. On the hydrofoil, Nal sat next to Vanessa. "That's my seat," grumbled a stout Fijian man in a bolo tie behind him, but Nal shrugged and gestured around the hold. "Looks like there are plenty of seats to go around, sir," he said, and was surprised when the big man floated on like some bad weather he'd dispelled with native magic. He could feel Vanessa radiating warmth beside him and was afraid to turn.

"Hey, you," Vanessa said. "Thanks for letting me crash in your bed last night."

"Don't mention it. Always fun to be the maid service for my brother."

Vanessa regarded him quietly for a moment. "I like your hair."

"Oh," Nal said miserably, rolling his eyes upward. "This blue isn't really me—" and then he felt immediately stupid, because just who did he think he was, anyway? Cousin Steve refused to shave it off, saying that to do so would be a violation of the Hippocratic Oath of Beauty Professionals. "Unfortunately you have an extremely lumpy head," Cousin Steve had informed him, stern as a physician. "You need that blue to hide the contours. It's like you've got golf balls buried up there." But Vanessa, he saw with a rush of gratitude, was nodding at him.

"I know it's not you," she said. "But it's a good disguise."

Nal nodded, wondering what she might be referring to. He

was thrilled by the idea that Vanessa saw past this camouflage to something hidden in him, so secret that even he didn't know what she was seeing there.

On the long ride to Whitsunday, they talked about their families. Vanessa was the youngest of five girls, and, from what she was telling Nal, it sounded as if her adolescence had been both accelerated and prolonged. She was still playing with dolls when she watched her eldest sister, Rue Ann, guide her boyfriend to their bedroom. "We have to leave the lights on, or Vanessa will be scared. It's fine, she's still tiny. She doesn't understand." The boyfriend grinning into her playpen, twaddling his fingers. Vanessa watched with eyes round as moon pies as her sister disrobed, draping her black T-shirt over the lampshade to dim it. But she had also been babied by her four sisters, and her questions about their activities got smothered beneath a blanket of care. Her parents began treating her like the baby of the family again once the other girls were gone. Her father was a Qantas mechanic and her mother worked a series of housekeeping jobs even though she didn't strictly need to, greeting Vanessa with a nervous "Hello!" at the end of each day.

"Which is funny, because our own house is always a mess now . . ."

Nal watched the way her mouth twitched; his heart and his stomach were staging some weird circus inside him.

"Yeah, that's pretty funny." Nal frowned. "Except that, I mean, it sounds really awful, too . . ."

He tried to get one arm around Vanessa's left shoulder but felt too cowardly to lower it all the way; he stared in horror at where his arm had stopped, about an inch above Vanessa's skin, like a malfunctioning bar in a theme park ride. When he lifted his arm again he noticed a gauzy stripe peeking out of Vanessa's shirt.

"I'm sorry," Nal interrupted, "Vanessa? Uh, your shirt is falling down . . ."

"Yeah." She tugged at it, unconcerned. "This was Brianne's, and she was never what you'd call petite. She's an air hostess now and my dad always jokes that he doesn't know how she maneuvers the aisles." Vanessa hooked a clear nail under her neckline. "My dad can be pretty mean. He's mad at her for leaving."

Nal couldn't take his eyes off the white binding. "Is that . . . is that a bandage?"

"Yes," she said simply. "It's my disguise."

Vanessa said she still held on to some childlike habits because they seemed to calm her parents. "I had to pretend I believed in Santa Claus until I was twelve," she said. "Did Sam tell you that I was accepted to LMASS, too?"

"Oh, wow. Congratulations. When do you leave?"

"I'm not going. I mentioned that the dorms at Lake Marion were coed and my father didn't speak to me for days." Why her development of breasts should terrify her parents Vanessa didn't understand, but she began wearing bulky, loose shirts and wrapping Ace bandages over her bras all the same. "I got the idea from English class," she said. "Shakespeare's Rosalind." Her voice changed when she talked about this—she let out a hot, embarrassed laugh and then dove into a whisper, as if she'd been trying to make a joke and suddenly switched gears.

"Isn't that a little weird?" Nal said.

Vanessa shrugged. "Less friction with my parents. The tape doesn't work as good as it did last year but it's sort of become this habit?"

Nal couldn't figure out where he was supposed to look; he was having a hard time staying focused in the midst of all this overt discussion of Vanessa's breasts.

"So you're stuck there now?"

"I don't see how I could leave my folks. I'm their last."

Vanessa wanted out but said she felt as though the exits had vanished with her sisters. They'd each schemed or blundered their way out of Athertown—early pregnancy, nursing school, marriage, the Service Corps. Now Vanessa rumbled around the house like its last working part. Nal got an image of Mr. and Mrs. Grigalunas sitting in their kitchen with their backs to the whirlwind void opened by their daughters' absence: reading the paper; sipping orange juice; collecting these old clothes like the shed skins of their former daughters and dressing Vanessa in them. He thought about her gloopy makeup and the urgency with which she'd kissed his brother, her thin legs knifing over the dune. Maybe she doesn't actually like my brother at all, Nal thought, encouraged by a new theory. Maybe she treats sex like oxidizing air. Aging rapidly wherever she can manage it, like a cut apple left on a counter.

"That's why it's easy to be with your brother," she said. "It's a relief to . . . to get out of there, to be with someone older. But it's not like we're serious, you know?" She brightened as she said this last part, as if it were a wonderful idea that had just occurred to her.

What do I say now? Nal wondered. Should I ask her to explain what she means? Should I tell her Samson doesn't love her, but I do? The homunculus typed up frantic speeches, discarded them, tore at his green sweater in anguish, gnashed the typewriter ribbon between his buckteeth. Nal could hear himself babbling—they talked about the insufferable stupidity of this year's ninth-graders, his harem of geezers at Penny's, Dr. J's jump hook, Cousin Steve's bewildering mullet. More than once, Nal watched her tug her sister's tentlike shirt up. They spent the rest of the afternoon exploring Whitsunday Island together, cracking jokes as they filed past the flowery enclosure full of crocodiles; the dry pool of Komodo dragons with their wispy beards; and finally, just before the park's exit, the koala who looked like a raddled veteran of war, gumming leaves at twilight. They talked about how maybe it wasn't such a terrible thing that they'd both missed out on Lake Marion, and on the way back up the waffled ramp to the hydrofoil Vanessa let her hand slide inside Nal's sweating palm.

That night Nal had a nightmare about the seagulls. Millions of them flew out of a bloodred sunset and began to resettle the town, snapping telephone wires and sinking small boats beneath their collective weight. Gulls covered the fence posts and rooftops of Athertown, drew a white caul over the marina, muffled every window with the static of their bodies—and each gull had a burgled object twinkling in its split beak. Warping people's futures into some new and terrible shapes, just by stealing these smallest linchpins from the present.

THE NEXT DAY, Nal went to the Athertown library to research omen birds. He was the only patron in the reading room. Beneath the painting of the full orange moon and the plastic bamboo, he read a book called *Avian Auspices* by Dr. Carlos Ramirez. Things looked pretty grim:

CROW: an omen of death, disease
RAVEN: an omen of death, disease
ALBATROSS: an omen of death at sea

Screech owls, Old World vultures, even the innocuous-sounding cuckoo, all harbingers of doom. Terrific, Nal thought, and if an enormous seagull followed you around and appeared to be making a blithe feast of your life, pecking at squares of paper and erasing whole futures, what did that mean? Coleridge and Audubon were no help here, either. Seagulls were scavengers, kleptoparasites. And, according to the books he found, they didn't portend a thing.

Nal began going to the nest every day. He woke at dawn and walked barefoot on the chilly sand down to the hollow. By

the second week he'd collected an impressive array of objects:
a tuxedo button, a scrap of paper with a phone number (out of
service—Nal tried it), a penny with a mint date one year in the
future. On Friday, he found what appeared to be the disgorged,
shimmering innards of a hundred cassette tapes, disguised at
first against the slick weeds. The seagulls had many victims,
then—they weren't just stealing from Nal. He wondered if the
gulls had different caches, in caves or distant forests. Whenever he
swept his hand over the damp nest he found new stuff:

An eviction notice, neatly halved by the gull's beak
Half a dozen keys of various sizes—car keys, big skeleton
    keys and tiny ones for safes and mailboxes, a John Deere
    tractor key, one jangling janitor's ring
A cheap fountain pen
A stamp from a country Nal didn't recognize
An empty vial of pills, the label soaking and illegible
Most disturbingly, on the soggy bottom of the nest, beneath
    a web of green eider, he found the disconnected wires of
    a child's gleaming retainer

Nal lined these objects up and pushed them around on the
sand. He felt like the paleontologist of some poor sod's stolen
fate—somewhere a man or a woman's life continued without
these tiny vertebrae, curving like a spine knocked out of align-
ment. Suddenly the ordinary shine of the plastic and aluminum
bits began to really frighten him. He drew the tiny fangs of the
tractor key through the sand and tried to imagine the objects'
owners: A shy child without his retainer, with a smile that would
now go unchaperoned. A redhead with pale eyelashes succumb-
ing to fever. A farmer on his belly in a field of corn, hunting for
this key. What new directions would their lives take? In Nal's
imagination, dark stalks swayed and knit together, obliterat-

ing the stranger from view. Somewhere the huge tractor wheels began to groan and squeal backward, trampling his extant rows of corn. A new crop was pushing into the spaces that the tractor had abandoned—husks hissing out of the earth, bristling and green, like the future sprouting new fur.

We have to alert the authorities, he decided. He zipped the future into his backpack and walked down to the police station.

"What do you want me to do with this sack of crap, son?" Sheila, the Athertown policewoman, wanted to know. "The pawnshop moved; it's down by the esplanade now. Why don't you take this stuff over there, see if Mr. Tarak will give you some quarters for it. Play you some video games."

"But it belongs to somebody." Nal hadn't found the courage to tell her his theory that the foreign flock of gulls were cosmic scavengers. He tried to imagine saying this out loud: "The seagulls are stealing scraps of our lives to feather this weird nest I found in a tree hollow on Strong Beach. These birds are messing with our futures." Sheila, who had a red lioness's mane of curls bursting from an alligator clip and bigger triceps than Nal's, did not look as if she suffered fools gladly. She was the kind of woman who would put DDT in the nest and call it a day.

"So leave it here then." She shrugged. "When somebody comes to report the theft of their number two pencil, I'll let you know."

On Saturday he found a wedding invitation for Bruce and Nancy, in an envelope the color of lilac icing. There was no return address. On Tuesday he checked the nest and found the wrinkled passport of one Dodi Watts. Did that mean he was dead, or never was? Nal shuddered. Or just that he'd missed his flight?

His guesswork was beginning to feel stupid. Pens and keys and train tickets, so what? Now what? Sheila was right. How was he supposed to make anything out of this sack of crap?

The giant seagull, which Nal now thought of as his not-conscience, appeared to be the colony's dominant gull. Today it was screaming in wide circles over the sea. Nal sat on a canted rock and watched something tiny fall from its beak into the waves, glinting all the way down. Beneath him the waves had turned a foam-blistered violet, and the sky growled. The whole bowl of the bay seethed around the rocks like a cauldron. Nal shuddered; when he squinted he could see something fine as salt shaking into the sea. Rain, he thought, watching the seagull ride the thermals, maybe it's only raining . . .

Later, when the sky above Strong Beach was riddled with stars, Nal got up on shaky legs and entered the woods. The gulls had vanished, and it was hard for him to find the tree with the hollow. He stumbled around with his flashlight for what felt like hours looking for it, growing increasingly frantic until he felt near-hysterical, his heart drumming. Even after he'd found what he thought was the right tree Nal couldn't be sure, because the nest inside was damp and empty. He sank his hands into the old leaves and at first felt nothing, but digging down he began to find an older stratum of plunder: a leather bookmark, a baby's rusting spoon. The gulls must have stolen this stuff a while ago, Nal thought, from a future that was now peeling away in ribbons, a future that had already been perverted or lost, a past. At the very bottom of the nest he saw a wink of light. Nal pinched at the wink, pulled it out.

"Oh God," he groaned. When he saw what he was holding he almost dropped it. "Is this some kind of joke?"

It was nothing, really. It was just a dull knuckle of metal. A screw.

Nal closed his fist around the screw, opened it. Here was something indigestible. It was a stop screw—he knew this from the diagram that had run with the local paper's story "Allegations of Nursing Home Negligence," next to a photograph of the two-inch chasm in the Paradise window made lurid by the journalist's ink. They'd also run a bad photo of his mother. Her face had been washed out by the fluorescent light. She was old, Nal realized. It looked like the "scandal" had aged her. Nal had stared at his mother's gray face and seen a certain future, something you didn't need a bird to augur.

He wouldn't even show her, he decided. What was the point of coming back here? The screw couldn't shut that window now.

NAL WAS SHOOTING hoops on the public court half a mile from Mr. McGowen's house when Samson found him. A fine dust from the nearby construction site kept blowing over in clouds whenever the wind picked up. Nal had to kick a crust of gravel off the asphalt so that he could dribble the ball.

"Hey, buddy, I've been looking everywhere for you. Mom says you two had a fight?"

Nal shoots, whispered the homunculus. He turned away from Samson and planted his feet on the asphalt. Shooter's roll—the ball teetered on the edge and at the last moment fell into the basket. "It was nothing; it was about college again. What do you need?"

"Just a tiny loan so I can buy Vanessa a ring. Mr. Tarak's going to let me do it in installments."

"Mr. Tarak said that?" Nal had always thought of Mr. Tarak as a CASH ONLY!!! sort of merchant. He had a spleeny hatred of everyone under thirty-five and liked telling Nal his new haircut made him look like the Antichrist.

Samson laughed. "Yeah, well, he knows I'm good for it." Sam was used to the fact that people went out of their way for him. It made strangers happy to see Samson happy and so they'd give him things, let him run up a tab with them, just to buoy that feeling.

"What kind of ring? A wedding ring?"

"Nah, it's just . . . I dunno. She'll like it. Tiny flowers on the inside part, what do you call that . . ."

"The band." Nal's eyes were on the red square on the backboard; he squatted into his thin calves. "Are you in love?"

Samson snorted. "We're having fun, Nal. We're having a good time." He shrugged. "It's her birthday, help me out."

"Sorry," Nal said, shooting again. "I got nothing."

"You've got nothing, huh?" Samson leaned in and made a playful grab for the ball, and Nal slugged him in the stomach.

"Jesus! What's wrong with you?"

Nal stared at his fist in amazement. He'd had no idea that swing was in the works. Wind pushed the ball downcourt and he flexed his empty hands. When his brother took a step toward him he swung wide and slammed his fist into the left shoulder—pain sprang into his knuckles and Nal had time to cock his fist back again. He thought, *I am going to really mess you up here,* right before Samson shoved him down onto the gravel. He stared down at Nal with an open mouth, his bare chest contracting. No signs of injury there, Nal saw with something close to disappointment. The basket craned above them. Blood and pebbled pits colored Nal's palms and raked up the sides of his legs. He could feel, strangest of all, a grin spreading on his face.

"Did I hurt you?" Nal asked. He was still sitting on the blacktop. He noticed that Samson was wearing his socks.

"What's your problem?" Samson said. He wasn't looking at Nal. One hand shielded his eyes, the sun pleating his forehead, and he looked like a sailor scouting for land beyond the blue gravel. "You don't want to help me out, just say so. Fucking learn to behave like a normal person."

"I can't help you," Nal called after him.

Later that afternoon, when Strong Beach was turning a hundred sorbet colors in the sun, Nal walked down the esplanade to

Mr. Tarak's pawnshop. He saw the ring right away—it was in the front display, nested in a cheap navy box between old radios and men's watches, a quarter-full bottle of Chanel.

"Repent," said Mr. Tarak without looking up from his newspaper. "Get a man's haircut."

"I'd like to buy this ring here," Nal tapped on the glass.

"On hold."

"I can make the payment right now, sir. In full."

Mr. Tarak shoved up off his stool and took it out. It didn't look like a wedding band; it was a simple wrought-iron thing with a floral design etched on the inside. Nal found he didn't care about the first woman who had pawned or lost it, or Samson who wanted to buy it. Nal was the owner now. He paid and pocketed the ring.

Before he went to catch the 3:03 bus to Vanessa's house, Nal returned to the pinewoods. If he was really going through with this, he didn't want to take any chances that these birds would sabotage his plan. He took his basketball and fitted it in the hollow. The gulls were back, circumnavigating the pine at different velocities, screeching irritably. He watched with some satisfaction as one scraped its wing against the ball. He patted the ring in his pocket. He knew this was just a temporary fix. There was no protecting against the voracity of the gulls. If fate was just a tapestry with a shifting design—some fraying skein that the gulls were tearing right this second—then Nal didn't see why he couldn't also find a loose thread, and pull.

VANESSA'S HOUSE WAS part of a new community on the outskirts of Athertown. The bus drove past the long neck of a crane rising out of an exposed gravel pit, the slate glistening with recent rain. A summer shower had rolled in from the east and tripped some of the streetlights prematurely. The gulls had not made it this far inland yet; the only birds here were sparrows and a few doll-like cockatoos along the fences.

Vanessa seemed surprised and happy to see him. "Come in," she said, her thin face filling the doorway. She looked scrubbed and plain, not the way she did with Samson. "Nobody's home but me. Is Sam with you?"

"No," said Nal. For years he'd been planning to say to her, *I think we're meant to be,* but now that he was here he didn't say anything; his heart was going, and he almost had to stop himself from shoving his way inside.

"I brought you this," he said, pushing the ring at her. "I've been saving up for it."

"Nal!" she said, turning the ring over in her hands. "But this is really beautiful . . ."

It was easy. What had he worried about? He just stepped in and kissed her, touched her neck. Suddenly he was feeling every temperature at once, the coolness of her skin and the wet warmth of her mouth and even the tepid slide of sweat over his knuckles. She kissed him back, and Nal slid his hand beneath the neckline of her blouse and touched the bandage there. The Grigalunases' house was dark and still inside, the walls lined with framed pictures of dark-haired girls who looked like funhouse images of Vanessa, her sisters or her former selves. An orange cat darted under the stairwell.

"Nal? Do you want to sit down?" She addressed this to her own face in the foyer mirror, a glass crescent above the door, and when she turned back to Nal her eyes had brightened, charged with some anticipation that almost didn't seem to include him. Nal kissed her again and started steering her toward the living room. A rope was pulling him forward, a buried cable, and he was able to relax into it now only because he had spent his short lifetime doing up all the knots. Perhaps this is how the future works,

Nal thought—nothing fated or inevitable but just these knots like fists that you could tighten or undo.

Nal and Vanessa sat down on the green sofa, a little stiffly. Nal had never so much as grazed a girl's knee, but somehow he was kissing her neck, he was sliding a hand up her leg, beneath the elastic band of her underwear.

Vanessa struggled to undo Nal's belt and the tab of his jeans, and now she looked up at him; his zipper was stuck. He was trapped inside his pants. Thanks to his recent weight loss, he was able to wriggle out of them, tugging furiously at the denim. At last he got them off with a grunt of satisfaction and, breathless and red-faced, flung them to the floor. The zipper liner left a nasty scratch down his skin. Nal began to unroll his socks, hunching over and angling his hipbones. It was strange to see the splay of his dark toes on the Grigalunases' carpet, Vanessa half-naked beyond it.

She could have whinnied with laughter at him; instead, with a kindness that you can't teach people, she had walked over to the windows while Nal hopped and writhed. She had taken off her shirt and unwound the bandage and was shimmying out of her bra. The glass had gone dark with thunderheads. The smell of rain had crept into the house. She drew the curtains and slid out of the rest of her clothes. The living room was now a blue cave—Nal could see the soft curve of the sofa's back in the dark. Was he supposed to turn the light on? Which way was more romantic? "Sorry," he said as they both walked back to the sofa, their eyes flicking all over each other. Vanessa slid a hand over Nal's torso.

"You and Samson have the same boxer shorts," she said.

"Our mother buys them for us."

Maybe this isn't going to happen, Nal thought.

But then he saw a glint of silver and felt recommitted. Vanessa had slipped the pawnshop ring on—it was huge on her. She caught him looking and held her hand up, letting the ring slide over her knuckle, and they both let out jumpy laughs. Nal could feel sweat collecting on the back of his neck. They tried kissing again for a while. Vanessa's dark hair slid through his hands like palmfuls of oil as he fumbled his way inside her, started to move. He wanted to ask: Is this right? Is this okay? It wasn't at all what he'd imagined. Nal, moving on top of Vanessa, was still Nal, still cloaked with consciousness and inescapably himself. He didn't feel invincible—he felt clumsy, guilty. Vanessa was trying to help him find his rhythm, her hands just above his bony hips.

"Hey," Vanessa said at one point, turning her face to the side. "The cat's watching."

The orange tabby was licking its paws on the first stair, beneath the clock. The cat had somehow gotten hold of the stop screw—it must have fallen out of his pocket—and was batting it around.

The feeling of arrival Nal was after kept receding like a charcoal line on bright water. This was not the time or the place but he kept picturing the gulls, screaming and wheeling in a vortex just beyond him, and he groaned and sped up his motions. "Don't stop," Vanessa said, and there was such a catch to her voice that Nal said, "I won't, I won't," with real seriousness, like a parent reassuring a child. Although very soon, Nal could feel, he would have to.

Proving Up

"Go tack up, Miles!" says Mr. Johannes Zegner of the Blue Sink Zegners, pioneer of the tallgrass prairie and future owner of 160 acres of Nebraska. In most weathers, I am permitted to call him Pa.

"See if your mother's got the Window ready. The Inspector is coming tonight. He's already on the train, can you imagine!"

A thrill moves in me; if I had a tail I would shake it. So I will have to leave within the hour, and ride quickly—because if the one-eyed Inspector really is getting off at the spur line in Beatrice, he'll hire a stagecoach and be halfway to the Hox River Settlement by one o'clock; he could be at our farm by nightfall! I think Jesus Himself would cause less of a stir stepping off that train; He'd find a tough bunch to impress in this droughty place, with no water anywhere for Him to walk on.

"Miles, listen fast," Pa continues. "Your brother is coming—"

Sure enough, Peter is galumphing toward us through the puddled glow of the winter wheat. It came in too sparse this year to make a crop, wisping out of the sod like the thin blond hairs on

Pa's hand. My father has the "settler's scar," a pink star scored into the brown leather of his palm by the handle of the moldboard plow. Peter's got one, too, a raw brand behind his knuckles that never heals—and so will I when I prove up as a man. (As yet I am the Zegner runt, with eleven years to my name and only five of those West; I cannot grow a beard any quicker than Mr. Johannes can conjure wheat, but I can *ride*.)

Pa kneels low and clasps his dirt-colored hands onto my shoulders. "Your brother is coming, but it's you I want to send to our neighbors in need. Boy, it's *you*. I trust you on a horse. I know you'll tend to that Window as if it were your own life."

"I will, sir."

"I just got word from Bud Sticksel—you got two stops. The Inspector's making two visits. The Florissants and then the Sticksels. Let's pray he keeps to that schedule, anyhow, because if he decides to go to the Sticksels first . . ."

I shiver and nod, imagining the Sticksels' stricken faces in their hole.

"The Sticksels don't have one shard of glass. You cannot fail them, Miles."

"I know, Pa."

"And once they prove up, you know what to do?"

"Yes, Pa. This time I will—"

"You take the Window back. Bundle it in burlap. Get Bud's wife to help. Then you push that Inspector's toes into stirrups—do unto others, Miles—and you bring that man to our door."

"But what if the Inspector sees me reclaiming the Window from Mr. Sticksel? He'll know how we fooled him. Won't he cancel their title?"

Pa looks at me hard, and I can hear the gears in his head clicking. "You want to be a man, don't you, Miles?"

"Yes, sir. Very much."

"So use your wits, son. Some sleight of hand. I can't think of everything."

Increasingly time matters. I can feel it speeding up in my chest, in rhythm with my pounding heart. A flock of cliff swallows lifts off the grassy bank of our house, and my eyes fly with them into the gray light.

"Hey," says Peter. He comes up behind me and shovels my head under his arm—he smells sour, all vinegary sweat and bones. "What's this fuss?"

So Pa has to explain again that when the sun next rises, we'll have our autographed title. Peter's grin is as wide and handsome and full of teeth as our father's, and I smile into the mirror they make.

"Tomorrow?"

"Or even tonight."

Behind them, Ma seeps out of the dugout in her blue dress. She sees us gathered and runs down the powdery furrow like a tear—I think she would turn to water if she could.

No rain on our land since the seventh of September. That midnight we got half an inch and Pa drilled in the wheat at dawn. Most of it cooked in the ground; what came up has got only two or three leaves to a plant. Last week the stalks started turning ivory, like pieces of light. "Water," Pa growls at the blue mouth of heaven—the one mouth distant enough to ignore his fists.

He mutters that this weather will dry us all to tinder, lightning fodder, and he's spent every day since that last glorious hour of rainfall plowing firebreaks until he's too tired to stand. Ma's begun to talk to the shriveling sheaves in a crazy way, as if they were her thousand thirsty children. My brother pretends not to hear her.

"Inspection day," Pa booms at Ma's approach. "He's on the train now."

"The Inspector? Says who? Who thinks they're proving up?"

"Bud says. And we are. Daniel Florissant, Bud, the Zegners."

Pa leans in as if to kiss her, whispering; she unlatches her ear from his mouth.

"*No!* Are you crazy, Jo? The Inspector is a rumor, he's smoke! I can make you a promise: no such person is ever coming out here. How long do we have to wait before you believe that? A decade? What you want to risk—" She looks over at me and her voice gets quieter.

A silence falls over the Zegner family homestead, which Pa splits with his thundering hymn:

"You faithless woman! How can you talk like that after we have lived on this land for five years? Built our *home* here, held out through drought and hail, through locusts, Vera—"

Peter is nodding along. I have to tiptoe around the half-moon of my family to get to the sod barn. As I tack up Nore I can hear Ma worrying my father: "Oh, I am not deaf, I hear you lying to our child—'*It's verified.*'"

"Bud Sticksel is no liar," I reassure Nore's quivering rump. "Don't be scared. Ma's crazy. We'll find the Inspector."

After the defections and deaths of several settlers, the Sticksels have become our closest neighbors. Their farm is eighteen miles away. Bud used to work as a hired hand in Salmon, Ohio, says Pa. Came here the same year as our family, 1872. He's an eyeblink from being eligible to prove up and get his section title: 1. Bud's land by the lake is in grain. 2. He's put a claim shanty on the property, ten feet by twenty. 3. He has resided on his land for five years, held on through four shining seasons of drought. ("Where is God's rain?" Mrs. Sticksel murmurs to Ma.) 4. He has raised sixty acres of emerald lucerne, two beautiful daughters, and thirty evil turkeys that have heads like scratched mosquito bites. The Sticksels have met every Homestead Act requirement save one, its final strangeness, what Pa calls "the wink in the bureaucrats' wall": a glass window.

Farther south, on the new rail lines, barbed wire and crystal lamps and precut shingles fire in on the freight trains, but in the Hox River Settlement a leaded pane is as yet an unimaginable good. Almost rarer than the rain. Yet all the Hox settlers have left holes in the walls of their sod houses, squares and ovals where they intend to put their future windows. Some use waxed paper to cover these openings; the Sticksels curtained up with an oiled buffalo skin. The one time I slept at their dugout that hide flapped all night like it was trying to talk to me: *Blab blab blab*.

"I know you don't belong here," I replied—I was sympathetic— "but there isn't any glass for that empty place. There's one Window in this blue-gray ocean of tallgrass, and it's ours."

"Now, Miles," both my parents preach at me continually, in the same tone with which they recite the wishful Bible rules, "you know the Window must benefit every settler out here. We are only its stewards." Pa long ago christened it the Hox River Window and swore it to any claimant in need. (I sometimes think my parents use me to stimulate goodness and to remind themselves of this oath, the same way I untangle my greedy thoughts by talking to the animals, Louma and Nore—because it's easy to catch oneself wanting to hoard all the prairie's violet light on the Hox panes.) He says our own walls cannot wear the Window until we prove up—it's too precious, too fragile. So we keep it hidden in the sod cave like a diamond.

Our house is a dugout in a grassy hill—I've sent three letters to my cross-eyed Cousin Bailey in Blue Sink, Pennsylvania, and in each one I fail to explain our new house to his satisfaction. Cousin Bailey uses his fingers to sum numbers; once he asked me if the winged angels in heaven eat birdseed or "man-food" like chocolate pie. The idea of a house made of sod defeats him. He writes back with questions about bedrooms and doors, closets and attics. "No, Bailey, we live in one room," I reply impatiently. "A ball of pure earth. Not enough timber for building walls on the prairie so we dug right into the sod. It's a cave, where we now live."

"A grave," says Peter, a joke I don't like one bit. It's our home, although it does look like a hiccup in the earth. The floor is sod, the roof is sod, hardened by the red Nebraska sun—if it ever rains again, water will sheet in on our heads for days. The mattress sits on a raised cage of wild plum poles. My mother covers the cookstove with her mother's pilled linen tablecloth to keep the lizards and field mice and moles and rattlesnakes and yellow spiders from falling into our supper. (Although she threatens to pull the cloth if we get cheated out of another harvest, and let every plaguey creature into our soup: "The wheat's not getting any taller, Jo, but our boys are. They need meat.")

Pa and Peter and I dug out the room. Pa used the breaking plow to sculpt the sod into six-inch slabs of what folks here call Nebraska marble. He stacked these into our walls, arranging each third layer in a cross-grained pattern with the grass side down. In summer, this room can get as hot as the held breath of the world. We dug a sod stable for the team of horses, the hogs, and Louma, our heat-demented cow. She's got the Hereford lightning up her red flanks—it looks like somebody nailed her with a bucket of scalding paint. She chews slop with a look of ancient shock, her vexed eyes staring out from a white face. In truth, her eyes look a little like Ma's.

My horse is Nore, who I've been riding since she was a two-year-old filly. She's jet-black and broody and doesn't fit with my father's team. Up on her back I'm taller than any man out here, taller than a pancake stack of Peters. I saddle Nore, explain the day to her, her ears flattening at the word *Inspector*.

Behind the stalls, my father is shaking my mother like a doll.

"He's a rumor, huh? Then I'm going to shove the fellow's arms through the coat sleeves of that rumor! He's real, and so are we Zegners. By sunrise we'll own our home, if you can muster faith. Faith the size of one—damn! One seed of some kind. It moves mountains. How's that go, Vera, in the Bible? Apple? Pumpkin?"

"It's a mustard seed, Jo. Yahweh is not baking any pies." Ma's voice is shaking now, too. "Miles is eleven years old," she says slowly. "The Sticksels are a half day's ride for you . . ."

Pa catches sight of me, and I duck his gaze. I hope he shakes the looniness right out of her. I'm ready to ride.

Ma never yells at me. But lately her voice is dreadful even when it's cheerful, singing out of the well mouth of our house. Hoarse, so that it sounds as if the very sod is gargling sand. She's not sick, or no sicker than anybody else—it's the dust. I hate the strain in her voice as she tries to make a happy tune for me and my brother, when her yellowish eyes are sunk deep in her face and every long note she holds shoves her ribs through her dress. She hasn't been fat for two years.

I was the last Zegner born in Pennsylvania. The three girls were born here, and buried in a little plot under the tufting gama grass, next to the sixty acres we have in wheat. Aside from salt thistle and the big sunflowers in July, nothing grows on top of the girls. Ma won't allow it. She's of the opinion that each of her daughters would have lived had we stayed in Blue Sink. Long-nosed and blue-eyed—"like you, Miles." Tall and pin-thin, like the women in her family.

That's how my sisters look to me, too. Glowing taller and taller. White legs twining moonward, like swords of wheat. They sprout after dark. Some nights the heat is suffocating and it wakes me. Through the hole in our kitchen where the Window will go I watch my mother kneeling in their field, weeding thistle. The three sisters sway behind her back. They stare at me with their hundred-year-old faces. They know they missed their chance to be girls. The middle one smiles at me, and her white teeth outshine the harrow. She gives me a little wave. I wonder if she knows I'm her brother.

When red dawn comes Ma's at the cookstove with her face to the leaping flame, and I'm afraid to ask her if I was dreaming.

I cannot tell Pa or Peter about the sisters, of course. And not Nore—she's a horse, she spooks. Lately I won't even pray on it, because what if God tells them up in heaven that I'm terrified to meet them? Sometimes I talk to the pig, who'll be butchered anyhow come Christmas Eve.

"I'll be fine, Ma."

"He'll be fine."

"Jo!"

"Do you want me to send Peter, then?" Pa says coolly.

"Oh, Jo. He *can't*. You know that." Ma chews at her lip, Louma-like.

Something is going wrong with my brother. He's not reliable. A few weeks ago, when the clouds dispersed again without releasing one drop of rain, he disappeared for three days; when he rode home his hands were wet. "Not my blood," he reassured Pa. Ma sent me on the four-mile walk to the well to haul for a bath, even though our washing day wasn't until the following Wednesday, and we boys go last—after a draw for drinking and cooking, after a draw for the garden.

Peter is sixteen, but that night he let Ma sponge the black blood off him like a child, and I almost cried like a kid myself when he splashed clean water in waves over the sides of the trough.

I am a little afraid of my brother.

"I'll go, then." Pa's whole body draws back like a viper in its gold burnoose. I close my eyes and see the shadow of his secret self throbbing along the wall of our sod barn: his head rolling to its own music and sloshing with poisons. Even in the quiet I can hear him rattling.

"Jo."

"No, sweetheart, you're right. Pete can't go, we can't spare Miles—who does that leave? I go or we forfeit our chance. We don't prove up. We don't own the land where our girls are buried."

Ma leaves to get the Window.

We nightly pray for everyone in Hox to prove up, the titles from the Land Office framed on their walls. The purple and scarlet tongue of my mother's bookmark used to move around the Bible chapters with the weather, but for the past year and a half it's been stuck on Psalm 68:9. On that page, says Ma, it rains reliably.

Through the empty socket in our sod, I can see her hunched over in the deepest shadows. Dust whirls around the floor in little twisters, scraping her ankles raw. She bends over the glass, and a rail of vertebrae jumps out. My mother is thirty-one years old, but the land out here paints old age onto her. All day she travels this room, sweeping a floor that is already dirt, scrubbing the dinner plates into white ovals, shaking out rugs. Ma is humming a stubborn song and won't look up from the Window on her lap. She polishes the glass by licking the end of her braid into a fine point and whisking it over the surface, like a watercolorist. Now the Window is the only clean thing in our house. It's the size of a hanging painting, with an inch border of stained glass. Two channeled lead strips run orange and jewel-blue light around it. But the inner panels are the most beautiful, I think: perfectly transparent.

Ma wraps it in some scatter rugs and penny burlap. "Good-bye, Miles," she says simply.

We fix my cargo to the horse's flank, half a dozen ropes raveling to one knot at the saddle horn. Pa hitches my leg at a painful angle, warns me not to put weight anywhere near the Window. Already I'm eager for the crystal risk of riding at a gallop. Then he gives me an envelope and kisses up to my ear like he does Ma's.

"A little bribe," he says. "Tell the Inspector there's more waiting at the Zegner place."

"Okay." I frown. "Is there?"

Pa thumps Nore on the rump.

When we reach the fence line a very bad thought occurs to me: "Pa! What if they don't give the Window back?" I call out. "The Sticksels—what if they try to keep it?"

"Then you'd better run fast, because those aren't our neighbors. Those are monsters, pretending to be the Sticksels. But before you run, grab the Window."

I might as well have asked him, *What if Ma leaves us? What if Peter never gets better?*

I don't look back as I glide Nore around the oak—the only tree for miles of prairie. The wind blows us forward, sends the last leaves raining around us and the October clouds flashing like horseshoes. I duck underneath the branches and touch the lowermost one for luck. When I turn to salute my father, I see that he and Ma are swaying together in the stunted wheat like a dance, his big hands tight around the spindle of her waist and her face buried in his neck, her black hair waterfalling across the caked grime on his shirt. It's only later that I realize Ma was sobbing.

THE FIRST FAMILY of landowners we met in Nebraska were the Henry Yotherses. Five years ago, a few weeks after our migration to the Hox River Settlement, we arrived at their July picnic "one hour shy of serendipity," as Mrs. Yothers immediately announced—too late but only just to meet the Inspector. I was a pipsqueak then, and so I remember everything: the glowering sunset and an army of Turkey Red wheat mustered by the Yotherses to support their claim, the whaleback hump of the sod house rising above the grassy sea—and Mr. Henry Yothers himself, a new king in possession of his title.

"A proven man," Pa whistled.

"Christ in heaven, love must glue you to him every fortnight," Ma joked to Mrs. Yothers—but in a hushed voice, surrounded as they were by what seemed like thousands of Yothers children. Ten thousand tiny mouths feeding on that quarter section of land, and dressed for the occasion like midget undertakers, in black trousers and bowties.

"That Inspector shook each of my children's hands," boasted Henry Yothers. "Congratulated each one of them on being 'landed gentry.' He's a curious fellow, Johannes. Lost an eye in the war. He wears a patch of dark green silk over the socket. It's no coincidence, I'm sure, that he's obsessed with the Glass Requirement."

And then we got our first look at the Hox River Window: that magical glass fusing their inner room to the outside world, gracing their home with light. Back in Blue Sink there were thousands of windows, but we only looked *through* them, never *at* them. We gasped.

Remembering this, I feel queasy all over again. Something about the big grins on everybody's faces, and all that pomp: the Inspector's checklist, the ten-dollar filing fee, the U.S. president's counterfeit autograph in an inky loop. Through the glass we watched Mrs. Yothers slide the title into its birch frame and dutifully applauded. The general mood confused me. We were going to slave and starve and wait five years to get a piece of paper so thin? Why? To prove what? Who cares what Washington, D.C., thinks?

"Congratulations!" my mother beamed at Mrs. Yothers, with a girlishness I'd never seen before, and then embarrassed us all by bursting into tears. "Oh, boys, they *proved* it to them."

"To who?"

"Who? Everybody, Miles! The people back East, who said they'd never make it a year on the frontier. The men in Washington. The Inspector will forward their papers on to the president himself. Now you come say a prayer with me—"

Back then, Ma never mentioned Pennsylvania except to say "good riddance." We'd traveled west under juicy clouds that clustered like grapes. My sisters weren't alive in her belly or dead under the thistle and sod. Our plow gleamed. Furniture from Blue Sink was still in boxes.

"Miles, if we're to make this place our home, we need it official. Same as any claimant out here. You can't understand that?"

With Pa out of earshot, I said, "No, ma'am. I really cannot."

"The Yotherses survived the grasshoppers of 1868, got hailed out twice, burned corn for fuel. They took over from the Nunemakers. Did you know that, Miles? A bunch that fled. But the Henry Yothers family prevailed—they held on to their claim. Your heart's so stingy you can't celebrate that?"

But, Ma, I wanted to say. Because I guessed that a few hours earlier, before the Inspection, the Yotherses' farm had looked no different from the proven place we'd leave—with the same children running barefoot around their cave, and in the distance the same wheat blowing. And the whole scene sliding through that Window, as real or as unreal as it had ever been.

WHAT WE DIDN'T know then, as we filed our own preempt in the white beehive of the Federal Land Office: the long droughts were coming. Since that July day, over half the Hox River homesteaders have forfeited their claims and left, dozens of families withdrawing back east. And the men and women who stayed, says Pa with teeth in his words, who sowed and abided, "We are the victors, Miles. Our roots reach deep. We Zegners were green when we came here, but now we're dust brown, the color of Hox. Proving up means you stand your ground, you win your title—a hundred and sixty acres go from public to private. Clear and free, you hold it. Nobody can ever run you off. It's home."

Over the years, my father's reasoning has been whittled to its core, like everything else out here. At times he wanders around our homestead shouting at random intervals, "I know a hunger stronger than thirst!" His voice booms like thunder in my brain as we light out. Nore digs into the dry earth, happy to be running.

"Nore?" Like Pa, I whisper into the pink cone of her ear. "We'll get the Inspector, but I'll tell you a secret: I don't understand why they need that piece of paper. This place has been home for years."

AT FIRST it is a fine morning. Nore strikes a square trot and I goose her to a canter. Pocket gophers and kangaroo rats scramble in front of our lunging shadow; the horned larks are singing in the grasses, plumping like vain old Minister Fudd back in Blue Sink. Soon nothing but crimson bluestem is blazing all around us. Coyotes go mousing in this meadow but today I count none. Twice I have seen eagles back here. Three miles of dead grass pass, tickling Nore's hindquarters. Whenever she sneezes I let go of the reins and grab ahold of the Window's wrought-iron frame, which feels as slender and bony as a deer's leg through the burlap case. Pa could have a million sons and none would be a better steward.

We sink into the tallgrass, happy to get swallowed and escape the midday sun. But when we emerge the sky is seamless and black, and the last yellow stitching goes dark. Something is shifting, I think. We reach a timber belt of cottonwood and Siberian elms—species not uncommon to Nebraska, yet I've never seen examples of such overpowering heights. Atmospheric salts spill through the air as birds scatter in fantastic numbers before us. The charge pucks the horse's huge nostrils, causes her devil's ears to cup around. A chill races down her bony shoulders and prickles up my neck. Between noon and one o'clock, the temperature must plummet some twenty degrees. A sound I barely recognize claps in the distance. "Oh, Nore," I mumble into her ear, sick with hope. The black sky grows blacker still.

Rain?

I dig into her soft belly too meanly, as if the moons of my spurs could burst the clouds, and maybe they can: The miracle sounds again as if the sky's been shot, and rain gushes all over us. Unstoppably, like blood from a body. I stick out my tongue to catch it. Over my scalp and Nore's coarse hair it runs and glimmers, crystal clear and *clean*. Sheets of water hammer the tallgrass flat, and we go whooping on, Nore and I whinnying in a duet:

Rain!

Rain!

Rain!

Deeper into the storm I begin to get a picture in my mind of water flooding down the Hox glass. Rain shining the Window. "Oh, God, I want to see that, Nore," I whisper to her. It's a scene I've imagined a thousand times through all the dry years.

I slow her to a stop and dismount. The red stump I use as Nore's hitching post is boiling with water; she stares at me, her great eyes running. I undo the knot, loosen the burlap. Rain soaks over my trembling hands; I move the scatter rugs and expose a triangle of the Hox glass. The first drop hits with a beautiful *plink,* and I feel like an artist. Soon this corner of the Window is jeweled with water, and I uncover the rest of the glass, floating the whole blurred world through it.

I close my eyes and see my mother and father drenched outside the soddy, still dancing but joyously now; Louma in the barn rolling her twinkling eyes at real lightning; the sod crumbling from our ceiling; the house turning into a mudslide. We'll sleep outdoors and watch the wheat growing and leafing, heading out and reseeding. I angle the Window and funnel the cold rain onto my boot toes. Feelings billow and surge in me to a phenomenal height, a green joy that I wish I could share with my mother.

By now a whole river must have fallen out of heaven and into the sod, and I don't know how long I've been standing here. Then I look up and see it's not only rainfall sweeping over the prairie: a shape slips through the bluestem just ahead of us, disappears.

"Mr. Florissant?"

But the Florissant claim is still an hour from us at a gallop. And if that shape belonged to Daniel Florissant, well, he has changed considerably since the Easter picnic.

Quickly I rebundle and rope up the Window and get astride Nore, wishing for Peter's .22 rifle or even a pocketknife as I scan the ground for flat rocks, sticks.

"Hello?"

The black figure is moving through the switchgrass. I turn Nore around and try to give chase until I realize it's not escaping through the rain at all but rather circling *us,* like a hawk or the hand of a clock.

"Mr. Florissant? Is that you?" I swallow. "Inspector . . . ?"

I wheel inside the shadow's wheeling, each of us moving against the rotation of the other like cogs, the stranger occasionally walking into sight and then vanishing again; and if he *is* the Inspector, he does not seem in any hurry to meet me. Perhaps this is part of some extra test—as if our patience requires further proof. Five years, three daughters, half an inch of rain, and no wheat crop last winter—even Cousin Bailey can sum those numbers. "Inspector!" I holler again over the thunder. Nore trembles, and I imagine that she, too, can feel the pull of this fellow's gaze, the noose he's drawing around us.

I realize that I'm shivering out of my clothes, my hands raw. Then a cold flake hits my nose. The rain is turning to snow.

Can a blizzard strike this early, in late October? Does that happen on the prairie? Immediately I regret putting the question to the sky, which seems eager to answer, suddenly very attentive to the questions of humans. "Run, Nore," I tell her. We still have to pass the Yotherses' place.

ONLY I KNOW where the Hox River Window really came from. Pa told me by accident after a pint of beer and made me pledge my silence. It's a scary story: One December night, almost two years ago now, we believed the Inspector was coming to visit our farm. We were eighteen months short of the residency requirement, and we had no window. Frantic, Pa rode out to the Yotherses' to beg for a square of glass and found their claim abandoned.

Tack was scattered all over the barn floor. Outside, three half-starved Sauceman hogs were masticating the pale red fibers of Mrs. Yothers's dress; piles of clothing lay trampled into the sod—bouquets of children's bow ties. The dugout was dark. A family of spotted black jackrabbits were licking their long feet under the table. A tarantula had closed around the bedpost like a small, gloved hand. The Window was still shining in the wall.

So Pa took it. He rode home and told Ma that he'd bartered for the Window from a man moving back to ranch West Texas.

What a whopper! I thought, and almost laughed out loud, guessing that Pa must be teasing us. Straightaway I'd recognized our neighbors' glass.

I waited for Ma to dispute the story, yet she surprised me by breathing, "Oh, *thank you*—" in a little girl's voice and reaching out to the Window with dreamy eyes. Peter, too, chuckled softly and touched the glass like it was a piece of new luck, and no one ever mentioned our friends the Yotherses again. As we carried the Window down to our dugout in a Zegner parade—Ma singing and Peter's smile lighting even his eyes—those thousand kids were everywhere in my imagination, asking me why I kept quiet, asking why I was trying with all my might to forget them.

To me only, Pa confessed to coveting their title, still posted on the dirt wall—but he took the Window instead, not wanting to risk our own claim by squatting on another man's haunted land. This scared me worse than anything else: Who would leave 160 acres to which they held title? What happened to them? "What's the difference, Miles?" My father had drunk himself into a moon-squint, his eyes glowing crescents. "Dead is gone."

Now whenever he mentions "West Texas," he winks at me, and I think of my sisters under the sod, silently winking back.

"What puzzles me, Miles," he slurred at the end of the night, "is that before he left, Mr. Yothers had drilled in a new crop. At first I saw the rows behind the wheat and thought, *Ah, Henry knows how starved we are for timber, he's planted trees*—dozens of queer little trees, shaped like crosses. Just a single branch right through their middles. Saplings, sure. Only one grew about a foot and a half, and the rest were much smaller. The thin trunks were the funniest shade of milky white, my son, like no tree's wood I've ever seen; and there wasn't a leaf in that bleached grove. And who plants anything in the dead of winter, in frozen ground? On my knees I discovered that each horizontal branch was roped to its base by a hitching knot, and these white branches were knobby at the ends, almost like animal—or even human . . ."

But Pa saw my face and trailed off, and soon he began to snore, and I was left alone to fret over his riddle. Now I think we must be very near to this milky white grove, and I am grateful for the dark sky and the snowflakes on Nore's reins—because there is no time for me to dismount and wander into the rows, to prove my guess right or wrong.

Forgive us, forgive us, I think as I race Nore past the Yotherses' bleak dugout, where the empty window frame leers on, and snow swirls in lovely patterns.

We detour five miles around a carmine streambed filled with ice, where dozens of black snakes draw S shapes like a slow, strange current, spooking Nore; and afterward I'm no longer sure of our direction. Like us, the sun is lost. The temperature continues to fall. We come upon a dam I've never seen, the Window rattling like a saber against Nore's belly.

"Oh, God, where are we, Nore?" I coax her up a low hill, and it's around then that the blizzard hits.

The wind attacks our naked skin like knives; I can nearly hear Ma's voice in it, calling me home. But I'm too brave to turn the horse around, and anyhow I wouldn't know which way to go. White octaves of snow shriek from the tallgrass to the great descending blank of the heavens. "Go, go, go," I moan into Nore's ear, wanting her to decide. A part of me is already at the Florissants', warming up by the fire, sharing a meal of drumsticks and cider and biscuits with the Inspector. Their title drying on the kitchen table. "Well, sir," I tell him, "we did have a little trouble getting here, but it was certainly worth the risk . . ." A chokecherry branch cuts my left eyelid, and the eye fills with blood. The more I rub at it the denser the red gel gets. Outside of my mind I can barely see. We go flickering through the snow, until it becomes difficult to say which colors and temperatures are inner or outer weather, where one leaves off and the other picks up. I tighten my knee's grip on the Window frame. When Nore breaks into a gallop I drop the reins and grab her neck. Snow is eating our tracks: when I look back, it's as if we no longer exist.

She shoots through the tempest like an arrow for its target, and I think, *Thank God, she must smell a barn*—but when her jaw jerks around, I see that ice coats her eyes. She's been galloping completely blind.

I am sure we're being punished—I should never have unwrapped the Window, not even for one second. Snow pummels us with its million knuckles. "Oh, my darling, oh, poor darling," I tell Nore—I don't recognize my own voice anymore; Peter would caw with laughter if he could hear my tone, my father would be sickened—"Nore, my sweet one, my love . . ." Tender words pour out of me, my grandmother Aura's words, the kind I haven't heard since she spoke them on the cousins' rose sofa in Blue Sink, and I wish I could use them like a compass needle to lead me back.

I grab ahold of the bridle and tug Nore forward with the wind at our backs, blowing more snow in on gales. I think of trying to guide her by the reins, but the snow's banked too deep to walk. Nore's sides heave, covered in freezing lather. Her eyelashes are stiff. I can't feel my toes inside my boots.

The horse keeps going blind, and I can't stop it—the ice coating the dark circles of her purply-black eyes. She moans whenever I attempt to pry and crack them clear. The reins wriggle snakily down her back and she jumps sideways. Hatred shivers along her spine; I've got one eyelid in a pinch when she peels back her lips and tries to bite me but misses and rears. As if in slow motion I watch the Window coming loose, thumping against her side in the snow-furred burlap; I feel myself rolling, falling out of the saddle and somehow beneath her churning hooves, reaching up as the Window slides slantwise, one point angled at my chest—and then I'm lying in the snow with the Window in my arms, stunned, watching as Nore disappears.

Now I understand: this is a nightmare. She flies into the white heart of the storm while I pant all raggedy in the drifts with the Window hard against my chest, sucking my frozen thumb. Screaming turns out to be an agility I've taken for granted; "Nore," I try to shout, but hear nothing. For one moment more I can see her running: a black match head tearing against a wall of snow. It's a wonder the gales don't catch alight and burn.

Mr. Inspector, sir, I hope you're stuck in the weather, too. And, Mrs. Florissant, do not let us hold you up for dinner, please eat, and should you spy a man through the open socket in your wall, won't you tell him that I'm lost . . .

Suddenly I realize what I'm holding on to—did I shatter it? I'm terrified to look. (What I see instead is Louma's skeleton in dust, my fingers threading through the open sockets in her skull.) As I pry at the burlap I learn something surprising about my future, something I hadn't guessed: If the Hox glass is in pieces, I won't ever go back home. I'd rather die here than return to our dugout without it.

Oh, Father, thank you—it's intact. I push my palms down the smooth length of it twice before sealing the burlap, then roll onto my back. High above me the black sky withdraws forever into an upside-down horizon—not a blue prairie line but a cone of snows. Wind wolves go on howling. Each of my eyelids feels heavier than iron, but sleep isn't what's beckoning me; the snow is teaching me a deeper way to breathe: long spaces open up behind each inhalation, followed by a very colorful spell of coughing. There's blood on the back of my hand—I knocked loose several teeth when I fell. One is lying near my left eye in its own smeary puddle. Snow falls and falls. Tomorrow, I think, the thirsty sod will drink this storm up, guzzle the red runoff from my chin. Acres of gold wheat wave at me from the future: March, April.

Hold on to your claim, Pa hisses, and I wipe my eyes.

What am I supposed to be doing out here again? Where am I taking the glass? And wasn't there a horse? For the life of me I cannot remember the horse's name.

More than anything I want to get the Window through the storm. I crouch over the burlap like something feeding—my skin becoming one more layer of protection for the glass. Soon my clothes are soaked through. The elements seal my eyes, so that I have to keep watch over the Window blindly with my arms. I clutch at it like a raft as the prairie pitches in icy waves. Images swirl through my mind of animals freezing in their stalls, black fingers lost to doctors' saws. *Think of a Bible verse, a hymn!* What enters my head instead is my mother's humming, a weedy drone that has no tune. Hours pass, or maybe minutes or whole days; the clock of my body breaks down. The world is pitch-black.

WHEN I WAKE, water is running in spring rivers down my face; my eyelids unravel and crack open. The temperature has risen, and a sunbeam fixes an *X* on my hand, which burns when I flex it. The hard pillow of the Window comes into focus under my cheek. I turn my head and find I'm surrounded by leafless skeletons of trees and the sapphire ice—and a man, watching me.

I sit up. Fifty yards ahead, a willowy man takes one sideways step through the golden haze and is somehow suddenly upon me. *I'm saved!* I think—but just as quickly my cry for help dissolves. This man looks even worse off than me. His gaunt face is entirely black except for the wet cracks of his eyes and mouth and pink lesions on his cheeks, as if he has just survived some kind of explosion. At first I think the skin is charred, but then the light gives it a riverbed glow and I realize he's covered in mud—soil, sod. His shirt and trousers are stiff with the same black filth, and the dirt on his collar isn't dried at all, but oozing. A dim saucer at each knee shows he's been genuflecting in the fields. Only, what sort of man is out farming in a blizzard? Not even my father is that crazy. What would drive a person into this weather?

He shuffles toward me, removing his hat.

"Inspector?"

We shout this at the exact same moment. Then we're left to gape at each other. White frogs of breath leap from my mouth. He doesn't seem to breathe at all.

"Hello, sir," I manage, and hold out a numb hand. The feeling returns to my stiff arm, and I bite down as pain rips along the bone—the polite smile, by some miracle, still on my face. "I guess we are both mistaken, sir." ("Etiquette will take possession of you at the oddest times, won't it, Miles?" Ma murmured once, when I caught her apologizing to a cupful of grasshoppers before drowning them in kerosene.)

Well, the stranger doesn't return any of my friendliness. *I'm Miles Zegner,* I was about to offer, but I swallow it back. And I don't ask for his name, either; a queasiness stirring in my gut warns me that I might not want to know it.

I'm certain that I've never seen this man on any homestead around here—but he's dressed for the work, with his cuffs pushed to the elbows like any man in Hox; and like Pa he has the settler's scar from the moldboard plow. He's a southpaw. A sodbuster. One of us. A newcomer to the Hox River Settlement? (*No, no,* a little voice in me whispers, *not new.*) His eyes have the half-moon markings of a pronghorn antelope. He looks like he's been awake for generations.

"You did not see a horse come through here, sir?"

"No horses. No Inspectors on horseback. No bats hanging from Inspectors' noses." He giggles.

"Are you all right, sir? Are you lost, too?"

Then the man says something in a jangly tone that I can barely understand, it's so reedy and high. His voice is almost female, or animal, and the words make no sense whatsoever.

"Green me that wheel!"

"Pardon, sir?"

"Grease me that doe!"

I swallow hard.

"Sir, I am not understanding you."

He draws a rectangle in the snow-dotted air and laughs; I swear I see a nugget of earth tumble out of his mouth. His lips are plush and smeared.

"But we need to wake up now, don't we, boy? This is quite a day! It sounds like you and I are on the hunt for the same fellow.

The Inspector is coming shortly, you see. Yes. I believe that he will be coming very soon."

A fine gray ash is blowing from his curly hair, which looks like it is or once might have been yellow. The wind shifts and my nose wrinkles—there's a smell, a putrescence, a mix of silage and marrow and a hideous sweetness, like the time a family of rats suffocated in our sod walls. One hand keeps fussing with his trousers, which he's belted with a double loop of rope—his rib cage is almost impossibly narrow. If he were any thinner I swear he'd disappear. My mother's voice drifts into my ear: "He's a rumor, he's smoke . . ." But his eyes are solid marbles, and his fingernails are real enough to be broken. His left hand closes on the handle of a hay knife.

"That's a beautiful knife."

He smiles at me.

"And you say you are also"—I cough—"waiting on the Inspector? You've been here for the five years, then?"

The handle of the knife is some kind of clover-toned wood. The blade looks like a long tooth.

"Oh!" The man laughs. "Even longer. Long enough to lose track of the days and seasons entirely. Suns, moons, droughts, famines—who's counting?" He laughs again. The sun is stronger now. It shifts above us but never seems to settle anywhere on him.

"Where is your quarter section?"

"You're standing on it."

"Oh." *But where are we?* "Is anyone else here? Don't you have a family?"

"I may have." He frowns and licks his black lips, as if he truly cannot remember. "Yes! I did have a family. Parents, certainly. They are buried back east. And a wife . . . yes!" He beams at me. "I *did* have one. A wife, but she wasn't worth much. Women can be so impatient, Miles. And children—I believe we had several of them."

He begins to shake his thin shoulders in the silvery *h-yuk, h-yuk, h-yuk* of a coyote. His tongue surprises me—I guess part of me thought he was a ghost, a creature like my sisters. But his tongue is as red as sunrise in his dark face. He is alive, no question. I feel relieved, then scared for fresh reasons.

"Ah, children—*that* was a wash." This time when he opens his mouth, his voice is all throat.

"You shouldn't laugh at that."

"What's the matter?" He grins, trying to rib me with his elbow. "Out here we need a sense of humor, isn't that so?"

The violence of his laughter sprays dirt into the air; I cough again and think with horror that I'm breathing a powder from his body.

"Your kids all died?"

He shrugs.

"Sons or daughters?"

"Sons and daughters, yes. Sicklings. Weak ones. None lasted."

"What happened to your wife?"

"She lost faith." He lets out a theatrical sigh. "Lost her will to prosper. Became a madwoman, if you want to know. I had to make a break with her. Had to make a fresh start"—I wince; he's talking just like Pa now—"drove her off. Or rather, plowed her under. The West is a land of infinite beginnings, isn't that right, Miles Zegner? Pick up, embark again, file a preempt, stake a new claim"—*Did I tell him my name?*—"and after many lonely seasons, I have fulfilled each of the Act's stipulations. See this?"

He's holding something out to me—half a piece of paper. I take it with a trembling hand and recognize the text of the Homestead Act. I marvel at the document's creamy white color, its ink-bleeding signature—if I didn't know better I'd swear it was the original writ. How did this dirt-streaked stranger acquire such a thing—a law that looks like it was snatched from the president's own desk?

SEC. 3. And be it further enacted, that the Register of the Land Office shall note all such applications on the tract books and plats of his office, and keep a register of all such entries, and make return thereof to the General Land Office, together with the proof upon which they have been founded . . .

The man trails a slushy finger down to the word *glass*. Every claim shanty or dugout must have a real glass window, a whimsical clause that has cost lives out here. I stare at the sod and the black ribbon of blood under his nail.

"So you see that I'm in real need here, Miles. All the other proof I have ready for this Register, the Inspector. The last thing I need is a window." He contorts his mouth into a terrible smile.

My father's instructions move my jaw, push out my breath: "Listen, sir. I have a Window. If the Inspector is coming, I can loan it to you. We can fix it so it looks like it belongs to your dugout. So you can prove up."

"You would do that? For me?"

His eyes brighten fervidly in his grimy face, but not with happiness—it's more like watching sickness take root and germinate, blazing into a wildfire fever.

I nod, thinking about Pa. For all his charity with the Hox glass, I'm the one who bears the risk of it.

Without my awareness, we have begun moving; and our march feels almost like a pleasant walk, just a normal trip to deliver the Window to a neighbor. I picture the Florissants' claim swimming toward me out of the plains. The sun casts itself like a spell across the land—as if the blizzard never happened, as if Nore was not lost. The sky out west has so many tricks to make a person forget what he's just lived through.

We enter a clearing. Shortgrass and green ash are planted in tiers as a windbreak, and I can see what must be his dugout.

There are no bones in his fingers. He is made of dust. If it ever rains again he will seep back into the earth.

Before us a wall of sod bulges and heaves—every inch of it covered with flies. Doorless and stolidly black, studded through with reddish roots; there is not one thing this heap of earth has in common with a home. The snow stops abruptly fifty yards in every direction from the structure's foundation. No grass grows on it or near it; no birds sing; the smell of death makes my nostrils burn and my eyes stream.

Dear Bailey, I write in my mind, *if you thought our sod house was difficult to understand, you'll find it impossible to imagine this one. Bailey, I might not make it out of here alive.*

"Gosh, sir" is all that squeaks out of me.

"Now, would you like to see my crops, Miles? The acres I have cultivated? They're behind the house."

"And what crops might those be, sir?"

I want his words to give me the familiar pictures. Say: *corn.* Say: *wheat, milo, hay, lucerne.* But he only smiles and replies, "Come take a look."

I let the man lead me by my elbow, and when we turn a corner I shut my eyes. I wonder if he'll pry them open—like I did Nore's.

"Quite a harvest, eh?" he's saying. "And I grew them without a drop of water."

Sometimes I dream that dark rains fall and my sisters rise out of the sod, as tall as the ten-foot wheat, shaking the midges and the dust from their tangled hair. Like rain, they thunder and moan. Their pale mouths open and they hiss. Their faces aren't like any faces I know. *Stay in the ground,* I plead. *Oh, God, please let only wheat rise up.*

Even when my eyes open, I can't stop rubbing at them—I feel like I'm still held in that dream. The scene before me is familiar and terrifying: white crosses, hundreds or maybe thousands of them, rolling outward on the prairie sea. A shovel head glints in a freshly plowed furrow, where a yellowish knob the size of an onion sticks out of the sod. And I see now why Pa was so troubled by their milky hue, because these trees aren't made of wood at all, but bone. My sisters go on hissing in my mind.

"So you see," the man says, as brightly as any western noon, "as soon as the Inspector comes, I'll own the land—a hundred and sixty acres, and not one yard less."

No, you are mistaken, sir. The land owns you.

He takes my arm and guides me back toward the sod mound. "Now, if you'll just kindly help me put the window in—"

"And when do you think the Inspector is coming?" I ask in a mild voice.

The man smiles and rakes at his black eyes.

As we unpeel the snowy burlap from the Window, I find myself thinking about my home: Once, when I was nearly sleeping, a fleecy tarantula with a torso as thick as a deck of cards crawled across my mouth, and Peter laughed so hard that I started laughing, too. My father took three months to finish a table and paint it lake blue, just because he thought the color would be a relief to Ma. My mother pieced a quilt for each of her daughters in the dark. Often, at night, I wake into the perfect blankness of the dugout and watch our dreams braid together along the low ceiling. It would take lifetimes to explain to this wretched creature why our Zegner soddy is a home, even without any Inspector's stamp, while this place is a . . . tomb.

I step back and let him do the last work to widen the aperture meant to frame the Window. He grunts and scrapes at the pegs holding the shape of the breach and snows sod down all around us. He spits sootily on the glass and rubs in broad strokes with his sleeve.

"When the Inspector comes and sees my window—" he begins prattling, and a quagmire opens up in my chest, deep in its center—a terror like the suck of soft earth. And like a quagmire the terror won't release me, because the man is speaking in the voice of my own father, and of every sodbuster in the Hox River

Settlement—a voice that can live for eons on dust and thimble-fuls of water, that can be plowed under, hailed out, and go on whispering madly forever about *spring,* about *tomorrow,* a voice of a hope beyond the reach of reason or exhaustion (*oh, Ma, that's going to be my voice soon*)—a voice that will never let us quit the land.

"Give it back."

"It's too late for that, Miles."

"I have money," I say, remembering Pa's envelope. "Give me the glass, take the money, and I'll be on my way."

The man looks down at me, amused; he fingers a dollar bill as if it were the feather of a foreign bird, and I think that he must be even older than our country, as old as the sod itself. "What use would I have for *that*? That isn't the paper I require. And anyway, this window isn't yours. You stole it."

I reply in a daze: "You're acquainted with the Yotherses?"

"I was, in a way, but only at the end."

"I didn't steal the Window."

"No, but your father did."

"You know my father?"

"Where do you think I was coming from when I happened upon you?"

My eyes swim and land on the clover glow of his hay knife.

"When the Inspector comes and sees my window—" he's say-ing again, in the tone that sparkles. His back is to me, and I watch the knife bob on his hip. My legs tremble as I spread them to a wide base and get ready to lunge. In a moment, I'll have to grab his knife and stab him in the back, then reclaim the Window from the wall of his tomb and run for the Florissants' place. I can feel the nearness of these events—feel the tearing of his skin, the tug of his muscle tissue as the knife rips between his twitching shoul-der blades—and I powerfully wish that I could crawl through the window of my Blue Sink bedroom, where such apprehensions would be unimaginable, and drift into a dreamless sleep in my childhood bed.

As I crouch stiffly into my soles, the stranger says gently, "I thought you said you weren't a thief."

"Excuse me?" I look up—and find my image reflected in the glass.

"That's the thing with windows, isn't it, Miles?" he says. "Sometimes we see things we don't want to see."

He turns to me then, and his eyes are bottomless.

MRS. STICKSEL PEERS through the hole in her wall at a tall shape coming on a long trot through the wheat—the complex moving silhouette of a horse and rider. She breaks into a smile, relieved, and moves to stand in the doorway, the children fluttering around her. It's only then that she notices the soreness of her jaw, tense from all the anxious waiting. She waves a pale arm beneath the black night sky, beneath the still-falling snow, and thinks, *That Zegner child sure did shoot up this year,* as the rider's profile grows. The face is still a blank mask.

"Well, look who made it!" she calls. "Oh praise God, lost lamb, we've been so worried about you. We had just about given you up—"

A slice of moonlight falls across the horse's flank.

"Say, isn't that the Florissants' mare? What happened to Nore?"

When the Zegner boy doesn't answer, she loosens the grip on her smile and tries a hot little laugh.

"That's you, ain't it, Miles? In this weather I can scarcely see out—"

And just as the children go rushing out to greet the rider, she has the dark feeling she should call them back.

The Barn at the End
of Our Term

The girl

The girl is back. She stands silhouetted against the sunshine, the great Barn doors thrown open. Wisps of newly mown hay lift and scatter. Light floods into the stalls.

"Hi horsies!" The girl is holding a cloth napkin full of peaches. She walks up to the first stall and holds out a pale yellow fruit.

Rutherford arches his neck toward her outstretched hand. Freckles of light float across his patchy hindquarters. He licks the girl's palm according to a code that he's worked out: - - - -, which means that he is Rutherford Birchard Hayes, the nineteenth president of the United States of America, and that she should alert the local officials.

"Ha-ha!" the girl laughs. "That tickles."

Rebirth

When Rutherford woke up inside the horse's body, he was tied to a stout flag post. He couldn't focus his new eyes. He was wearing blinders. A flag was whipping above him, but Rutherford was tethered so tightly to the post that he couldn't twist his neck to count the stars. He could hear a clock gonging somewhere nearby, a sound that rattled through his chest in waves. That clock must be broken, Rutherford thought. It struck upwards of twelve times, of twenty, more gongs than there were hours in a day. After a certain number of repetitions, it ceased to mean anything.

Rutherford stared down into a drainage ditch and saw a horse's broody face staring back at him. His hooves were rough, unfeeling endings. He stamped, and he couldn't feel the ground beneath him. The gonging wasn't a clock at all, he realized with a warm, spreading horror, but the thudding of his giant equine heart.

A man with a prim mustache and a mean slouch blundered toward him, streaked fire up Rutherford's sides with a forked quirt, shoved Rutherford into a dark trailer. The quirt lashed out again and again, until he felt certain that he had been damned to a rural Hell.

The Devil! Rutherford thought as the man drew closer. He shied away, horrified. But then the man reached up and gave him a gentle ear-scratch and an amber cube of sugar, confounding things further.

"God?"

The man seemed a little on the short side to be God. His fly was down, his polka-dotted underclothes exposed. Surely God would not have faded crimson dots on his underclothes? Surely God would wear a belt? The man kept stroking his blond mustache. His voice sounded thick and wrong to Rutherford's ears: "He's in, hyuh-hyuh. Give her the gas, Phyllis!"

The trailer rolled forward, and in three days' time Rutherford reached the Barn. He has been stabled there ever since.

The Barn

The Barn is part of a modest horse farm, its pastures rolling forward into a blank, mist-cloaked horizon. The landscape is flat and corn-yellow and empty of people. In fact, the prairies look a lot like the grasslands of Kentucky. There are anthills everywhere, impossibly huge, heaped like dirt monsters.

There are twenty-two stalls in the Barn. Eleven of the stabled horses are, as far as Rutherford can ascertain, former presidents of the United States of America. The other stalls are occupied by regular horses, who give the presidents suspicious, sidelong looks. Rutherford B. Hayes is a skewbald pinto with a golden cowlick and a cross-eyed stare. Rutherford hasn't made many inroads with these regular horses. The Clydesdales are cliquish and pink-gummed, and the palominos are inbred buffoons.

The ratio of presidents to normal horses in the Barn appears to be constant, eleven:eleven. Rutherford keeps trying and failing to make these numbers add up to some explanation (*Let's see, if I am the nineteenth president but the fourth to arrive in the Barn, and if eleven divided by eleven is one, then . . . hrm, let me start again . . .*). He's still no closer to figuring out the algorithm that determined their rebirth here. "Just because a ratio's stable doesn't make it meaningful," says James Garfield, a tranquil gray Percheron, and Rutherford agrees. Then he goes back to his frantic cosmic arithmetic.

The presidents feel certain that they are still in America, although there's no way for them to confirm this. The year—time still advances the way it did when they were president—is indeterminate. A day gets measured in different increments out here. Grass brightens, and grass dims. Glass cobwebs spread across the tractor's window at dawn. Eisenhower claims that they are stabled in the past: "The skies are empty," he nickers. "Not a B-52 in sight."

To Rutherford, this new life hums with the strangeness of the future. The man has a cavalry of electric beasts that he rides over his acreage: ruby tractors and combines that would have caused Rutherford's constituents to fall off their buggies with shock. The man climbs into the high tractor seat and turns a tiny key, and then the engine roars and groans with an unintelligible hymn. Cherubs strumming harps couldn't have impressed Rutherford more than these baritone plows of the hereafter.

"Come back! That's not holy music, you dummy!" Eisenhower yells. "It's just diesel!"

The man goes by the name of Fitzgibbons. The girl appears to be Fitzgibbons's niece. (Rutherford used to think the girl was an Angel of Mercy, but that was before the incident with the wasps.) She refers to the man as "Uncle Fitzy," a moniker that many of the presidents find frankly alarming. Rutherford, for his part, feels only relief. "Fitzy" certainly doesn't seem so bad when you consider the many infernal alternatives: Beelzebub, Mephistopheles, old Serpent, the Prince of Darkness, the Author of Evil, Mister Scratch. Even if Fitzgibbons does turn out to be the Devil, Rutherford thinks, there is something strangely comforting about his Irish surname.

At first many of the presidents assumed that Fitzgibbons was God, but there's been plenty of evidence to suggest that their reverence was misplaced. Fitzgibbons is not a good shepherd. He sleeps in and lets his spring lambs toddle into ditches. The presidents have watched a drunken Fitzgibbons fall off the roof of the shed. They have listened to Fitzgibbons cursing his dead mother. If Fitzgibbons is God, then every citizen of the Union is in dire jeopardy.

"Well, I for one have great faith in Fitzgibbons. I think he is a just and merciful Lord." James Buchanan can only deduce, given his administration's many accomplishments, that this Barn must be Heaven. Buchanan has been reborn as a fastidious bay, a gelding sired by that racing great Caspian Rickleberry. "Do you know that I have an entry in the Royal Ledger of Equine Blood-lines, Rutherford? It's true." His nostrils flare with self-regard. "I am being rewarded," Buchanan insists, "for annexing Oregon."

"But don't you think Heaven would smell better, Mr. Buchanan?" Warren Harding is a flatulent roan pony who can't digest grass. "The presidency was Hell," he hiccups. "All I wanted was to get out of that damn White House, and now look where I've ended up. Dispatch for Mr. Dante: Hell doesn't happen in circles. This Barn is one square acre of Hell and Fitzgibbons is the Devil!"

Rutherford lately tries to avoid the question. All the explana-tions that the other presidents have come up with for what has befallen them, and why, feel too simple to Rutherford. Heaven or Hell, every president gets the same ration of wormy apples. Every president is stabled in a 12' by 12' stall.

Maybe we have the whole question reversed, mixed up. Rutherford sighs. At night the wind goes tearing through the Barn's invis-ible eaves and he wonders. Maybe the man is Heaven, the mobile hand that brings them grain and water. Maybe the Barn itself is God. If Rutherford lops his ears outward, the Barn's rafters snap with the reverb of something celestial. At dusk, Fitzgibbons feeds them, waters them, shuts the door. Then the Barn breathes with the promise of fire. Stars pinwheel behind the black gaps in the roof. Rutherford can hear the splinters groaning inside wood, waiting to ignite. *Perhaps that will be the way to our next life,* Rutherford thinks, *the lick of blue lightning that sets the Barn ablaze and changes us more finally.*

Perhaps in his next body Rutherford will find his wife, Lucy.

The runaway

One day, at the end of an otherwise unremarkable afternoon, James Garfield makes it over the Fence. Nobody sees him jump it. Fitzgibbons and the girl come in to groom the horses, and Rutherford B. Hayes overhears them talking about it. Shouting, really: "Well, I'll be sweetly pickled! A runaway!" Fitzgibbons's face looks blood-pulsed, flushed from the search. But his eyes crinkle up with delight. Sunup, sundown, Fitzgibbons follows the same routine. Surprise is a rare and precious feeling on the farm.

"How do you like that, angel? We've never had a runaway before . . ."

"But where did he run to, Uncle Fitzy?"

Fitzgibbons grins down at her. "I don't know."

Fitzgibbons doesn't seem at all put out by the loss. Something about the way that he squints into the green mist beyond the Fence makes Rutherford think that Fitzgibbons is rooting for Garfield's escape.

"Do you think that Garfield will return?" James Buchanan asks now, looking nervous. "Because he must return, for the good of the Barn. We elected Garfield to represent the mallards. Who is going to speak out on behalf of the mallards at our next Convention? You can't just shirk a duty like that. You can't just abandon your post!"

Apparently, you can, thinks Rutherford. The other presidents all stare at the dark and rippling air in James Garfield's vacant stall.

The next incumbent

The following morning, Fitzgibbons comes in early to muck out Garfield's stall. The Barn buzzes with speculation about the next president to join the ranks. Millard Fillmore is nervous enough for all of them. "Do you think he will be an agreeable sort of man? Do you think he will be a Republican? Why, what if he's just a regular stud horse, and not a president at all . . . ?"

Nobody answers him. Every man is scheming in the privacy of his own horse-body. Andrew Jackson, a stocky black quarter horse stabled next to Rutherford, can barely contain his ambitions in his deep ribs. You can feel his human cunning quiver from the fetlock up. "Whoever the newcomer is, I will defeat him," he says. Jackson has been lonely for an adversary. Every spring he runs uncontested for the office of Spokeshorse of the Western Territories. Many of the presidents have sworn themselves in to similarly foolish titles: Governor of the Cow Pastures, Commanding General of the Standing Chickens. They reminisce about their political opponents like old lovers. There's a creeping emptiness to winning an office that nobody else is seeking.

At noon, Fitzgibbons leads the new soul in. He's a thoroughbred with four white socks and a cranberry tint to his mane. Buchanan recognizes him right away: "John Adams!"

Adams lets out a whinny so raw with relief that it dislodges sleeping bats from the rafters: "You know me!" Adams woke up just yesterday, in the dark, close trailer that he assumed was a roomy coffin. "Excepting that I could see sunshine through the slats," he says in a voice still striped with fear. He seems grateful when Buchanan gives him a friendly bite on the shoulder.

"Are we dead?"

Ten horses nod their heads.

"Is this Heaven?"

It's an awkward question. Ears flatten; nostrils dilate as wide as a man's fist. Rutherford unleashes a warm, diplomatic sneeze to ease the tension.

"That depends," shrugs Ulysses. A series of bleary battle-weary lines cross-hatches his black nose. "Do you want this to be Heaven? Does this look like Heaven to you?"

Adams studies the dark whorls of mildew, the frizz of lofted hay, his own hooves. He goes stiff in the ears, considering. "That also depends. Is Jefferson here?"

Jefferson is not. There are many absences in the Barn of unknown significance: Washington, Lincoln, Nixon, Harrison. The presidents haven't arrived in the order of their deaths, either. Woodrow Wilson got here before Andrew Jackson, and Eisenhower has been here since the beginning.

"But we can't live out our afterlives as common beasts!" Adams's eyes shine with horror. "There must be some way back to Washington! I am still alive, and I am certainly no horse."

There is always this period of denial when new presidents first arrive in the Barn. Eisenhower still refuses to own up to his own mane and tail. "I'm not dead, either, John Adams," Eisenhower says. "I'm just incognito. The Secret Service must have found some way to hide me here, until such time as I can return to my body and resume governance of this country. I can't speak for the rest of you, but I'm no horse."

"'I'm no horse!'" Andrew Jackson mimics. He butts Eisenhower with the flat of his head. "What the Christ are you, then?"

"The thirty-fourth president of the United States." Eisenhower shakes burrs from his tail in a thorny maelstrom.

Adams is rolling his eyes around the Barn, on the verge of rearing. His gums go purple: "Gentlemen, we must get out of here! Help me out of this body!" By the looks of things, Adams will be a stall-kicker. He kicks again and again, until splinters go flying. "We need to alert our constituents to what has befallen us. Gentlemen, rally! What's keeping us here? The doors to the Barn stand wide open."

"Rutherford," says Ulysses. He stands sixteen hands high and retains his general's authority. "Why don't you show our good fellow Adams the Fence?"

The Fence

Rutherford and Adams trot out of the dark Barn into a light, silvery rain. The fence wood is rotted with age, braided through with wild weeds. Each sharpened post rises a level four feet tall, midway up the horses' thick chests. Fitzgibbons put it up to discourage the fat blue geese from flight.

"This is the Fence? This is what keeps us prisoners here? Why, I could jump it this moment!"

Rutherford regards Adams sadly. "Go ahead, then. Give it a try."

Adams charges the Fence. His forelegs lift clean off the ground as he runs. At the last second, he groans and turns sharply to the left. It looks as if he is shying away from the edge of a cliff. He shakes his small head, stamps and whinnies, and charges again. Again he is repelled by some invisible thicket of fear. Sweat glistens on his dark coat.

"Blast, what is it?" Adams cries. "Why can't I jump it?"

"We don't know." The presidents have tried and failed to get over the Fence every day of their new lives. Rutherford thinks it's an ophthalmological problem. A blind spot in the mind's eye that forces a sharp turn.

"How did James Garfield manage it? And where did he run to?"

Garfield's hoofprints disappear at the edge of the paddock. The fence posts point at the blue sky. Adams and Rutherford stare at the trackless black mud on the other side of the Fence. There are two deep crescents where Garfield began the jump, and then nothing. It's as if Garfield vanished into the cool morning air.

"Good question."

Animal memories and past administrations

Woodrow Wilson is giving speeches in his sleep again: *Ah, ah, these are very serious and pregnant questions,* Woodrow mumbles, his voice thick with an old nightmare. Upon the answer to them depends the peace of the world.

Poor Wilson, Rutherford thinks, watching as he addresses the questions of a phantom nation. Wilson paws at the stall floor as he dreams, his lips still moving. The world is drafting new questions, new answers, without him.

In his own dreams, Rutherford never returns to the White House. Instead his memory takes him back to his Ohio home of Spiegel Grove, back to the rainy morning of his death. Unlike the other presidents, Rutherford's dreams find him paralyzed, power-less. He remembers watching the moisture pearl on his bedroom window, the crows lining the curved white rail of his veranda. Lucy's half of the huge pine bed had been empty four years. In the end, divested of all decisions, he had only an old thick-waisted nurse opening his mouth, filling it with tastes, urging him to swallow. Boyhood tastes, blood-pumpkin stew and sugared beets. His son and his youngest daughter were two smudges above the bedside. The boy quietly endeavored to blink good-bye. Then Rutherford's throat began to close, shutting him off from all words, and he felt himself filling with silence. The silence was a field of cotton growing white and forever inside him. Rutherford wasn't afraid to die. *My Lucy,* he remembers thinking, *will be waiting for me on the other side.*

The first First Lady

Lucy Webb Hayes was the first president's wife to be referred to as a First Lady. Nobody besides Rutherford and a few balding

White House archivists remembers her. Rutherford wishes that he was still a man and that she was still a Lady. He wishes that he had a hand to put on her waist. "Lucy?" he hisses at a passing mallard. "Lucy Webb?" Women revert to their maiden names in Heaven, Rutherford feels fairly certain. He can't remember where he learned this—France or the Bible.

"Lucy Webb!"

The duck goes waddling away from him, raising the green tips of its wings in alarm. When Rutherford looks up, Fitzgibbons and the girl are standing at the edge of the pasture, looking at him strangely.

"Uncle Fitzy? Does it sound like that horsie is *quacking* to you?"

Rutherford and Fitzgibbons stare at each other for a long moment.

"You know, Sarge has been acting up lately. All the horses have been behaving mighty queer. Worms, maybe. We ought to get the vet out here. We ought to get them some of those hydrangea shots."

After Fitzgibbons and the girl disappear behind the house, Rutherford continues on his quest to find the soul of his wife. There is a sheep that Rutherford has noticed grazing on the north pasture, slightly apart from the others. The sheep perks up when Rutherford trots over. It might be his imagination, but he thinks he sees a fleck of recognition, ice-blue, floating in her misty iris.

"President Wilson?" Rutherford nudges him excitedly. "Could I trouble you to take a look at one of the ewes?" Rutherford has heard that Woodrow Wilson grazed sheep on the South Lawn. He hopes that Woodrow will be able to confirm his suspicion.

"Your wife, you say?" Wilson exchanges glances with the other horses. "Well, I will gladly take a look, President Hayes." His voice is pleasant enough, but his ears peak up into derisive triangles. Rutherford's shame grows with each hoof-fall. The closer they get to the sheep pasture, the more preposterous his hope begins to seem. His trot hastens into a canter until Woodrow is breathless, struggling to keep pace with him. "Slow down, man," he grumbles. They stand in the rain and stare at the sheep. She's taking placid bites of grass, ignoring the downpour. Her white fleece is pasted to her side. "Uh-oh," says Woodrow. "Hate to break it to you, but I think that's just your standard sheep. Not, er, not a First Lady, no."

"Her eyes, though . . ."

"Yes, I see what you mean. Cataracts. Unfortunate."

Rutherford thanks him for his assessment.

"President Hayes?" Eisenhower is smirking at them from across the field. "Pardon, am I interrupting something? The other presidents have all gathered behind the bunny hutch. You are late again, sir."

Rutherford straightens abruptly, his cowlick flopping into the black saucers of his eyes. He takes an instinctual step in front of sheep-Lucy to shield her from Eisenhower's purple sneer.

"Late for what? Not another caucus on that apple tax."

"We voted that into law two weeks ago, Rutherford," Eisenhower sighs. "Tonight it's the Adams referendum. On the proposed return to Washington? We are leaving in three days' time."

Washington or oblivion

Secret deals get brokered behind the Barn, just north of the red sloop of the bunny hutch. A number of the presidents are planning their escape for a day they are calling the Fourth of July.

"The country is drowning in sorrow," Adams snorts. It's high summer. Oats fall around him like float-down snow. "Our country needs us."

After several months of nickered rhetoric, Adams has convinced a half dozen of the former presidents to be his running mates in a charge on Washington. Whig, Federalist, Democrat, Republican—Adams urges his fellow horses to put aside these partisan politics and join him in the push for liberty. He wants the world to know that they have returned. "It is obvious, gentlemen: of course we're meant to lead again. It is the only thing that makes sense. What other purpose could we have been reborn for? What other—"

Adams is interrupted by a storm of hiccups. Behind him, Fitzgibbons is hitching Harding to a child-size wagon. He helps the girl into the wooden wagon bed. Fitzgibbons grins as he hands the child the reins, avuncular and unconcerned, his big arms crossed against his suspendered chest.

"And tell me," Rutherford asks quietly, "tell me, what evidence do you have that the country needs us to lead again? They seem to be getting on just fine without us."

Now Harding is pulling the girl in miserable rectangles around the bare dirt yard, hiccupping madly. "*This*—hiccup!—*is*—hiccup!—*Hell*." The girl waves a dandelion at him like a wilted yellow scepter. "Giddy-up, horsie!" She laughs.

Aside from Rutherford and Harding, the other presidents are in ecstasies. "Surely the term limits of the Twenty-second Amendment won't apply to me anymore. This rebirth is the loophole that will let me run again, Rutherford." Eisenhower grins for some invisible camera, exposing his huge buck teeth. "And win."

Oh *dear,* thinks Rutherford. That smile is not going to play well on the campaign trail.

"With all due respect, sir, I fear you might be seeking the wrong office? I think there are some, er, obstacles to your run that you perhaps haven't considered?"

"Obstacles?" A fly buzzes drowsily between them and lands on one trembling whisker. "Now, give me some credit, Rutherford. I've put a lot of thought into this. Let me outline my campaign strategy for you . . ." Eisenhower has made this speech before.

"And what about you, Rutherford? What are you, a stallion incumbent or a spineless nag?"

Rutherford blinks slowly and doesn't answer Eisenhower. Both options are depressing. He doesn't want to return to Washington, if there even is a Washington. He just wants a baaa of recognition out of this one ewe.

"Neither. I'm not going anywhere. I'm not leaving my wife."

"Baaa!" says the sheep. She is standing right behind him. Her head is a black triangle floating on the huge cloud of her body. Rutherford has been training the sheep who might be Lucy to follow him. He holds his own supper in his mouth and then drops clumps of millet and wet apple cores to coax her forward. "Come on, sweet Lucy, let's go back to the Barn."

The other presidents mock him openly, their ears pivoting with laughter. The sheep trails him like a pet delusion. *Or like a wife who hasn't woken up to the fact of our love yet!* Rutherford tells himself, tempting her with another chewed-up apple. White apples stud the slick grass behind him. The sheep that might be his wife follows him into the Barn, blinking her long lashes like a deranged starlet.

Dirt memoirs

The girl comes again later that evening with a currycomb and six leafy carrots. Her arrival causes riotous stirring in the Barn.

"Does the child have her book bag?" Buchanan inches forward in his stall and cranes his neck, trying to see around the child's narrow back.

"Yes!" Adams crows. "To arms, gentlemen!"

The horses have been trying to get hold of the girl's schoolbooks for some time. Every president wants to find out how history regards him. Fitzgibbons is no help; he is maddeningly apolitical. He'll spend hours musing out loud about fertilizer or the toughness of bean hulls. But Fitzgibbons never complains about property taxes. He never mentions a treaty or a war. He seems curiously removed from the issues of his day.

"Get her book bag," Eisenhower hisses. There's something sinister about the angle at which his lips curl over his rubbery gums. The girl's schoolbag is leaning against the Barn door frame.

Van Buren tries to hypnotize the child by rhythmically swishing his tail. "Look over here, girlie! Swish! Swish!" He shakes his head from side to side. Eisenhower steps gingerly into the looped strap of the child's bag and drags it with his foreleg. He has it almost to the edge of his stall before she notices.

"Uncle Fitzy!" the girl yells. "Gingersnap is being bad!" Eisenhower hates it when she calls him Gingersnap. He complains about it with a statesman's pomp: "Gentlemen, there exists no more odious appellation than"—nose crumpling, black lips curling—"Gingersnap."

The girl walks forward and snatches her book bag back, but not before Eisenhower has shaken it upside down and kicked several of the books under a clump of hay. "Hurry," he hisses, "before Fitzgibbons comes with the whip!"

The presidents crowd around the books. Literature, mathematics, science, cursive. No history book. The cursive book has fallen open to a page thick with hundreds of lowercase *b*s. Eisenhower sends the books flying with a swift kick from his right foreleg, disgusted. "Every subject but American history! What has become of our education system? What are they teaching children in schools these days?!" It's an urgent question. What *are* they teaching children these days? And how is each president remembered? That's the afterlife the presidents are interested in. Not this anonymous, fly-swatting limbo.

James Buchanan is busy rewriting his memoirs, *Mr. Buchanan's Administration on the Eve of the Rebellion*. He is furious that none of the other presidents ever read the original while they were alive. "Yeah, about that," coughs Harding. "Pretty sure that's out of print."

It's a labored process. Equine anatomy severely limits the kinds of letters the presidents can straight-leg into the dirt. Buchanan can draw an *H*, an *F*, an *E*, an *A*, a *T*, an *I*, an *X* with the meticulous action of his right hoof. *Z*, once you get the hang of it, is also quite easy. *O*s and *U*s and *S*s are impossible. *K*s and *W*s leave him shuddery and spent. Buchanan never questions his own record of the past; commas are tough enough, and he would have to break his leg to make a question mark. He is just now putting the finishing touches to Chapter Four. "Voilà, gentlemen! And now I will add a final paragraph of summation and then on to chapter . . . *oh no!*"

Fitzgibbons rolls one of his red fleet of tractors over Buchanan's sod parchment, erasing even the prologue.

Rutherford used to believe it was the civic duty of every elected official to preserve a full record of his administration. While in office, he was a compulsive memoirist who filled dozens of journals with his painstaking schoolboy script. But now he has only a single use for the human alphabet. He hoofs messages in the rich loam behind the coop, too, but they are for one woman instead of posterity. *L-L-L-L*, he writes, by which he means *Lucy*.

Hunger and restraint

Rutherford is losing weight. He keeps the sheep near him all the time now, crooning to her through closed gums: "Lucy, Lucy, give me your answer, do, I'm half crazy . . ."

"Pipe down, Rutherford," snaps Harding. "Stop giving that

sheep your food, you idiot. You will starve to death if you keep it up."

Rutherford ignores the other presidents and kneels next to the sheep. He smiles at the blue fleck of evidence that his wife is hiding somewhere inside this fleecy body. I know you, he whispers. He lets a brown apple plop into the sawdust between them. The sheep eats it with gusto, and Rutherford hopes this means his love is requited. In the morning, Fitzgibbons yelps when he discovers the sheep in the stall with Rutherford. "Sarge!" Fitzgibbons smacks a palm against his bald head. "What in the hell are you doing with that blind ewe? That is spooky, Sarge. That is goddamn unnatural. You feeling sick, Sarge? You get into some rat poison or something?" Fitzgibbons approaches Rutherford with the oiled halter. "Come along now," he grunts. "Open up . . ." He jostles a carrot around Rutherford's stubbornly pursed lips. A second later the carrot has disappeared and Fitzgibbons is cursing and hopping on one foot. "Jesus!" he growls. "Sarge, you old fleabag, you bit me!"

I am becoming very clever at getting the carrot without opening up for the bit, Rutherford thinks. He keeps the carrot in a pouch in his cheek, a gift for Lucy. *At the games of hunger and restraint, my fellow countrymen, I am becoming excellent.*

Campaign promises

In the yard, the other presidents are still hungry for power. They are practicing for the return to Washington. Adams is so starved for dominion that he begs the girl to allow him to represent her interests to her uncle Fitzgibbons. "Elect me to take part in the public life of your Barn, young lady, and I shall act a fearless, intrepid, undaunted part, at all hazards . . ."

"Ha-ha, Mister Pretty, you are so noisy today!" The girl hums a nonsense tune as she plaits Adams's tail with geraniums.

Martin Van Buren is barn sour but even he shouts out impossible promises at the turkeys from the dim interior of his stall: "You are my constituents, my turkeys," Van Buren neighs, "and the love I feel for you is forever." The turkeys promenade around the yard and ignore him. Rutherford wonders if they, too, have human biographies hidden beneath their black feathers. The presidents spend a lot of time talking about where the other citizens of the Union might have ended up. Wilson thinks the suffragettes probably came back as kicky rabbits.

"I don't understand," Rutherford says. "Don't you gentlemen realize that you are stumping for nothing? What sort of power could you hope to achieve out here?"

Rutherford was ready for his term to be over. He was happy to keep his promise not to run for reelection. He had been a reluctant incumbent in the first place, unwilling to leave his war post to take a furlough for the stump. Mark Twain campaigned for him, and still he never expected to win. Rutherford never knew a generous margin in the whole of his life. His victory was the most disputed in American history. A single electoral vote would have given the presidency to Samuel J. Tilden. "It was a squeaker." Eisenhower nods. "I remember studying it in school." Often, Rutherford wonders what would have happened if Tilden had won. He wonders if he has unjustly displaced Tilden from this stall in the blank country sun of the afterlife.

If we could just reach a consensus that this is Heaven, Rutherford snorts, *we could submit to it, the joy of wind and canter and the stubbed ashy sweetness of trough carrots, burnished moons, nosing the secret smells out of grass. I would be free to gallop.* The only heaven that Rutherford has known in the Barn comes in single moments: a warm palm on his nose, fresh hay, a tiny feast of green thistle made nearly invisible by the sun. At dawn, Heaven is a feeling that comes when the wind sweeps the fields. Heaven is this wind, Rutherford knows for an instant, bending a million yellow heads of wheat.

By nightfall, though, the wheat has straightened, and the whole notion of an afterlife strikes Rutherford as preposterous. "All these arguments are nonsense," he confides to Lucy. "We are all still alive. This is still America. The stars look the same," he continues, "and we are fed. We are here."

Shorn

One afternoon, the sheep is not waiting for him in his stall.

"Rutherford," Jackson sniggers from the pasture, "take a gander at this. Looks like Fitzgibbons is doing something very untoward to your wife."

Fitzgibbons is kneeling in the center of the field, shearing the sheep that might be Lucy. Wool flies up and parachutes down in the sun. Fitzgibbons clips off first one clump of fleece and then another, until the sheep is standing shorn and pink before him. All of a sudden Rutherford's body feels too heavy for his coltish knees. He stares at the growing pile of fleece, heart pounding, and for a crazy moment Rutherford thinks that he can still salvage what's left of his Lucy. Perhaps there's some way to put this wool back on the sheep's body, to cover her up again? He paws frantically at the white curls with his hoof.

The sheep rises up out of the green grass completely bald. Now the fleck in her eye looks bright and inhuman. Worse than meaningless, Rutherford thinks. A symptom of illness, cataracts, just like Woodrow first said. Rutherford hangs his head and keeps his eyes on the ugly dandelions. He swallows the grainy pear that he has been holding to feed the sheep with. "That is not my wife."

Independence day

On the eve of the other presidents' push for liberty, with a whistling nonchalance, Fitzgibbons leaves Rutherford's stall door open. The latch bangs in the wind, a sound like *open,* a song like *no accident.*

Rutherford strolls through the doors into the dusk light.

"The Fence is just a wooden afterthought," Rutherford thinks, coming as close to its rough posts as he dares. "We're imprisoned already." He can feel the walls of his new body expand and contract. Tonight it's not an altogether unpleasant sort of Heaven to be trapped in. The stars are out, and for the first time in months Rutherford has swallowed his whole ration of grain at the trough. He can feel a forgotten strength pulsing through his body. "It's our suspicion that there's another, better Heaven behind the cumulus screen," he murmurs into the grass, bending and tearing at a root that tastes beautifully yellow. "That's the trouble. That's what keeps us trapped here, minds in animals."

Rutherford begins to run, lightly at first. *What am I,* Rutherford wonders, *a horse's body or a human mind?* Both options are twining together like a rope, then fraying. They are disappearing, the faster he runs. The sound of his hoofbeats doesn't trouble him now; it doesn't even register. They thud and they vanish. His tail is still attached to him at the root. But Rutherford isn't trying to outrun his horse tail anymore. It sails out like a black flag behind him, its edges in tatters.

Rutherford turns and starts running again, and this time he finds that he cannot stop. The Fence is right in front of him now. It takes on a second life inside his mind, a thick gray barrier. His blood feels hot and electric inside him, and Rutherford knows from the certainty of his heartbeat that he is alive, that there isn't any "after." There is no reason to believe that anything better or greener waits on the other side of the Fence. There is nothing to prevent him from jumping it. There it is, Rutherford thinks, the blue lick of lightning. His eyes still refuse to focus, but now he finds that he is no longer afraid of the blind spot. *This is for the Union,* Rutherford whinnies, and suddenly he stops worrying about cause and effect, about the impossibility that his hoofbeats could hold any Union together, or why any of this should matter, one horse running in an empty field: none of his speed, none of his grandeur, no droplets of sweat streaming off his hide like wings, and he runs. And nobody is watching when he clears the Fence.

Dougbert Shackleton's Rules for Antarctic Tailgating

Perhaps it is odd to have rules for tailgating when the Food Chain Games themselves are a lawless bloodbath. And that is what a lot of fans love about the games: no rules, no refs, no box seats, and no hot pretzels—not below the Ross Ice Shelf! So take these rules of mine with a grain of salt. That said, I've seen too many senseless deaths over the years. Some people think they can just hop down to the South Pole with a six-pack of Natural Ice and a sweater from the Gap, and that is just not the way we do it for the Food Chain Games. The Team Krill vs. Team Whale match takes place every summer in the most dangerous and remote tailgating site in the world. With the -89°F temperatures and the solar radiation, not to mention the strong katabatic winds off the polar plateau, it can be easy to lose faith, and fingers.

Antarctic tailgaters know exactly how *hard* it is to party.

So: how to get ready for the big game? Say farewell to your loved ones. Notarize your will. Transfer what money you've got into a trust for the kids. You'll probably want to put on some weight for the ride down to the ice caves; a beer gut has made the difference between life and death at the blue bottom of the world. Eat a lot at Shoney's and Big Boy and say your prayers. Take an eight-month leave of absence, minimum, from your office job. Kill your plants, release your cat, stop your mail. It's time to hit the high seas.

Rule One: Make friends with your death

Tailgating in the Antarctic is no joke. We are trying to do nothing less ambitious than reverse the course of history. We want Team Krill to defeat Team Whale.

Look, if you want to tailgate in comfort, don't get on a boat. You can buy some quail eggs or snails or whatever you people eat and you can watch the Food Chain Games on your flat TV. Stay in Los Angeles. Hug your wife on your plush banquette. Cheer for the Antarctic minke whales, like every other asshole.

No, wait a second, here comes the real Rule One: if you are a supporter of Team Whale, you can go fuck yourself, my fine sir. This list is for the fans of Team Krill.

Rule Two: Plan to arrive early

Honestly, for the March game I like to get down to the Ross Ice Shelf by mid-January. The cousins will joke that I'm a little bit of a stickler for punctuality, but I don't see the harm in reaching the ice caves early. I've seen too many Antarctic tailgaters killed in the Drake Passage over the years—even I get choked up when I see a Team Whale vessel cracked to bits on a 'berg, its flags faded so bad you can't read them.

So plan for frostbite and Aeolian terror. Personally, I don't like to risk the easterlies in the Gerlache Strait any later than

November—the pack ice is on the move, a bad traffic. All those gentoo penguins looking at you, frizzy and ruby-eyed. It's uncanny. Team Gentoo is a decent franchise but I've never been a fan. They beat Team Squid again last season but got smoked by Team Orca and Team Elephant Seal.

Another reason to haul ass is that all the good spots in the harbor outside the ice caves go by Valentine's Day. You don't want to have to motor in sixty miles on your Zodiac boat come game day.

A note on etiquette: People have to do terrible, terrible things to arrive there on time. When you make small talk, use your judgment. Keep it light. Nobody wants to kill the spirit in the ice caves with some downer questions about the recently deceased. Be prepared to see a black-nosed victim of frostbite; a boatload of probable cannibals, suspiciously fat and sheepish in their snug parkas; a scurvy-riddled tailgater in a lifeboat, vestless and begging oranges. Don't ask questions. Maybe offer the guy a nectarine, if he's wearing Team Krill gear.

Rule Three: Before you leave for the big game,
make a tailgating checklist

At minimum, you will need to bring Zodiac boots and gaiters; first-aid kits; survival bags; both VHF and HF solar-powered radios; a SeaRover Remotely Operated Vehicle with sonar imager; a fluorometer; a Conductivity, Temperature, and Depth Sensor; a Bio-Optical Multifrequency Acoustical and Physical Environment Recorder; an Acoustic Doppler Current Profiler; nachos.

And of course the tailgate is not just potentially fatal glacial navigation—there is also a fun component. Inspired by our brethren in the football stadium parking lots of Florida and Alabama, some Antarctic tailgaters have brought ale tankards in recent years, although this is not requisite. You might also choose to prioritize more of the room in your hold for auxiliary drinking supplies, like sea-sickness bags and barrels of aspirin.

If you're not a drinker, you'll still be in good company. For example, I was sober as a judge until recently, when Maureen took off and I discovered that rye whiskey is a terrific complement to every meal at sea. Plenty of Team Krill tailgaters party "dry" during the voyage to avoid accidents; if you're abstaining, you could bring orange juice or seltzer or melt big bricks of ice for fishy-tasting water. In fact, you will almost definitely have to do this at one of the army stations, unless you want to go the pricey Reverse Osmosis Desalinator route and get your water supply directly from the sea. Tip: this water will taste a little like movie popcorn unless you doctor it with Tang or Crystal Light lemonade.

Here is a recipe we like for Team Krill Kool-Aid Punch:

1. Pina-Pineapple, Pink Swimmingo, or Double Double Cherry Kool-Aid brand flavored drink mix
2. Glacial ice blocks (Lake Fryxell is a reliable source)
3. Vodka (Russian crew members are an excellent source)
4. Plastic Krill stirrers

You may have heard of pemmican, the Spam of Antarctica? A big favorite with the early polar explorers? Pemmican consists of a repugnant arithmetic of dried beef + beef fat. We don't eat that dog food on my ship.

Dehydrated foods, nonperishables—these are Antarctic tailgating staples. Apocalypse food is appropriate for the Antarctic tailgate, the sort of stuff you'd find in a Cold War bunker: jerky, canned tuna, powdered milk, soups in envelopes. If you're a health nut, don't tailgate in the Antarctic. You can always put balsamic vinaigrette on salted meat and sort of pretend it's a salad.

The tailgaters for Team Whale employ a wicked stratagem of culinary intimidation: they feast on krill cocktail, on krill risotto, on a humongous red velvet cake shaped to look like a krill with chocolate eyestalks. It's a macabre business. You are aware it's just icing, but still: the cake *looks* like a krill. Those Team Whale pricks have a five-star French-Guyanese chef on board.

Of course, those bastards are probably also pouring liquid gold onto their organic arugula leaves or something. Well, fuck them. Potato flakes and ham-in-a-can and army MREs from mid-century wars are plenty fine for Team Krill.

Rule Four: Pack a Victory Cooler

When Team Krill defeats Team Whale, you'll want to have the provisions for a true Antarctic feast. I've been tailgating around the Frozen Continent with these items in my Victory Cooler since Ronald Reagan was in office: Arm & Hammer baking soda, Crisco, Nestlé Quik (powdered), a sack of sugar, dried corn, dried prunes, Hormel corned beef, astronaut candy, air horn. On the day that our team finally wins, it will be a bacchanalia. That said, rookie tailgaters, take note! You can get caught up in the moment in those ice caves and then—boom!—botulism.

Rule Five: Wear Team Krill colors—but insulate

In the katabatic winds, a "balmy" game day is 0.5°F. You are going to want to cover your extremities. Put your Team Krill outer shell over your Team Krill neck gaiter. Buy a pair of badass goggles.

Science hasn't proven the efficacy of tailgating in costume (yet) but we believe that the visible support we provide to Team Krill by dressing up and moving our antennae and plastic krill thoraxes in the characteristic undulant motion of a school of krill is *vital* to their eventual victory against Team Whale. Through mists of ice, we tailgaters lean over the gunwales of our boats and shake our pinky-beige swimmerets, tracing moody shapes onto the dark surface. What does this do for Team Krill? Skeptics, marine biologists, and my ex-wife, Maureen, will tell you: nothing. Can the krill hear us cheering for them? Probably not. Do they understand what they are seeing with their shrimpy compound eyes? Yes. Definitely. After seventeen seasons I am sure of this. I've seen the magic of cheering, in costume, for the almost invisible, indefatigable krill. I've seen krill accelerate toward the maw of Team Whale, streaming bubbles, a mute shrimp battle cry. It's a beautiful sight, and beautiful to feel you were a part of it. That our screaming and our gyrations on the surface reach down to them, to the tiny, tumbling bodies deep below the ice: our team.

In fact, sometimes the little guys wave their plentiful legs back at us, as if they are cheering on our cheering.

If you're really serious about tailgating, like my cousins and me, you'll want to sequester yourself in your bedroom for two to three months prevoyage with old National Geographic footage and practice swishing. Most people lead with their hips, but for me it's all in the ribs.

Denny Fitzpatrick, who is like the commissioner of our tailgates down there—this red-nosed Irishman who looks a little like a krill himself, whiskery and furious, and who started tailgating around the South Pole when I was still in diapers—Denny can do this one waggly thing, with his elbow. It really seems to get them going.

I mean, you really should try to look as much like a krill as you can.

Rule Five-A: If your wife leaves you for a millionaire motel-chain-owning douchebag fan of Team Whale, make sure you get your beloved mock-bioluminescent Team Krill eyestalks out of the trunk of her Civic before she takes off

Rule Six: Tip the Russians well

I'm assuming that you rented a boat crewed by Russians. They control a lot of the Antarctic tailgating industry, so treat them well. We usually tip 5 percent of the charter cost of the ex-polar navigator. If and when you make it to the ice caves, you'll be family.

Team Whale tailgaters fly into Ushuaia, Argentina. Typically, they roll into the harbor of the ice caves on the day of the game, their fleet puttering through the blue archways as lazily as a series of yawns, all those hundreds of Team Whale fans looking so smugly upholstered in their Disney-manufactured whale suits. I hear those cushioned baleens are as comfortable as pajamas. Just the fin portion costs three thousand dollars. Good for you, Team Whale tailgaters! It must be nice for you, to have that kind of money. It must be *real tough,* you cetaceous fucks, to support the best team in the league.

Excuse me.

Your average Team Krill tailgater can't afford that kind of luxury. He wouldn't want to. We like to travel in our own style. For example, my cousins and I have converted a Russian schooner into *The Krill Cruiser,* whose only purpose is to visually and audibly support Team Krill. Cousin Larry is an electrician and he did just an incredible job on the cabin. Strobe lights, a birch bar for beers and "hot" peanuts. The Russians love that little flourish, though theirs is not a culture of tailgaters. I sometimes get the sense the Russians think us a little silly.

You might also want to bring a little gift for the mailman at Port Lockroy. They had some British guy installed there last time we sailed through. Young guy. He gets so lonely. Some magazines, some chocolate mints. It's really just the thought.

Rule Seven: Tailgating is all about sharing

Quick and easy cooking is a must for the Antarctic tailgater. Here is a family recipe that will give your Antarctic tailgate some "regional flavor":

1. Whale meat
2. Fire

Salt to taste and all that.

Although, typically, I don't bother with salt. I don't really bother with forks and such, either. I like to pluck the meat from the burning coals and bare my teeth and let out a piercing, unearthly howl at the Team Whale tailgaters moored across the ice floes, personally. Just to razz them a little.

Rule Eight: Be a good sport—but watch your back!

You want to have a sportsmanlike attitude while tailgating in the Antarctic, even when it is difficult (e.g., snow-blind/mourning a loss/drunk on Crown Royal). Show those Team Whale fans that even though their players weigh ten tons to our players' .038 grams, we krill supporters are the bigger people. Some of the tailgaters for the minke whales are homicidally devoted to their team. Rich psychopaths. You're likely to find the rowdiest bands of them near the Grytviken whaling station, drinking cabernet and hissing across the calved icebergs at us.

Pull your rubberized Krill earflaps down—that's what I do. Be civil. Tragedies happen in the lower latitudes, particularly when some of the younger guys get their blood up. Fights seem to spike about a month or two before the Big Game, when you hit that traffic in the Bismarck Strait.

One sad example, from a coupla seasons ago: This teenager called the minke whale fans "dickriders." A poor freckled kid from Decatur City, Iowa. God, we all liked him. He wasn't the brightest bulb but somehow he'd memorized every Krill statistic going back to the Cretaceous Food Chain Games—he just loved the franchise. It was his first tailgate, he told us—his first time below the equator. Sweet kid. We all liked him but we kept forgetting his name.

Anyway, the dawn after the whole "dickriders" altercation? Our Krill boats were all still at anchor but the Team Whale tailgaters were long gone. We found the kid's body floating amid blocks of ice, already meat, three blue skua jawing on it. An orca sailed by him like a sunken moon, its wake engulfing the kid in black ripples. His feet were bare, I remember that. Those monsters took his Krill feet and his Krill Scamper-socks. Can you imagine that level of evil—sock robbers? We could see the boats of his murderers like a line of ants in the distance, entering the hole of the midnight sun.

You can lose at tailgating, too, just as devastatingly as Team Krill keeps losing to Team Whale.

Rule Nine: Should you have to bury your dead, do so in the proper receptacles

Nobody likes a litterbug. You can't get much lower class than a boat of tailgaters who just leave their dead around.

Rule Ten: Don't fall overboard

The game lasts twenty seconds, tops. You don't want to come all that way and miss the game.

Rule Eleven: Don't stop believin'

Some (like my ex) will tell you that it's a special sort of masochist who supports Team Krill, since all evidence suggests that they have been consistently losing the Food Chain Games for eons. Paleobiologists' molecular-dating methods reveal that the krill have never won a game. Team Krill loses to Team Blue Whale, Team Humpback Whale, Team Fin Whale, Team Sei Whale, Team Skua, and Team Albatross.

To this, I say: sure, it takes a special kind of fan to love the league underdog. Something Maureen would know very little about. Listen. The krill are in a rebuilding year. The krill are always in a rebuilding year. Every year the whole franchise of 60,000,000,000 krill gets eaten. Team Whale sucks Team Krill into the primordial combs of its baleen plates at twenty-eight knots. We've got a decent offense but we've got a pretty dismal record on defense.

But this is going to be our season. With all your might, try to believe that.

The greatest feeling in the world is getting there. Rowing over to the ice caves on game night, after all that travel. Krill will surge along either side of your boat in a rosy pregame warm-up. Lots of excitement in the frozen air. Inside the ice caves, you can glimpse the minke whales grouping into pods.

"Surge, krill!" Denny Fitzpatrick always screams at this juncture; you can bet that he's been drunk since April. "Surge, you godless bastards!"

Antarctic tailgating is such a nice way of socializing on a balmy evening, when the sun goes down in flames behind the caves, while you share the end of your two-year supply of liquor and chips (how did it last only eight months?) with the Russians. We wear our costumes on the stern of the boat, our Krill eye-stalks ogling the polar stars, huddled, shivering, convulsing with victory dreams. We munch and munch in the most extraordinary silence.

The New Veterans

When Beverly enters the room, the first thing she notices is her new patient's tattoo. A cape of ink stretches from the nape of the man's neck to his hip bones. His entire back is covered with blues and greens, patches of pale brown. But—what the hell is it a tattoo *of*, anyways? Light hops the fence of its design. So many colors go waterfalling down the man's spine that, at first glance, she can't make any sense of the picture.

Compared to this tattoo, the rest of the man's skin—the backs of his legs and his arms, his neck—looks almost too blank. He's so tall that his large feet dangle off the massage table, his bony heels pointing up at her. Everything else is lean and rippling, sculpted by pressures she can only guess at. Beverly scans the patient's intake form: male, a smoker, 6'2", 195 lbs., eye color: brown, hair color: black, age: 25. Sgt. Derek Zeiger, U.S. Army, Company B, 1st Battalion, 66th Armor Regiment, 4th Infantry Division. In the billing section, he's scribbled: *This is free for me, I hope and pray . . . ? I'm one of the veterans.*

And it is free—once she fills out and faxes in an intimidating stack of new forms. Ten sessions, 100 percent covered by military insurance. Sergeant Zeiger is her first referral under the program created by Representative Eule Wolly's H.R. 1722 bill, his latest triumph for his constituency: Direct Access for U.S. Veterans to Massage Therapist Services.

At the Dedos Mágicos massage clinic, they'd all been excited by the new law; they'd watched a TV interview with the blue-eyed congressman in the office break room. Representative Wolly enumerated the many benefits of massage therapy for soldiers returning home from "the most stressful environments imaginable." Massage will ease their transition back to civilian life. "Well, he's sure preaching to our choir!" joked Dmitri, one of the oldest therapists on staff. But Beverly had been surprised to discover her own cellular, flower-to-sun hunger for exactly this sort of preaching—in the course of a day, it was easy to lose faith in the idea that your two hands could change anything.

On the table, her first referral from the VA hospital has yet to budge. She wonders how long this soldier has been home for—a month? Less? Dark curls are filling in his crew cut. Only the back of his skull is visible, because he is lying facedown on the table with his head fitted in a U-shaped pillow. She can't tell if he's really asleep or just pretending to be completely calm for her; often new patients *try* to relax, a ruse that never works—they just disperse their nervousness, springload their bones with guile. Rocky outcroppings of "relaxation" shelve and heave under their backs, while their minds become a tangle of will.

With the man's bright tattoo for contrast, the rest of the room looks suddenly miserably generic. The walls are bare except for a clock lipped in red plastic, which feels like a glowing proxy for Ed's mouth, silently screaming at her not to go a penny over the hour. The young sergeant's clothes are wadded on the floor, and she shakes out and folds them as she imagines a mother might do.

"Sir? Ah—Sergeant Zeiger . . . ?"

"Unh," moans the soldier, shivering inside a good or a bad dream, and the whole universe of the tattoo writhes with him.

"Hullo!" She walks around to the front of the table. "Did you fall asleep, sir?"

"Oh, God. Sorry, ma'am," says the soldier. He lifts his face stiffly out of the headrest and rolls onto his side, sits up. "Guess I zoinked."

"Zoinked?"

"Passed out. You know, I haven't been sleeping at night. A lot of pain in my lower back, ma'am."

"Sorry to hear it." She pats his shoulder, notes that he immediately tenses. "Well, let's get you some help with that."

How old was Sergeant Derek Zeiger when he enlisted? Seventeen? Twenty? As she heats the oils for his massage, Beverly becomes very interested in this question. Legally, nowadays, at what age can you do business with your life's time—barter your years for goods and services? A new truck, a Hawaii honeymoon, a foot surgery for your mother, a college degree in history? When can you sell your future on the free market? In Esau, Wisconsin, you have to be eighteen to vote, to smoke cigarettes, to legally accept a marriage proposal or a stranger's invitation to undress; at twenty-one, you can order a Cherry-Popper wine cooler and pull a slot lever; at twenty-five, you can rent a family sedan from Hertz. At any age, it seems, you can obtain a room by the hour at the Jamaica Me Crazy! theme motel next to the airport, which boasts the world's dirtiest indoor waterfall in the lobby. The gift store sells padded bras and thongs and a "Caribbean wand" that looks like a stick of cotton candy with tiny helicopter rotors, for some erotic purpose that Beverly, at forty-four, still feels too young to guess at.

At eighteen, Beverly had no plans for her future. She had zero plans to make a plan. To even think that word, the "future," caused a bile that tasted like black licorice to rise in the back of Beverly's throat. All that year her mother had been dying, and then in April, two months before her high school graduation, her haunted-eyed father had been diagnosed with stomach cancer, a double hex on the McFadden household. Six months to a year, the doctors said. Mr. Blaise McFadden was a first-generation Irish-man with hair like a lion's and prizefighter fists, whose pugilist exterior concealed a vast calm, a country of calm of which Beverly secretly believed herself to be a fellow citizen, although she had never found a way to talk to her dad about their green interior worlds or compare passports. His death was not the one for which she'd been preparing. What a joke! Pop quiz, everybody! She'd spent her senior year cramming for the wrong test: Mrs. Marcy McFadden's passing.

"Go to school," said Janet, Beverly's older sister. "Daddy doesn't need you underfoot. They can take care of themselves. Nobody wants you to stay."

But Beverly didn't see how she could leave them alone with the Thing in the house. Beverly's parents were coy, demurring people. If they heard Death mounting the stairs at night, footsteps that the teenage Beverly swore she could feel vibrating through the floorboards at three a.m., nobody mentioned this intrusion at breakfast.

Beverly enrolled in the "Techniques of Massage" certificate program at the Esau Annex because it required the fewest credit hours to complete. She'd surprised herself and her instructors by excelling in her night classes. Beverly felt that she was learning a second language. As a child she'd been excruciatingly shy, stiffening in even her parents' embraces, but suddenly she had a whole choreography of movements and touched people with a purpose. *I can't believe I'm telling you this,* a body might confide to her. Spasming and relaxing. Pain unwound itself under her palms, and this put wonderful pictures in her head: a charmed snake sinking back into its basket, a noose shaking out its knots. In less than six months, Beverly had passed her tests, gotten her state certification, and found a job in downtown Esau; she was working at Dedos Mágicos before her twentieth birthday. At twenty, she'd felt smugly certain that she'd made the right choice.

Six months after his diagnosis of stomach cancer, right on schedule, Beverly's father died; her mother hung on for another decade. She'd flummoxed her oncologists with her fickle acrobatics, swinging over the void and back into her body on the hospital bed while the life-recording machines telegraphed their silent electronic applause. Beverly arranged for the sale of the farmhouse and used the proceeds to pay down her mother's staggering medical bills. For three years her mother lived in Beverly's apartment. In remission, then under attack again; in and out of the Esau County Hospital. Beverly tracked the rise and fall of her blood cell counts, her pendulous vitals. Twenty-nine when her mother entered her final coma, she was accustomed by that time to a twilight zone split between work and the ward.

In her mother's final days, massage was the last message to reach down to her—when her sickness had pushed her to a frontier where she could no longer recognize Beverly, when she didn't know her own face in a mirror, she could still respond with childlike pleasure to a strong massage. Beverly visited the mute woman in the hospital gown every day. She gave this suffering person a scalp-and-neck massage, and swore she could feel her real mother in the shell of the stranger smiling up at her. Marcy McFadden was gone. But Beverly could read the Braille of her mother's curved spine—it was composed in the unspeakable, skeletal language that she had learned at school.

Beverly smiles down at him, rubbing the oil between her hands. She pulls at his trapezius muscles, which are dyed sky-blue. His tattoo is the stuff of Dutch masters. Beverly is amazed that this level of detail is possible on a canvas of skin. Practically every pore on his back is covered: in the east, under his bony shoulder, there's an entire village of squat huts, their walls crackled white-and-black with the granular precision of cigarette ash. South of the village there is a grove of palm trees, short and fat. A telephone pole! Beverly grins, as proudly happy as a child to identify nouns. A river dips and rises through the valley of his lower back. Tiny cattle with dolorous anatomies are grazing and bathing in it, bent under black humps and scimitar-horns. The sky is gas-flame blue, and right in the center of his back a little V of birds tapers to a point, creating the illusion of a retreating horizon. Several soldiers occupy the base of Zeiger's spine. What kind of ink did this tattoo artist use? What special needles? The artist dotted desert camouflage onto the men—their uniforms are so infinitesimally petaled in duns and olives that they are, indeed, nearly invisible against Sergeant Zeiger's skin. Now that she's spotted them once, though, she can't stop seeing them: their brown faces are the size of sunflower hulls. Somewhere a microscope must exist under which a tattoo like this would reveal ever-finer details—freckles, sweat beads, bootlaces. Windows that open onto sleeping infants. The cows' tails swatting mosquitoes. Something about the rice-grain scale of this world catches at Beverly's throat.

"What's the name of this river back here?"

She traces the blue ink.

"That's the Diyala, ma'am."

"And this village, does it have a name?"

"Fedaliyah."

"That's in Iraq, I'm assuming?"

"Yup. New Baghdad. Fourteen miles from the FOB. We were sent there to emplace a reverse osmosis water purification unit at JSS Al Khansa. To help the Iraqi farmers feed their *jammous*."

"*Jammous?*"

"Their word. Arabic for 'water buffalo.' We're probably mispronouncing it." He wiggles his hips to make the bulls dance. "That was a big part of my war contribution—helping Iraqi farmers get some feed for their buffaloes. No hamburgers and fries in Fedaliyah, Bev, in case you're curious. Just *jammous*."

"Well, you've got some museum-quality . . . *jammous* back here, Sergeant." She smiles, tracing one's ear. She can see red veins along the pink interior. Sunlight licks at each sudsy curl.

"Yeah. Thanks. My artist is legendary. Tat shop just outside Fort Hood."

The brightest, largest object in the tattoo is a red star in the palm grove—a *fire,* Derek Zeiger tells her, feeling her tracing its edges. He doesn't offer any further explanation, and she doesn't ask.

She begins *effleurage,* drawing circles with her palms, stroking the oil onto his skin. The goal is to produce a tingling, preparatory warmth—a gentle prelude to the sometimes uncomfortably strong pressure required for deep tissue work. Most everyone enjoys this fluttery feeling, but not so Sergeant Zeiger. Sergeant Zeiger is thrashing around under her hands like Linda Blair's understudy.

"Christ, lady," he grumbles, "you want to hurt me that bad, just reach around and twist my nuts."

Effleurage is a skimming technique, invented by Swedes.

"Sergeant, please. I am barely applying any pressure. Forgive me for saying this but you are behaving like my nieces."

"Yeah?" he snarls. "Do you twist their nuts, too?"

Healing is a magical art, said the pamphlet that first attracted the nineteen-year-old Beverly to this career. *Healing hands change lives.*

"Healing hurts sometimes," Beverly tells the soldier briskly. "And if you cannot hold still, we can't continue. So, please—"

People can do bad damage to themselves while trying to Houdini out of pain. Beverly has seen it happen. Recently, on a volunteer visit at the county hospital, Beverly watched an elderly woman on a gurney dislocate a bone while trying to butterfly away from the pins of her doctors' hands.

But ten minutes into their session, Beverly can feel the good change happening—Zeiger's breathing slows, and she feels her thoughts slowing, too, shrinking into the drumbeat of his pulse. Her mind grows quieter and quieter within the swelling bubble of her body, until all her attention is siphoned into her two hands. The oil becomes warm and fragrant. A sticky, glue-yellow sheet stretches between her palms and the sergeant's tattoo. Each body, Beverly believes, has a secret language candled inside it, something inexpressibly bright that can be transmitted truly only via touch.

"How does that feel now? Too much pressure?"

"It's fine. It's all good."

"Are you comfortable?"

"No," he grunts. "But keep going. This is free, right? So I'm getting my money's worth."

Bulls stare up at her from the river. Their silver horns curl like eyelashes. Under her lamp, the river actually twinkles. It's amazing that a tattoo needle this fine exists. Beverly, feeling a bit ridiculous, is nonetheless genuinely afraid to touch it. She has to force herself to roll and knead the skin. For all its crystalline precision, the soldier's tattoo has a fragile quality—like an ice cube floating in a glass. She supposes it's got something to do with the very vibrancy of the ink. Decay being foreshadowed by everything bright. Zeiger is young, but he'll age, he'll fade—and he's the canvas. Zeiger is now breathing deeply and regularly, the village rising and falling.

At a quarter to four, Beverly begins to wind down. She makes a few last long strokes along his spine's meridian. "Time's up," she's about to say, when she notices something stuck beneath her pinky. When she moves her hand she slides the thing across the sky on Zeiger's shoulder, still tethered to her finger like a refrigerator magnet. Only it's flat—it's inside the tattoo. No, she thinks, impossible, as she continues floating it around his upper back. An orange circle no larger than a grocery SALE sticker. It's the sun. Beverly swallows hard and blinks, as if that might correct the problem. She draws her pinky halfway down his spine, and the sun moves with it. When she lifts her little finger, the sun stays put. She can't stop touching it, like an idiot child at a stovetop—well, this is trouble, this is a real madhouse puzzle. The sun slides around, but the rest of the tattoo stays frozen. The cows stare at the grass, unalarmed, as it zings cometlike over their horns. The soldiers' faces remain stiffly turned to the west, war-blasé, as the sun grazes their helmets . . .

She gasps, just once, and Sergeant Zeiger says in a polite voice, "Thank you, ma'am. That feels nice."

"Time is *up*!" Ed raps at the door. "Bev, you got a four o'clock!"

The door begins to open.

"Ed!" she calls desperately, pushing the door back into its jamb. "He's changing!"

And when she turns around, Derek Zeiger *is* changing, standing behind the hamper and hopping into his pants. His arms lift and pull the world of Fedaliyah taut; Beverly gets a last glimpse at the sun, burning in its new location on the Diyala River.

Beverly swipes at her eyes. When she opens them, the tattoo is gone from view. Now Sergeant Derek Zeiger is standing in front of her, just as advertised on his intake form: 6'2", a foot taller than Beverly, and he is muddy-eyed indeed, squinting down at her through irises that are brown, almost black. He draws a hand from his pocket—

"Well, thank you, ma'am." Inexplicably, he laughs, scratching behind one ear. "I guess I don't feel any worse."

"Sergeant Zeiger—"

"Derek," he says. "Derek's good."

She notices that he winces a little, just walking around. He pushes a hand to the small of his back like a brace.

"Oh, it's been like this for months," he says, waving her concern away. "*You* didn't do this. You helped. It's a little better, I think."

And then she watches him straighten for her benefit, his face still taut and bloated with pain.

She can feel her face smiling and smiling at him, her hand shaking in his:

"Then you have got to call me Beverly. None of this *ma'am* stuff."

"Can I call you Bev?"

"Sure."

"What about Beav?" He grins into the distance, as if he's making a joke to people she can't see. "Beaver? Can I call you The Beav?"

"Beverly," she says. "Can you do me one favor, Derek? The next time you're in the shower—"

"Beverly!" He swivels to give her a big, real grin. "I'm shocked! It's only our first date here . . ."

"Haha. Well." Beverly can feel the blood tinting her cheeks. "Just be sure to get all the oil off. And should you notice—if you feel any pain? Or—anything? You can call me."

She's never given her home number out to a patient before. As the sergeant turns his back to leave, shouldering his jacket, she mumbles something about muscle adaptation to deep tissue massage, the acids that her hands have released from his trigger points. How "disruptions" can occasionally occur. The body unaccustomed.

At the Hoho's Family Restaurant, Beverly treats herself to peanut butter pancakes and world news. She grabs a menu and seats herself. She's a longtime patron, and waiting for service always gives her a crawling, uncomfortable feeling. Beverly often finds herself struggling to stay visible to waitstaff, taxi drivers, cashiers. She tries hard to spite the magazines and persist in her childhood belief that aging is honorable, to wear her face proudly, like a scratched medallion, the widening circles of purple under her eyes and the trenches on her brow. To be that kind of veteran. A woman aging "gracefully," like the church ladies she sees outside Berea Tenth Presbyterian, whose yellowed faces are shadowed by wigs like cloudbursts. In truth, Beverly can never quite adjust to her age on the calendar; most days, she still feels like an old child. She spends quite a lot of time trying to communicate to strangers and friends alike that her life situation is something she chose: "I never wanted anything like that, you know, serious, long-term. No kids, thank God. My patients keep me plenty busy."

But it's been years . . . Beverly thinks. And whatever need starts knuckling at her then is so frightening that she can't complete the sentence. It's been decades, maybe, since she's been really necessary to anybody.

That night, emerging from the fog of her own shower, Beverly wonders what the soldier is seeing in his mirror. Nothing out of the ordinary, probably. Or almost nothing.

She places her hand against the green tiles and cranes around to peer at her back. She can't remember the last time she's done this. Her skin is ghostly white, with a little penguin huddle of moles just above her hip, looking lost on that Arctic shelf. She can imagine her sister rolling her eyes at her, telling Beverly to get some color. Dmitri, whose skin is an even shade of gingerroot all year round, *tsk*ing at her: "Beeeverly, quit acting like the loneliest whale! Go to a tanning salon!"

Her hand glides along the curve of her spine, bumps along her tailbone. These are the "rudimentary vertebrae": the fishy, ancient coccygeal bones. The same spine that has been inside her since babyhood is hers today, the exact same bones from the womb, a thought that always fills her with a kind of thrilling claustrophobia. So much surface wrapped around that old stem. She watches her hands smear the water droplets on her stomach. It's strange to own anything, Beverly thinks, even your flesh, that nobody outside yourself ever touches or sees.

That night, under the coverlet, Beverly slides her hands under her T-shirt and lets them travel up and up, over her rib cage, over her small breasts and along the hard ridge of her collarbone, until she is gently wringing her own stiff neck.

Monday morning, Ed greets her with a can of diet soda. Eduardo Morales is the owner of Dedos Mágicos, and he's been Beverly's boss for nearly twenty-five years. He is a passionate masseur whose English is so-so.

"Beverly. Here. On accident, I receive the diet soda," Ed murmurs. "The machine made a mistake."

Beverly sighs and accepts the can.

"I hate it, you drink it." He says this with a holy formality, as if this transaction were underwritten by the teachings of Christ or Karl Marx.

"Okay. It's eight a.m. Thank you, Ed."

Ed beams at her. "I really, really hate that one. Hey, your first appointment is here! Zeiiiiger." He gives her a plainly lewd look. "Rhymes with *tiiiger.*"

"Very funny." She rolls her eyes. "You all love to give me a hard time."

But Beverly's hands are lifting like a teenager's to fix her hair. She hasn't felt this kind of nervousness in years.

Sergeant Derek Zeiger is waiting for her, lying shirtless on the table, facing the far wall, and once again the tattoo burns like a flare against the snowy window. The first thing Beverly does is lock the door. The second thing is to check his tattoo: all normal. The sun is back at its original o'clock. When she breathes in and rubs at it, the skin wrinkles but the sun does not move again.

Today, she tells Zeiger, she's trying "crossgrain techniques"— bearing down with her forearms, going against the grain of the trapezius muscles. He says he's game. Then he shouts a curse that would shock even Ed, apologizes, curses again. She tries to lift his left hip, and he nearly jumps off the table.

"It's not my fingers that are causing you the pain," she says a little sternly. "These muscles have been spasming, Sergeant. Working continuously. I'm just trying to release the tension. Okay? It's going to hurt a little, but it shouldn't *kill* you. On a scale of one to ten, it should never hurt worse than a six."

"Ding, ding, ding!" he yells. "Eleven!"

"Oh, come on." She can feel herself smiling, although her voice stays stern. "I'm not even touching you. Tell me if you're really hurting."

"Isn't that *your* job? To know that kind of stuff? I mean, you're the expert."

She exhales through her nostrils. Knots, she tells the sergeant, are "myofascial trigger points." Bony silos of pain. Deep tissue massage is a "seek-and-destroy" mission, according to one of her more macho instructors at the Annex, a big ex-cop named Federico—a guy who used to break up race riots in Chicago but then became a massage therapist, applied his muscle power to chasing pain out of tendons and ligaments. Her fingers feel for the knots in Zeiger's large muscle groups. Her thumbs skate over the oil, entering caves between his vertebrae and flushing the old stores of tension from them. She pushes down into the fascia, the Atlas bone that supports the skull, the top and center of each shoulder blade, the triangular bone of his sacrum, his gluteal muscles, his hamstrings. She massages the trigger points underneath the tattooed river, which seems to pour from his lowest lumbar vertebrae, as if the Diyala has been wired into him. Beverly imagines the *whoosh* of blue ink exploding into real blood . . .

Her fingers find a knot underneath this river and begin to pull outward. Out of the blue—so to speak—Sergeant Zeiger begins talking.

"The tattoo artist's name was Applejack. But everybody called him 'Cuz.' You ask him why, he'd tell you: 'Just Cuz.' Get it?"

Well, that *was a mistake, Applejack!* Beverly silently rolls her knuckles over Zeiger's shoulders. With a birth name like Applejack, shouldn't your nickname be something like Roger or Dennis? Something that makes you sound like a taxpayer?

"Cuz is the best. He charges a literal fortune. I blew two disability checks on this tattoo. What I couldn't pay, I borrowed from my friend's mom."

"I see." Her knuckles sink into a cloud over Fedaliyah. "Which friend?"

"Arlo Mackey. He died. That's what you're looking at, on the tattoo—it's a picture of his death day. April 14, 2009."

"His mother . . . paid for this?"

Under the oil the red star looks smeary and dark, like an infected cut.

"She lent each of us five hundred bucks. Four guys from Mackey's platoon—Vaczy, Grady, Belok, me, we all got the same tattoo. Grady draws real good, and he was there that day, so he made the source sketch for Applejack. After we got the tattoo, we paid a visit to Mrs. Mackey. We lined up side by side on her yard in Lifa, Texas. To make a wall, like. Mackey's memorial. And Mrs. Mackey took a photograph."

"I see. A memorial of Arlo. A sort of skin mural."

"Correct." He sounds pleased, perhaps mistaking her echo for an endorsement of the project. Beverly doesn't know how to feel about it.

"That must be some picture."

"Oh, it *is*. Mackey's mom decided she'd rather invest in our tattoos than some fancy stone for him—she knew we were his brothers."

The sergeant's head is still at ease in the U-shaped pillow. Facing the floor. Which makes it feel, eerily, as if the tattoo itself is telling her this story, the voice floating up in a floury cloud from underneath the sands of Fedaliyah. As he continues talking, she pushes into his muscles, and the tattoo seems to dilate and blur under the oil.

"She circled our names in his letters home—Mackey wrote real letters, not emails, he was good like that—to show us what he thought of us. He loved us," he says, in the apologetic tone of someone who feels that they are bragging. "Every one of us shows up in those letters. It was like we got to peel back his mind. She said, 'You were his family and so you're my family, too.' Grady told her all the details of the attack, she wanted them, and then she said, 'We will join together as a family to honor Arlo.' She said, 'Now, I want you boys to put the past behind you'—that was her joke."

"My God. That's a pretty dark joke."

Sick, she was about to say.

His shoulders draw together sharply.

"I guess it is."

Thanks to the tattoo, every shrug causes a fleeting apocalypse.

The V of birds gets swallowed between two rolls of blue flesh, springs loose again.

"And—stop me if I've told you this? Mackey's ma had another kid. A girl. Jilly. She's a minor, so Mrs. Mackey had to sign a piece of paper to let Applejack cut into her with his big powerdrill crayons."

"His sister got the tattoo? Her mother let her?"

"Hell yes! It was her mother's idea! Crazy, crazy. Fifteen years old, skinny as a cricket's leg, a sophomore in high school, and this little girl gets the same tattoo as us. April 14. Arlo in the red star. Except, you know, scaled down to her."

His scalp shakes slightly in the headrest, and Beverly wonders what exactly he's marveling at, Jilly Mackey's age or the size of the tragedy or the artist's ingenuity in shrinking the scenery of her brother's death day down to make a perfect fit.

He waits a beat, but Beverly cannot think of one word to say. She knows she's failed because she feels his muscles tense, the world of Fedaliyah stiffening all at once, like a lake freezing itself.

"Plenty of guys in my unit got tattoos like this, you know. It's how the dead live, and the dead walk, see? We have to honor his sacrifice."

Pride electrifies the sergeant's voice. Unexpectedly, he gets up on his elbows on the massage table, cranes around to meet her eye; when he says "the dead," she notes, his long face lights up. It's like some bitter burlesque of a boy in love.

"What does your own mother say about all this, if you don't mind me asking?"

He laughs. "I don't talk to those people."

"Which people? Your family?"

"My family, you're looking at them."

Beverly swallows. "Which one is Mackey? Is this him, in the palm grove?"

"No. That's Vaczy. Mackey's burning up."

Zeiger pudges out a hip bone.

"He's—this red star?"

"It's a *fire*." The sergeant's voice trembles with an almost child-ish indignation. "Mack's inside it. Only you can't see him."

The truck has just run over a remotely detonated bomb and exploded. Still burning inside the truck, he explains, is Specialist Arlo Mackey.

"Boom," he adds flatly.

Why on earth would you boys choose this moment to incarnate? Beverly wonders. *Why remember him—your good friend—dying—engulfed?*

"You were with him on the day he died, Derek? You were all together?"

"We were."

And then he fills in the stencil of April 14 for her.

At 6:05 a.m., on April 14, Sgt. Derek Zeiger and a convoy of four Humvees exited the wire of the FOB, traveling in the north-bound lane of Route Roses, tasked with bringing a generator and medical supplies to the farm of Uday al-Jumaili. The previous week, they had driven out to Fedaliyah to do a school assess-ment and clean up graffiti. As a goodwill gesture, they had helped Uday al-Jumaili's son, a twelve-year-old herder, to escort a dozen sweaty buffalo and one million black flies to the river.

Pfc. Vaczy and Sgt. Zeiger were in the lead truck.

Pfc. Mackey and Cpl. Al Grady were in the second vehicle.

From the right rear window of the Humvee, Sgt. Zei-ger watched telephone poles and crude walls sucked backward into the dust. Sleeping cats had slotted themselves between the stones, so that the walls themselves appeared to be breathing. An orangeish-gray goat watched the convoy pass from a ruined courtyard, heaving its ribs and crusty horns at the soldiers, its pink mouth bleating after them in the rearview like a cartoon without sound. At 6:22 a.m., a click away from the farm in Fedaliyah, the lead Humvee passed a palm grove within view of the Diyala River and the wise-stupid stares of the bathing *jammous*. Zeiger remembered watching one bull's tremendous head disappear beneath the dirty water. At 6:22, perhaps fifteen seconds later, an IED tore through the second Humvee, in which Pfc. Mackey was the gunner. Sgt. Zeiger watched in the mirrors as the engine compartment erupted in flames. Smoke flew into the gash of his mouth. Smoke blindfolded him. On his knees in the truck he gagged on smoke, its oily taste. Incinerated metal blew inside the vehicle, bright chunks raining through the window. His head slammed against the windscreen; immediately, his vision darkened; blood poured from his nostrils; a tooth, his own, went skidding across the truck floor.

"This front one is a fake," he tells Beverly, tapping his enamel. "Can't you tell? It's too perfect."

He remembered picking up the tooth, which was a shocking, foreign white, etched in space. He remembered grabbing the aid bag and the fire extinguisher and tumbling from the truck and screaming, directing these screams nowhere in particular, down at his own laced boots, then skyward—and then, when he got his head together, he remembered to scream for the intervention of a specific person, the medic, Spec. Belok. He saw the gunner from the third truck running over to the prone figure of Cpl. Al Grady and followed him.

"Well, okay: the bomb was a ten-inch copper plate, concave shape, remote-detonated, so when it blows there's about fifty pounds of explosives behind it. I heard over the radio 'There is blood everywhere,' and I could hear moaning in the background. The blast shot Corporal Grady completely into the air, out of the vehicle—and Grady is six foot five, Beverly . . ."

Beverly pulls at the wispiest clouds along the cords of his neck.

"Where's the triggerman? Are we about to get ambushed on the road? Nobody knows. There's no one around us, there's no one around us, and do you think maybe Uday al-Jumaili came running to help us? Guess again. His house is dead quiet, it's just our guys and the palm grove. Behind the truck, the *jammous* are staring at us. Three or four of them, looking as pissy as women, you know, like the attack interrupted their bathing plans. Grady is responsive, thank God. The door is hanging. Mackey is screaming and screaming, I'm kneeling right under him. Some of his blood gets in my mouth. Somehow even in my state I figured that one out: I'm coughing up Mack's blood. And whatever he's screaming, I don't understand it, it's not words, so I go, 'Mack, what're you saying, man? What are you saying?' I cut his pants to see if the femoral artery was severed. I remove his IBA looking for the chest wound. I wrap the wound to his head and his neck with a Kerlix . . ."

Zeiger's head is buried in the cushion—all this time, he hasn't looked up from the floor. Jigsaw cracks spread through the tattoo where his muscles keep tensing.

"Hours later, I'm still hearing the screaming. That night at the DFAC—the chow hall—we're all just staring at our food, and I'm telling people, 'I didn't catch his last words. I lost them, I didn't catch them.'

"And Lieutenant Norden, I didn't see him standing there, he goes: 'Hey, Zeiger, I'll translate: good-bye. He was saying: bye-bye.' Norden's like a robot, no feeling. And I almost get court-martialed for breaking Norden's jaw, Bev."

Bev, he says, like a strand of hair tucked behind her ear. Incredibly, in the midst of all this horror, she can still blush like a fool at the sound of her own name. She's terrified of setting him off again, knuckling down on the wrong spot, but at no point during his story does she halt the exploratory movements of her hands over the broad terrain of Zeiger's back.

"So now we all hump Mackey around like turtles. That day, April 14, it's frozen for all time back there."

"Well, for *your* lifetimes," Beverly hears herself blurt out.

"Right."

Zeiger scratches at a raw spot on his neck.

"Nobody has to live forever, thank God."

"Gotcha. My mistake."

Moisture clouds her eyes out of nowhere. *Forever,* just that word fills Beverly with an unaccountable, schoolmarmish sort of rage. Forever, that's got to be bad math, right? Such terrifying math. God, she does not want the kid to have to carry this forever.

"You know," she says, adjusting the pressure, "I think it's a beautiful thing you've done for your friend—" She traces the inky V below the tight cords of his neck. Silent birds migrating into the deeper blues. "You're giving him your, ah, your *portion* of eternity."

Portion of eternity, Christ, where did she get that one? A Hallmark mug? The Bible? Possibly she's plagiarizing the chalkboard Hoho's menu, some unbelievable deal: the bottomless soup bowl. Until doomsday, free refills on your coffee.

"No, you're right." He laughs sourly. "I guess I'm only good for a short ride."

A long silence follows. Fedaliyah heaves and falls.

"How long do you think, Bev?" he asks abruptly. "Fifty, sixty years?"

Beverly doesn't answer. After a while she says, "Are you still being treated at the VA down the road?"

"Yes, yes, yes—" His voice grows peevish, seems to scuff at the floor under the head support. "For PTSD, the same as everybody. Do I seem traumatized to you, Beverly? What's the story back there?"

Instead of answering his question, Beverly lets her hands slide down his back. "Breathe right here for me, Derek," she murmurs. She eagles her palms outward, pushes in opposite directions until she gets a tense spot above his sacrum to relax completely. Beneath the sheet of oil, the tattoo's colors seem to deepen. To glow, grow permeable. As if she could reach a finger into the landscape and swirl the *jammous* into black holes, whirlpools in the tattoo . . .

Soon Zeiger is snoring.

She works her fingertips into the skin around the fire, and she can smell the flowery scent of the oil becoming more powerful; just briefly, she lets her eyes close. Suddenly the jasmine smells of her room are replaced by burning rubber, diesel. Behind her closed eyelids, she sees a flash of beige light. Spidery black palms, a roadside stand. A pair of heat-blurred men waving at her as if from the other end of a telescope. Sand ticking at a windscreen.

Beverly hears herself gasp like someone emerging from a pool. When her eyes fly open, the first thing she sees are two hands, her own, rolling in circles through the oil on the sergeant's shoulders. She watches, astonished, as her two hands continue to massage on autopilot, rotating slickly all the way down the man's spine—has she been massaging him this whole time? She feels a disorientation that is very close to her childhood amazement during the ghostly performances of her uncle's player piano: the black keys and the white keys depressing in sequence, producing music. Sergeant Zeiger groans happily.

What just happened? *Nothing happened, Beverly,* she hears in the no-nonsense voice of her dead mother, the one her mind deploys to police its own sanity. But her nostrils are stinging from the burning petroleum. Her eyes are leaking. Tentatively, Beverly strokes the red star again.

This time when she shuts her eyes, the flashes she gets are up close: she sees the clear image of a face. Behind the long windscreen of a Humvee, a sunburned, helmeted soldier smiles vacantly at her. "Hey, Mackey—" someone yells, and the man turns. He is bobbing his chin to some distant music, drumming his knuckles against the stiff Kevlar vest, uneclipsed.

Beverly has to stop the massage to towel her eyes. Where are these pictures coming from? It feels like she's remembering a place she's never been before, reminiscing about a face she's never seen in her life. Somehow a loop of foreign experience seems to have slotted itself inside her brain, like her uncle's piano rolls. Zeiger's song, spinning wildly through her. She wonders if such a thing is possible. Music she hears on the radio lodges in Beverly for weeks at a stretch. All sorts of strange contagions sweep over this earth. Germs travel inside coughs and sewer rats, spores are cloaked in the bare wind.

A "flashback"—that was the word from the VA literature.

Beverly tries to concentrate on her two hands, their shape and weight in space, their real activity. If she closes her eyes for even a second, she's afraid that Humvee will roll into her mind and erupt in flames. She forces herself to massage Zeiger's shoulders, his buttocks, the tendons of his neck. Areas far afield of the "Arlo Mackey" trigger, the red star—the fatal fire, rendered down. The star seems to be the matchstick that strikes against her skin, combusts into the vision. And yet, in spite of herself, she watches her hands drawn down the tattoo. Now she feels she has some insight into the kind of trouble that April 14 must be giving Sergeant Derek Zeiger—there's a gravity she can't resist at work here. Her hands sweep around the red star like the long fingers of a clock, narrowing their orbit. Magnetized to that boy's last minute.

At the end of the massage, she pauses with the oily towel in her hand.

Her eyes feel as if there are little heated pins inside them.

A truck goes rolling slowly down Route Roses.

"Wake up!" she nearly screams.

"Goddamn it, Bev," Zeiger grumbles with his eyes shut. Beverly stands near his face on the pillow, and watches him open one reluctantly. Under her palms, his pulse jumps. "I was just resting my eyes for a sec. You scared me."

"You fell asleep again, Derek." It's an effort to ungrit her teeth. She can feel an explosion coming in their tingling roots. "And it seemed to me like you were stuck in a bad dream."

At home, Beverly licks at her chalky lips. Her heartbeat is back to normal but her ears are still roaring. Is she lying to herself? Possibly the flashback is really nothing but her own projection, a dark and greedy way to feel connected to him, to dig into his trauma. Perhaps all she is seeing is her own hunger for drama spooling around the sergeant's service, herself in hysterics, a devotee of that new genre, "the bleeding heart horror story." So named by Representative Eule Wolly in his latest rant on TV. He'd railed against the media coverage on the left and right alike: prurience, pawned off as compassion! The bloodlust of civilians. War-as-freak-show, war-as-snuff-film. "All the smoky footage on the seven a.m. news to titillate you viewers who are just waking up. Give you a jolt, right? Better than your Folger's."

Was it that? Was that all?

That week, Beverly sees her ordinary retinue of patients: a retired mailman with a herniated disk; a pregnant woman who lies curled on her side, cradling her unborn daughter, while Beverly works on her shoulders; sweet Jonas Black, her oldest patient, who softens like a cookie in milk before the massage has even begun. By Friday the intensity of her contact with Sergeant Derek Zeiger feels dreamily distant, and the memory of the tattoo itself has gone fuzzy on her, that picture no more and no less real to her than the war accounts she's seen on television or read. Next time she won't allow herself to get quite so worked up. Dmitri, who is working with several referrals from the VA hospital, tells her that he can't stop bawling after his sessions with them, and Beverly feels a twist of self-loathing every time she sees his puffy face. No doubt his compassion for the returning men and women is genuine, but there's something else afoot at Dedos Mágicos, too, isn't there? Some common need has been unlidded in all of them.

What a sorrowful category, Beverly thinks: the "new veteran." All those soldiers returning from Fallujah and Kandahar and Ramadi and Yahya Khel to a Wisconsin winter. Flash-frozen into citizens again. The phrase calls to mind a picture from her childhood Bible: "The Raising of Lazarus." The spine of the book was warped, so that it always fell open to this particular page. Lazarus, looking a little hungover, was blinking into a hard light. Sunbeams were fretted together around his forehead in jagged green and yellow blades. His sandaled pals had all gathered outside his tomb to greet him, like a birthday surprise party, but it seemed to be a tough social moment; Lazarus wasn't looking at anyone. He was staring into the cave mouth from which he had just been resurrected with an expression of sublime confusion.

When, fifteen minutes into his third massage, Sergeant Derek Zeiger begins to tell Beverly the same story about Pfc. Arlo Mackey and April 14, she pauses, unsure if she ought to interject—is the sergeant testing her? Does he want to see if she's been paying attention to him? Yet his voice sounds completely innocent of her knowledge. She supposes this could be a symptom of the trauma, memory loss; or maybe Derek is simply an old-fashioned blowhard. As her hands travel up and down his spine, he tells the same jokes about the *jammous*. His voice tightens when he introduces Arlo. His story careens onto Route Roses . . .

"Why did you call it that? Route Roses?"

"Because it smelled like shit."

"Oh." The flowers in her imagination shrink back into the road.

"Because Humvees were always getting blown to bits on it. I saw it happen right in front of me, fireballs swaying on these big fucking stems of smoke."

"Mmh." She squirts oil into one palm, greases the world of April 14. Just his voice makes her crave buckets and buckets of water.

"I killed him," comes the voice of Sergeant Derek Zeiger, almost shyly.

"What?" Beverly surprises both of them with her vehemence. "*No.* No, you didn't, Derek."

"I did. I killed him—"

Beverly's mouth feels dry and papery.

"The bomb killed him. The, ah, the *insurgents* . . ."

"How would you know, Beverly, what I did and didn't do?" His voice shakes with something that sounded like the precursor to a fit of laughter, or fury; it occurs to her that she really doesn't know this person well enough to say which is coming.

"You can't blame yourself."

"Listen: there are two colors on the road, green and brown. Two colors on the berm of Route Roses. There was a *red* wire. I didn't miss it, Bev—I saw it. I saw it, I practically *heard* that color, and I thought I probably ought to stop and check it out, only I figured it was some dumb thing, a candy wrapper, a piece of trash, and I didn't want to stop again, it was a thousand degrees in the shade, I just wanted to get the fucking generators delivered and get back to base, and we kept right on driving, and I didn't say anything, and guess who's dead?"

"Derek . . . You tried to save him. The blood loss killed him. The IED killed him."

"It was enough time," he says miserably. "We had fifteen, twenty seconds. I could have saved him."

"No—"

"Later, I remembered seeing it."

Beverly swallows. "Maybe you just imagined seeing it."

When Beverly's mother first started coughing, those fits were indistinguishable from a regular flu. Everybody in the family said so. Her doctors had long ago absolved them. At the wake, Janet and Beverly agreed that there was nothing to tip them off to her cancer. And their father's symptoms had been even less alarming: discomfort on one side of his body. Just an infrequent tingling. Death had waited in the dark for a long time, ringing the McFaddens' doorbell.

"You think it's hindsight, Derek, but it's not that. It's regret. It's false, you know, what you see when you look back—it's the *illusion* that you could have stopped it . . ."

Beverly falls silent, embarrassed. After a moment, Derek lets out a raucous laugh. He allows enough time to elapse so that she hears the laugh as a choice, as if many furious, rejected phrases are swirling around his head on the pillow.

"You trying to pick a fight with me, Bev? I saw it. Believe me. I looked out there and I saw something flash on the berm, and it was hot as hell that day, and I didn't want to stop." He laughs again. "Now I can't stop seeing it. It's like a punishment."

He lets his face slump into the headrest. On the tattoo, Fedali-yah is becoming weirdly distorted, pulled to Daliesque proportions by the energy of his shuddering. His shoulders clench—he's crying, she realizes. And right there in the middle of his back, a scar is swelling. Visibly lifting off the skin.

"Shhh," says Beverly, "shhh—"

At first, it's just a shiny ridge of skin, as slender as a lizard's tail.

Then it begins to darken and swell, as if plumping with liquid. Has it been there all along, this scar, disguised by the tattoo ink? Did the oils irritate it? She watches with ticklish horror as the scar continues to lengthen, rise.

"I saw it, I saw it there," he is saying. "I can see it now, just how that wire would have looked . . . why the *fuck* didn't I say anything, Beverly . . . ?"

Quickly, without thought, Beverly pushes down on it. An old, bad taste floods her mouth. When she lifts her hand, the thin, dark scar is still there, needling through the palm grove on the tattoo like something stitched onto Derek by a blotto doctor. She runs her thumbs over it, all reflex now, smoothing it with the compulsive speed that she tidies wrinkles on the white sheet. For a second, she succeeds in thumbing it under his skin. Has she burst it, will fluid seep out of it? She lifts her hands and the scar springs right back into place like a stubborn cowlick. Then she pushes harder, wincing as she does so, anticipating Zeiger's scream—but the sergeant doesn't react at all. She pushes down on the ridge of skin as urgently as any army medic doing chest compressions, and from a great distance a part of her is aware that this must look hilarious from the outside, like a Charlie Chaplin comedy, because the scale is all wrong here, she's using every ounce of her strength, and the red threat to Sergeant Zeiger is the width of a coffee stirrer.

And then the scar or blister, whatever it was, is gone. Really gone; she removes her hands to reveal smooth flesh. Zeiger's tattoo is a flat world again, ironed solidly onto him. This whole ordeal takes maybe twelve seconds.

"Boy, *that* was a new move," says the soldier. "That felt deep, all right. Do the Swedes do that one?" His voice is back to normal. "What did you do just now?"

Beverly feels woozy. Her mouth is cracker-dry. She keeps sweeping over his back to confirm that the swelling has stopped.

"Thank you!" he says at the end of their session. "I feel *great*. Better than I have since—since forever!"

She gives him a weak smile and pats his shoulder. Outside the window, the snow is really falling.

"See you next week," they say at the same time, although only Beverly's cheeks blaze up.

Beverly stands in the doorway and watches Zeiger scratching under his raggedy black shirt, swaying almost drunkenly down the hallway. Erasing it—she hadn't intended to do that! Medically, did she just make a terrible mistake? Should she have called a real doctor? Adrenaline pumps through her and pools in her stiff fingers, which ache from the effort of the massage.

Call him back. Tell Derek what just happened.

Tell him what, though? Not what she did to the scar, which seems loony. And surely not what she secretly believes: *I saw the wire and I acted. I saved you.*

The next time Sergeant Zeiger comes to see her he looks almost unrecognizable.

"You look wonderful!" she says, unable to keep a note of pleasure out of her voice. "Rested."

"Aw, thanks, Bev," he laughs. "You, too!" His voice lowers with a childlike pride. "I'm sleeping through the night, you know," he whispers. "Haven't had any pain in my lower back for over a week. Don't let it go to your head, Bev, but I'm telling all the doctors at the VA that you're some kind of miracle worker."

He walks into the room with an actual swagger, that sort of boastful indifference to gravity that Beverly associates with cats and Italian women. One week ago, he was hobbling.

"Are you done changing?" she calls from behind the door.

She knocks, enters, lightheaded with happiness. Her body feels so fiercely tugged in the boy's direction that she takes a step behind the counter, as if to correct for some gravitational imbalance. Derek rubs his hands together, makes as if to dive onto the table. "God, I've been looking forward to seeing you all week. Counting down. How many more of these do I get?"

Seven sessions, she tells him. But Beverly has already privately decided that she will keep seeing Zeiger indefinitely, for as long as he wants to continue.

She grabs a new bottle of lotion, really high-end stuff, just in case it was only the oil she used last time that provoked his reaction. Ever so lightly, she pushes into his skin. The little fronds of Fedaliyah seem to curl away from her probing fingers. Ten minutes into the massage, without prompting, he starts to talk about the day that Mackey died. As the story barrels onto Route Roses and approaches the intersection where the red wire is due to appear, Beverly's stomach muscles tighten. An animal premonition causes her to drape her hands over the spot on Zeiger's back where the scar appeared last time. She has to resist the urge to lift her hands and cover her eyes.

"Derek, you don't have to keep talking about this if you . . . if it makes you . . ."

But she has nothing to worry about, it turns out. In the new version of the story, on his first pass through the fields of Uday al-Jumaili, Zeiger *never sees a wire*. She listens as his Humvee rolls down the road, past the courtyard and the goat and the spot where the red wire used to appear. Only much later, over fifty minutes after Mackey's body has been medevaced out on a stretcher, does Daniel Vaczy locate the filthy grain sack that contains a black mask, a video camera, and detonation equipment for the ten-inch copper plate that kills Mackey, fragments of which they later recover.

"We almost missed it. All hidden in the mud like that. No triggerman in sight. Really, it's a miracle Vaczy uncovered it at all."

Beverly's hands keep up their regular clockwork. Her voice sounds remarkably steady to her ears: "You didn't see any sign of the bomb from your truck?"

"No," he says. "If I had, maybe Mackey would be alive."

He's free of it.

Elation sizzles through her before she's fully processed what she's hearing. She's *done* it. Exactly what she's done she isn't sure, and how it happened, she doesn't know, but it's a victory, isn't it? When the sergeant speaks, his voice is mournful, but there is not a hint of self-recrimination in it. Just a week ago last Tuesday, his sorrow had been shot through with a tremulous loathing—his guilt outlined by his grief. Beverly once read a science magazine article about bioluminescence, the natural glow emitted by organisms like fireflies and jellyfish, but she knows the dead also give off a strange illumination, a phosphor that can permanently damage the eyes of the living. Necroluminescence—the light of the vanished. A hindsight produced by the departed's body. Your failings backlit by the death of your loved ones. But now it seems the soldier's grief has become a matte block. Solid, opaque. And purified (she hopes) of his guilt. His own wary shadow.

Is it possible he's lying to her? Does the kid really not remember a red wire?

She plucks tentatively at a tendon in his arm.

"You can't blame yourself, Derek."

"I don't blame myself," he says coolly. "Did I plant the fucking bomb? It's a war, Bev. There was nothing anybody could have done."

Then Zeiger's neck tightens under her fingers, and she has to manually relax it. She massages the points where his jawbone meets his ears, imagines her thumbs dislodging the words she just spoke. Where did the wire go? Is it gone for good now? She leans onto her forearms, applying deeper pressure to his spinal meridian. The oil gives the pale sky on Zeiger's back a dangerous translucence, as if an extra second of heat might send the sunset-pink inks streaming. She has a terrible, irrational fear of her hand sinking through his skin and spine. All along his sacrum, her fingers are digging in sand.

"That feels incredible, Beverly," he murmurs. "Whatever you are doing back there, my God, don't stop."

And why *should* he feel guilty, anyway? Beverly wonders that night, under an early moon. And why should she?

Did it happen when I moved the sun? Beverly wonders sleepily. It's 11:12 p.m., claims the cool digital voice of time on her nightstand, 11:17 by the windup voice of her wristwatch. Did she alter some internal clock for him? Knock the truth off its orbit?

Memories are inoperable. They are fixed inside a person, they can't be smoothed or soothed with fingers. *Don't be nutty, Beverly,* she lectures herself in her mother's even voice. But if it turns out that she really can adjust them from without? Reshuffle the deck of his past, leave a few cards out, sub in several from a sunnier suit, where was the harm in that? Harm had to be the opposite, didn't it? Letting the earliest truth metastasize into something that might kill you? The gangrenous spread of one day throughout the life span of a body—wasn't that something worth stopping?

3:02 a.m. 3:07 a.m. Beverly rolls onto her belly and pushes her head between the pillows. She pictures the story migrating great distances, like a snake curling and unwinding under his skin. Shedding endlessly the husks of earlier versions of itself.

One thing she knows for certain: Derek Zeiger is a changed man. She can feel the results of her deep tissue work on his lower back, which Zeiger happily reports continues to be pain-free. And the changes aren't merely physical—over the next few weeks, his entire life appears to be straightening out. An army friend hooks him up with a part-time job doing IT for a law firm. He's sleeping and eating on a normal schedule; he's made plans to go on an ice fishing trip with a few men he's met at work. He has a date with a female Marine from one of his VA groups. The first pinch of jealousy she feels dissolves when she sees his excitement, gets a whiff of cologne. He rarely mentions Pfc. Arlo Mackey anymore, and he never talks about a wire.

All of a sudden Derek Zeiger, who is thawing faster than the rainbow ice he used to slurp at the state fair, wants to tell her about other parts of his past. Other days and nights and seasons. Battles with the school vice principal. Domestic dramas. She listens as all the former selves that have hovered, invisibly, around the epicenter of April 14 start coming to life again, becoming his life: Zeiger in school, Zeiger before the war. Funny, ruddy stories fill in his blanks.

Beverly feels a tiny sting as Derek ambles off. He looks like any ordinary twenty-five-year-old now, with his rehabilitated grin and his five o'clock shadow. It's the first time she's ever felt anything less than purely glad to see his progress. They have four more sessions together as part of his VA allotment. Soon he won't need her at all.

On Friday, Sergeant Zeiger interrupts a long and mostly silent massage to recount his recent dream:

"I had such a strange one, Beverly. It felt so real. You know how you can unspool the ribbon from a cassette tape? I found this wire, I had bunches and bunches of it in my arms, I walked for miles, right through the center of the village, it was Fedaliyah and it wasn't, you know how that goes in dreams, the houses kept multiplying and then withdrawing, like this *shimmering,* like a wave, I guess you would call it. A tidal wave, but going backward, sort of pulling the whole village away from me like a slingshot?—now, okay, that's how I knew I was dreaming? Because those houses we saw outside Fedaliyah were shanties, they had shit for houses, no electricity, but in my dream all the windows were glowing . . ."

These walls receded from him, sparklingly white and quick as comets, and then he was alone. There was no village anymore, no convoy, no radios, no brothers. There was only a featureless desert, and the wire.

"I kept tugging at it, spooling it around my hand. I wasn't wearing my gloves for some reason. I followed the wire to where it sprung off the ground and ran through the palms, and I knew I shouldn't leave the kill zone alone but I kept following it. I thought I was going to drop dead from exhaustion—when I woke up I ran to my bathroom and drank from the faucet."

"Did you ever get to the end of it?"

"No."

"You woke up?"

"I woke up. I remember the feeling, in the dream, of knowing that I wouldn't find him. I kept thinking, I'm a fool. The trigger-man has got to be long gone by now."

"What a strange dream," she murmurs.

"What do you think it means, Beverly?"

His tone is one of sincere mystification. He doesn't seem to connect this wire in his dream to the guilt he once felt about Arlo. Does this mean he's getting better—healing, recovering? Beverly's initial thrill gives way to a queasy feeling. There are child savants, she knows, who can recite answers to the thousandth decimal point without ever understanding the equations that produced them. If they continue these treatments, she worries that all his memories of the real sands of Iraq might get pushed into the hourglass of dreams, symbols.

Derek is still lying on his stomach with his face turned away from her. She rubs a drop of clear gel into the middle of his spine.

"You were looking for the triggerman, Derek. Isn't that obvious? But it was a nightmare. It doesn't mean anything."

"I guess you're right. But this dream, Bev—it was terrible." His voice cracks. "I was alone for miles and miles, and I had to keep walking."

She pictures a dream-small Zeiger retreating after the wire, growing more and more remote from the Derek Zeiger who's awake. And a part of her thinks, *Good. Let him forget that there ever was an April 14. Let that day disappear even from his nightmares.* If the wire ever comes up again, Beverly decides in that moment, she'll push it right back under his skin. As many times as it takes for Sergeant Derek Zeiger to heal, she will do this. With sincere apologies to Pfc. Arlo Mackey—whom she suspects she must also be erasing.

Working the dead boy out of Route Roses like a thorn.

She has a sensation like whiskey moving to the top of her brain. It leaves her feeling similarly impaired. Beverly pushes down and down and down into the muscles under his tattoo to release the knots. Muscle memory, her teacher used to say, that's what we're working against.

Off duty, at home, Beverly's own flashbacks are getting worse. Beverly shuts her eyes on the highway home, sees the mist of blood and matter on the Humvee windscreen, Mackey's head falling forward with an abominable serenity on the cut stem of his neck. At the diner, her pancake meals are interrupted by strange flashes, snatches of scenery. Fists are pounding on glass; someone's voice is screaming codes through a radio. Freckles sprinkle across a thin nose. A widow's peak goes pink with sunburn. Here comes the whole face again, rising up in her mind like a prodigal moon, miraculously restored to life inside the Humvee: the last, lost grin of Pfc. Arlo Mackey. Outside her window, the blue streetlight causes the sidewalk to shine like an empty microscope slide. Her bedroom is a black hole. Wherever she looks now, she sees Arlo's absence. At night, she sits up in bed and hears Derek's voice:

"So Belok gets on the radio. Blood is coming out of Mackey like a fucking hydrant . . ."

Now Beverly is afraid to go to sleep. A moot fear, it turns out: she can't sleep any longer.

Of course there is always the possibility that she is completely off her rocker. If Zeiger were to bring her a photograph of Mackey in his desert fatigues, would she recognize him as the soldier from her visions? Would he have a receding hairline, brown hair with a cranberry tint, a dimple in his chin? Or would he turn out to be a stranger to Beverly—a boy she doesn't recognize?

Derek she likes to picture in his new apartment across town, snoring loudly. There is something terribly attractive to Beverly about the idea that she is remembering this day *for* him, keeping it locked away in the vault of her head, while the sergeant goes on sleeping.

Despite her insomnia, and her growing suspicion that she might be losing her mind, Beverly spends the next month in the best mood of her life. Really, she can't account for this. She looks terrible—Ed never even yells at her anymore. Her regular patients have started making tentative inquiries about her health. She's lost twelve pounds; her eyes are still bloodshot at dusk. But so long as she can work with Derek, she feels invulnerable to the headaches and the sleep deprivation, to the bobbing head of Pfc. Mackey and the wire loose in the dirt. So long as only she can see it, and Derek's amnesia holds, and Derek continues to improve, she knows she can withstand infinite explosions, she can stand inside her mind and trip the red wire of April 14 forever. When Derek comes in for his eighth session, he brings her flowers. She thanks him, embarrassed by her extraordinary happiness, and then presses them immediately when she gets back to her apartment.

She stops wasting her time debating whether she's harming or helping him. Each time a session ends without any reappearance of the wire, she feels elated. That killing story, she excised from him. Now it's floating in her, like a tumor in a jar. Like happiness, laid up for the long winter after the boy heals completely and leaves her.

Derek misses three appointments in a row. Doesn't turn up outside Beverly's door again until the last day of February. He's wearing his unseasonably thin black T-shirt, sitting in a hard orange chair right outside her office. With his skullcap tugged down and his guilty grin he looks like a supersize version of the jug-eared kid waiting for the vice principal.

"Sorry I'm a little late, Bev," he says, like it's a joke.

"Your appointment was three weeks ago."

"I'm sorry. I forgot. Honestly, it just kept slipping my mind."

"I'll see you now," says Beverly through gritted teeth. "Right now. Don't move a muscle. I have to make some calls."

Through the crack in the door she watches Zeiger changing out of his shirt. Colors go pouring down his bunched bones. At this distance his tattoo is out of focus and only glorious.

"So, American Hero. Long time no see." She pauses, struggling to keep her voice controlled. She was so worried. "We called you."

"Yeah. Sorry. I was feeling too good to come in."

"The number was disconnected."

"I'm behind on my bills. Nah, it's not like that," he says hurriedly, studying her face. "Nothing serious." His mouth keeps twitching like an accordion. She realizes that he's trying to smile for her.

"You don't look too good," she says bluntly.

"Well, I'm still sleeping," he says, scratching his neck. "But some of the pain is back."

He climbs onto the table, smoothing his new cap of hair. It's grown and grown. Beverly is surprised the former soldier can tolerate it at this length. The black tuft of hair at his nape is clearly scheming to become a mullet.

"Is the pressure too much?"

"Yes. But no, it's fine. I mean, do what you gotta do back there to fix it, Bev." He takes a sharp breath. "Did I tell you what's happening to Jilly?"

Beverly swallows, immediately alarmed. Jilly Mackey, she remembers. Arlo's sister. Her first thought is that the girl must be seeing the pictures of April 14 herself now. "I don't think so . . ."

In Lifa, Texas, it turns out, Jilly has been having some trouble. Zeiger found out about this when he spoke on the phone with the Mackey women last night; he'd called for Arlo's birthday. "A respect call," he says, as if this is a generally understood term. She'll have to ask one of the other veterans if it's a military thing.

"Her mother's upset because I guess Jilly's been 'acting out,' whatever the fuck that means, and the teachers seem to think that somehow the tattoo is to blame—that she should have it removed. Laser removal, you know, they can do that now."

"I see. And what does Jilly say?"

"Of course she's not going to. That's her brother on the tattoo. She's starting at some new school in the fall. But the whole thing makes me sad, really sad, Beverly. I'm not even sure exactly why. I mean, I can see to where it would be hard for her—emotionally, or whatever—to have him back there . . ."

Beverly squeezes his shoulders. A minor-key melody has been looping through her head since he began talking, and she realizes that it's a song from one of her father's records that she'd loved as a child, a mysterious and slightly frightening one with wild trumpets and horns that sounded like they'd been recorded in a forest miles away, accidentally caught in the song's net: "The Frozen Chameleon."

"It's probably a weird thing to explain in the girls' locker room, you know? But on the other hand I almost can't believe the teachers would suggest that. It doesn't feel right, Bev. You want a tattoo to be, ah, ah . . ."

"Permanent?"

"Exactly. Like I said, it's a memorial for Arlo."

Grief freezing the picture onto him. Grief turning the sergeant into a frozen chameleon. Once a month Beverly leaves flowers in front of her parents' stones at St. Stephen's. Her sister got out twenty-five years ago, but she's still weeding for them, sprucing daffodils.

"You don't think the day might come when you want to erase it?"

"No! No way. Jesus, Beverly, weren't you listening? Just the thought makes me sick."

She smooths the sky between his shoulder blades. The picture book of Fedaliyah, stuck on that page he can't turn. After an instant, his shoulders flatten.

"I was listening. Relax." She shifts the pressure a few vertebrae lower. "There. That's better, isn't it?"

By March 10, she estimates she's survived hundreds of explosions. Alone in her apartment, she's watched Pfc. Mackey die and reincarnate with her eyes shut, massaging her own jaw.

From dusk until three or four a.m., in lieu of sleeping, she's started sitting through hundreds of hours of cable news, waiting for coverage of the wars. Of course Zeiger and Mackey won't be mentioned, they are ancient history, but she still catches herself listening nightly for their names. One night, spinning through the news roulette, she happens to stop on a photo still of a face that she recognizes: Representative Eule Wolly, the blue-eyed advocate of massage therapy for the new veterans.

Who, she learns, never served abroad during the Vietnam War. First Lieutenant Eule Wolly was honorably discharged from the navy while still stationed in San Francisco Bay. He lied about receiving a purple heart. The freckled news anchor reading these allegations sounds positively gleeful, as if he's barely suppressing a smile. Next comes footage of Representative Wolly himself, apologizing on a windy podium for misleading his constituents through his poor choice of wording and the "perhaps confusing" presentation of certain facts. Such as, to give one for instance, his alleged presence in the nation of Vietnam from 1969 to 1971. Currently he is being prosecuted under the Stolen Valor Act.

Beverly switches off the TV uneasily. Just that name, the "Stolen Valor Act," gets under her skin. She pushes down the thought that she's no better than the congressman, or the rest of the pack of liars and manipulators who parade across the television. In a way his crime is not so dissimilar to what she's been doing, is it? Encouraging Derek to twist his facts around as she loosens his muscles; trying to rub out his memories of the berm. Thinking she can live the boy's worst day for him.

"He's doing amazingly well," Beverly hears herself telling her sister, Janet, during their weekly telephone call. Bragging, really, but she can't help herself—Zeiger is making huge strides. His life is settling into an extraordinarily ordinary routine, she tells Jan, who by now has heard all about him.

"He's got a full-time job now, isn't that exciting? He signed the lease on a new apartment, too, much nicer than the cockroach convention where he's been living. I'm really so proud of him. Janet?"

She pauses, embarrassed—it's been whole minutes since her sister's said a word. "Are you still there?"

"Oh, I'm still here." Janet laughs angrily. "You think I don't know what you're doing? You want to throw it in my face?"

"What?"

"Nice to hear you're still taking such *excellent* care of everyone."

Fury causes her sister's voice to crackle in the receiver. For a second, Beverly is too stunned to speak.

"Janet. I have no idea what you're talking about."

"Don't pretend like I didn't do my part. I was there as often as I could be, Beverly. Once a month without fail—more, when I could get away. And not everybody thought it was a good idea to skip college, you know."

Beverly stares across her kitchen, half expecting to see the dishes rattling. Once a month? Is Janet joking?

"Do you want me to get the calendar out?" Beverly's voice is trembling so hard it's almost unintelligible. "From September to May one year," she says, "I was alone with her. Don't you dare deny it."

"It's been twenty goddamn years. Every other weekend, practically, I was there."

"You did *not*—"

"Dad thought you were crazy to stay, Mom practically begged you to go, so if you stayed, you did it for your own reasons. Okay? And I came to help plenty of times. I'm sorry if it wasn't every fucking weekday like you. I'm sorry we can't all be saints like you, Beverly. *Healers*—"

Now she sounds like the older sister that Beverly remembers, her voice high and wild, stung, making fun.

"And I had my own family."

"You had Stuart. The girls weren't even born yet." Beverly sputters. *You got the girls,* she manages not to say, although now her outrage is actually blinding.

"You're not remembering right," Janet insists. We were out there a bunch of times . . ."

"Janet! You can't be serious!"

"We *were* and you know it."

Beverly swallows. "But that's simply not true."

"I know I'll regret saying this, okay, I've held my tongue for twenty years, I should get a damn medal like your little buddy out there. But who else is going to tell you? You are like a dog, Beverly." Beverly can almost feel her sister's fingers clawing into the telephone, as if they are wrapped around Beverly's neck. "You're like a sad dog. Your masters aren't coming back. Sor-ry. Mom's been dead for over a decade, do you realize that? You need some new tricks."

Beverly takes a breath; it's as if she's been punched.

"You have no idea what I sacrificed—"

"Oh, give me a break. Die a martyr then. Jesus Christ."

For many years, Beverly will remember every word of this conversation while failing to recall, no matter how hard she tries, who hung up first.

Quaking alone in her apartment, Beverly's first impulse is to dial their old home phone number. *If you were alive, Mom,* she thinks, *you would set the record straight.* For years she's assumed that she and Janet agreed on this point, at least: the basic chronology of their mother's fight with cancer. What happened when. Who was present in which rooms. Beverly doesn't know how to make sense of who she is today without those facts in place. With a chill she realizes there are no witnesses left besides herself and Janet. She has a sense memory of steering her mother down a long corridor, her wheelchair spokes glinting. Janet missed knowing that version of their mother. If Beverly stops pushing her now, or loses her grip, she will roll out of sight.

With her hand still tangled in the telephone cord, Beverly decides that she doesn't want to be yet another of the cover-up artists. Can't. She won't go on encouraging the sergeant to lie to himself, just so he can sleep at night. She's warped the truth, she pushed the truth under his skin, but she won't allow it to go on changing. Suddenly it is vitally important to Beverly that Zeiger remember the original story, the one she has stolen from him.

Whatever she's wiped from his memory, she wants to restore. Immediately, if that's possible.

"Derek? It's Beverly. Can you come in tomorrow? I have a slot at nine . . ."

She gets a melting flash of an obscenely blue sky, blooming fire. A large bull is standing in a river, in chest-high green water, chains of mosquitoes twisting off its bony shoulders like tassels. Its eyes are vacuums. Placid and hugely empty. The animal continues lapping at its reddish shadow on the water, oblivious of the bomb behind it, while a thick smoke rolls over the desert.

When she sees Zeiger in person the following morning, with his big grin and his smooth, unlined face, she can feel her resolve fading. She knows she's got to help him to recover his original memory, to straighten out the timeline of April 14 now, before she loses her nerve completely. He lies down on the massage table, and she's glad his face is turned away from her.

"I was thinking about you a lot this weekend, Derek," she says. "I saw a news show where they interviewed an army general about IEDs . . . I thought of your friend Arlo, of course. That story you told me once, about April 14—"

Derek doesn't react, so she babbles on.

"This general said it was almost impossible to spot trip wires. He called them these 'tiny wires in the dirt.' And I thought, I'll have to ask Derek if that was, ah, his same experience . . ."

There is no warning contraction of his shoulder blades.

"Of course it's hard to spot the wires!" Derek explodes at her. He shakes off her hands, sits up. "You need TV to tell you that? You need to hear it from some general? Jesus Christ, it's nine a.m., and you're interrogating me?"

"Derek, please, there's no need to get so upset—"

"No? Then why the hell did you bring up Arlo?"

"I'm sorry if I—I was only curious, Derek—"

"That's right, that's everyone. You're 'only curious,'" he snarls. "None of you has any idea what it was like. Nobody gives a shit."

Derek rolls his legs away from her and stands, struggles into his shirt and pants, knocking into the massage table. Then he goes stumbling out of the room like a revenant, half dressed, trailing one sleeve of his jacket. Walking away from her so quickly that it's impossible to tell what, if anything, changed on the tattoo.

Six thirty a.m. on Monday: Beverly is brushing her teeth when the phone rings. It's Ed Morales, of course, who else would it be this early on a workday but Ed, his voice spuming through the receiver. Lance Corporal Oscar Ilana is dead, Ed tells her. Has been dead for two days. In the mirror, Beverly watches this information float on the surface of her gray eyes without penetrating them.

"Oh my God, Ed, I'm so sorry, how terrible . . ."

Not Derek is her only thought as she hangs up.

It remains that, beating in her head like a bat, a tiny monster of upside-down joy: *not-Derek, not-Derek*. Then the bat flies off and she's alone in a cave. Oscar. She remembers who he is—was, she corrects herself. Another of their VA referrals. One of Ed's patients. He'd survived three IED blasts in Rustamiyah. She'd chatted with him once in the waiting room, a lean man with glasses, complaining about how pale he'd gotten since coming home to Wisconsin although his skin was a beautiful maroon. He'd passed around a photograph of his two-year-old daughter. For a new veteran, he'd seemed remarkably relaxed. Cracking himself up.

The news of Lance Corporal Ilana's death turns out to be hidden in plain sight in her apartment, spread out on her countertop, gathering leaky drips from her ceiling. After Ed calls her, she finds the Saturday newspaper where his suicide was reported—

The soldier died in his car of an apparently self-inflicted gunshot wound to the head at 11:15 p.m. At 11:02 p.m., he reportedly sent a text message to his wife informing her of his plans to harm himself.

Beverly cancels every appointment in her book except for Derek Zeiger. Then Zeiger fails to show. For the first time in three years, Beverly skips work. Beds down straight through noon with the blinds half drawn, the sunbeams rattling onto her coverlet. Through the mesh of light she can still see Arlo Mackey's ruined face. *Go away,* she whispers. But the ghost is in her body, not her room, and scenes from his last day continue to invade her.

"It all came at you like you didn't have a brain," Derek told her once, describing the routine chaos of their patrols.

Beverly has never been a drinker. But after learning of Oscar Ilana's death she returns from the liquor store with six bottles of wine. Between Monday and Friday four bottles disappear. Into her, it seems, as unlikely as she finds these new hydraulics of her apartment. It turns out the dark cherry stuff doesn't help her to sleep, but it blurs the world she stays awake in. What a bargain for ten bucks, she thinks, on her tiptoes in the liquor store. Maybe she can fix the problem by moving the sun again. How far back would she have to rewind it, to instill a permanent serenity in Derek? Hours? Eons? She imagines blue glaciers sliding over Fedaliyah, the soldiers blanketed in ice. It seems incredible to her that she ever thought she might do this for him—wring the whole war from his tissue and bone. In Esau, night lightens into dawn. Cars begin to jump and whine across the intersection at six a.m. When an engine backfires, she flinches and grinds down on her molars and watches the Humvee erupt in flames.

Enough, she tells herself, *snap out of it, this is ridiculous, insane*—but it turns out these commands don't clear the smoke from her brain. Beverly uncorks a second bottle of wine. She cracks open her window, lights a cigarette pinched from Ed. Smoke exits her lips in a loose curl, joining the snow. She wonders if this will become a new habit, too.

Nobody blames massage therapy for the young soldier's suicide, exactly, but Representative Wolly's H.R. 1722 program gets scuttled, and plenty of the commentators add a rueful line about how the young lance corporal had been receiving state-funded deep tissue massages at a place called Dedos Mágicos.

At Dedos, it's surprising to see how deeply everyone is affected, even those on staff who only briefly met Ilana. There are lines of mourning on Ed's face. He spends the week following Oscar's death walking softly around the halls of the clinic in black socks, hugging his arms around his ice cream scoop of a belly. He doesn't curse or scream at anybody, not even the clock face. A gentle hum seems to be coming from deep in his throat.

And where is Derek? His phone is still disconnected. He's AWOL from his regular groups at the VA hospital. The counselor there reports that she hasn't heard a peep from him in five or six days. Beverly replays her last words to him until she feels sick. She keeps waiting for him to show up, staring down at the Dedos parking lot. It occurs to her that this vigil might merely be the foretaste of an interminable limbo, if Derek never comes back.

Outside the window, a dozen geese are flying west, sunlight pooling like wet paint on their wings. Beverly has been noticing many such flocks moving at fast speeds over Esau, and whenever she sees them they are as gracefully spaced as writing. She can't read any sense behind their dissolving bodies. Then the red parchment of the Wisconsin sunset melts, black space erases the geese, it's night.

Beverly learns that one prejudice that has been ordering her existence is that there *is* an order: that time exists, and that its movements are regular and ineluctable, migrating like any animal from sunup to sunset—red dawns molting their way into violet dusks, days flocking into weeks and months. Not: *April 14. April 14. April 14,* like raindrops plunking onto her head from a ceiling she can't see. Her "flashbacks," such as they are, do not conform to the timeline of Derek's first story anymore. They feel closer to dreams—in one of them, the red wire rises out of his back like a viper to strike at her hands. Sometimes Zeiger stops the truck and kneels in dirt, digging with his fingers, and Mackey survives, and sometimes Zeiger fails to see the wire and the bomb explodes. Sometimes every character in the story has been dead for half a century, and a gleaming herd of water buffalo is grazing on the empty land, which looks like a science-fiction moonscape in this epoch, and a team of archaeologists finds the bomb, spading into the dust of the old New Baghdad.

The wire is always present, though—that's the one constant. Curled loosely on top of the dirt, or almost completely buried. It's a surprise that keeps giving itself away, exposed in the ruby light of her jarred skull.

Sometimes her worries worm southward, and she finds herself thinking about Jilly Mackey. This tenth-grader with her brother's death day pinioned to her back like some large and trembling butterfly. She pictures the kid leaning over her homework in Lifa, Texas, pulling the red star taut under her shirt. What exactly were these "troubles" that Derek mentioned? Is the tattoo changing on her, too? What if something worse than a wire is lunging out of her canvas? Beverly has to fight down a crazy desire to telephone the Mackey women, offer her services. In another mood this would have struck Beverly as hilarious, the vision of herself boarding a plane to Texas with a duffel of massage oils. *My thumbs to the rescue!* How would she conduct that conversation with Mrs. Mackey? "Hello, I'm a massage therapist in Wisconsin, you don't know me from Adam but I've been mourning the death of your son? I'd like to help your daughter, Jilly, with her back pain?"

But that's a lunatic wish, of course; Beverly's concern for the Mackeys would fly through the telephone wires and mutate into something that stabbed at their ears. There's no etiquette for a call like that. No set of techniques or magical oils.

"You know, I wanted to save him," Ed confides to her. And Beverly thinks that she would have liked to save all of them—Arlo Mackey and Oscar Ilana and Derek Zeiger, Jilly Mackey and her mother, the Iraqi children of the *jammous* farmers getting poisoned by their swims in the polluted Diyala, her own mother and father.

"Me, too, Ed."

"But a man like that is beyond help," says Ed, patting Beverly's shoulders as he has never done before in their decades together, and it's a construction of such grammatical perfection that she knows he must have memorized it from the TV anchors.

Early Sunday morning, the phone startles Beverly awake.

This time, thank God, it's not Ed Morales. It's not Janet calling with the weather report from Sulko, Nevada, or the joyful percolations of her twin nieces, wearing their matching jammies under Gemini stars in the American desert. Nobody else calls her at home. No stranger has ever rung her at this hour.

"Hello?"

"Hi, Bev. Sorry to call so early."

"Derek."

Beverly sinks under her coverlet. The relief she feels is indescribable.

"Were you up? You sound wide-awake."

"You scared me. The last time I saw you—"

"I know. I'm really, really sorry. I didn't mean to explode on you like that. I honestly don't know why that happened. It's weird because I've been feeling so much better lately. And for that I wanted to say, you know: *thank you.* To be honest, I was never expecting much from you. My real doctor at the VA made me enroll in the program. Massage therapy, no offense, I was thinking: hookers. Happy endings, la-la beads."

"I see."

"But whatever you do back there *works.* I've been sleeping like a baby ever since. I sleep through the night."

The wall clock says 3:00 a.m.

"I sleep good," he maintains, as if wanting to forestall an argument. "Tonight is an exception to the rule, I guess." He laughs quietly, and Beverly feels like a spider clinging to one bouncing line—their connection seems that frail.

"Well, we're both awake now." She swallows. "Why are you calling me here, Derek?"

"I'm not cured, though."

"Well, Derek, of course you're not," she says, fighting to get control of a lunging pressure in her chest. "Massage doesn't 'cure' people, it's a process . . ."

"Beverly . . ." His voice breaks into a whimper. "Something's wrong—"

There are a few beats of silence. In the mysterious, unreal distances of her inner ear, Pfc. Arlo Mackey continues screaming and screaming inside the burning truck.

"I'm in pain, a lot of pain. I need to see you again. As soon as I can."

"I'll see you on Monday, Derek. Ten o'clock."

"No, Beverly. Now." And then there is shuffling on his end of the receiver, and an awful sound like half a laugh. "Please?"

Ed Morales has never fired anybody in his thirty-year tenure as the owner of Dedos Mágicos, and he always mentions this a little wistfully, as if it's a macho experience he's dreamed of having, the way some men want to summit Everest or bag a lion on safari. She doesn't doubt that he will fire her if he finds them out.

Still, where else are they supposed to go? Beverly is a professional. She is not going to confuse everything even further at this late hour by beginning to see patients in her home.

Beverly has keys to the building. She drives beneath a full, icy moon, following the chowdery line of the Esau River. All the highways are empty. When she pulls into her staff slot, the sergeant's blue jalopy is already there.

"Thank you," he mumbles as they climb out of their cars. His eyes are red hollows. "Don't be scared, promise? I don't know what went wrong the other day."

Beverly, who has some idea, says nothing.

"Are you afraid of me, Beverly?"

"Afraid! Why would I be? Are you angry at me?"

Kind *no*s are exchanged.

There is a fat moon behind him, one white ear eavesdropping brazenly in the midwestern sky.

Beverly fumbles with the car lock, gets them both inside the building. Something is moving under his shirt, on his back, she can see it, a dark shape. In the onlyness of moonlight, his snowy boots look almost silver. Nothing stirs in the long hallway; when they pass the crescent of the reception desk, she half expects Ed to leap up in a fountain of expletives. Their shoes mewl on the tiles, sucked along by slush. They speak at the same time—

"Lie down?"

"I'll go lie down—"

"Thank you for meeting me, Beverly," he says again, sounding so much like a boy about to cry. "Something's wrong, something's wrong, something's wrong, something's *wrong.*" He groans. "Ah, Bev! Something feels twisted around . . ."

He pulls off his shirt, lies down. Beverly sucks in her breath— his back is in terrible shape. The skin over his spine looks raw and abraded; deep blue and yellowish bruises darken the sky of Fedaliyah. And a long, bright welt, much thicker and nastier than the thin scar she erased, stretches diagonally from his hip bone to his shoulder.

"Jesus, Derek! Did someone do this to you? Did you do this to yourself?"

"No."

"Did you have some kind of accident?"

"I don't know," he says flatly. "I don't remember. It looked this way when I woke up two days ago. It's gotten worse."

Beverly touches his shoulder and they both wince. Maybe the welt did erupt from inside the tattoo. Maybe Derek vandalized the tattoo himself, and he's too ashamed or too frightened to tell her. She's surprised to discover how little the explanation matters to her. In the end, every possibility she can imagine arises from the same place—a spark drifting out of his past and catching, turning into this somatic conflagration. No matter how it happened, she is terrified for him.

She dips a Q-tip into a bottle of peroxide, stirs.

This time she abandons any pretension of getting the true story out of him. She doesn't try to grab hold of April 14 and reset it like a broken bone. She doesn't mention IEDs or Mackey. Her concerns about whether or not it would be better for the sergeant to forget the wire, wipe his slate clean, are gone; she thinks those debates must belong to a room without this boy hurting in it. All she wants to do right now is reduce his pain. If she can help him with that, she thinks, it will be miracle enough.

"Don't worry," she says. "We're going to fix you up. Hold still for me, Derek."

She begins at the base of his spine, rolling up, avoiding the most irritated areas. He whimpers only once. Through his neck, she can feel the strain of his gritted teeth.

"That fucking *kills,* Beverly—what are you doing?"

"Shh—you focus on relaxing. This is helping."

She defaults to what she knows. Eventually, as in the first sessions, she can feel something shifting under her hands. Her voice needles in and out of Zeiger's ears as she tells him where to move and bend and breathe. It's dark in the room, and she's barely looking at his back, letting his fascia and muscles guide her fingers. Gradually, and then with the speed of windblown sands, the story of the tattoo begins to change.

A little after five a.m., Beverly stops the massage to button her sweater up to her neck. It's the same baggy cerulean skin that she always puts on, her old-lady costume. Tonight her sleeves bunch at her elbows, so that she feels like a strange molting bird—eating keeps slipping her mind. The moon is out; their two cars, viewed through the clinic window, have acquired a sort of doomed mastodon glamour, shaggy with snow. A green light blinks ceaselessly above her, some after-hours alarm she's never here to see. She checks to make sure the windows are closed—the room feels ice-cold. Beverly moves to get Zeiger's shirt, towels. She's washed and dressed the damaged skin; the tattoo is almost completely hidden under gauze. Now she doesn't have to look at the red star. Beverly cotton-daubs more peroxide onto his neck, which feels wonderfully relaxed. Zeiger begins to talk. With his eyes still shut, he tours her through the landscape on his back; it's a version of April 14 that is completely different from any that's come before. She listens to this and she doesn't breathe a word. She has no desire to lift the gauze, check the tattoo against this new account.

When he's finished, Beverly asks him in a shaky voice, "Nobody died that day, Derek?"

"Nobody."

He sits up. Perched on the table's edge, with the blanket floating in a loose bunting around his shoulders, the sergeant flexes and relaxes his long bare toes.

"Nobody died, Bev. That's why I got the tattoo—it was a miracle day. Amazing fucking grace, you know? Fifty pounds of explosives detonate, and we all make it back to the FOB alive."

Beverly smooths a wrinkle in a square of gauze, tracing the path of what was, the last time she looked, the Diyala River.

"Nobody died. I lost a chunk of my hearing, but I just listen harder now."

His face is beaming. "I love telling that story. You're looking at the proof of a miracle. My tattoo, it should hang in a church."

Then he slides toward her and cups one big hand behind her head. He sinks his fingers through the gray roots of her hair and holds her face there. It's a strange gesture, more gruff than romantic, his little unconscious parody of how she feels toward him, maybe—it makes her think, of all things, of a mother bear cuffing its cub. He digs his fingers into her left cheek.

"Thank you, Beverly." Zeiger talks in a telephone whisper, as if their connection is about to be cut off at any moment by some maniacal, monitoring operator. "You can't even imagine what you've done for me here—"

For what is certainly too long an interval Beverly lets her head rest against his neck.

"Oh, you're very welcome," she says into a muzzle of skin.

What happens next is nothing anyone could properly call a kiss; she turns in to him, and his lips go slack against her mouth; when this happens, whatever tension remains in him seems to flood into her. She fights down a choking sensation and turns her head, reaches for his hand.

"Beverly—"

"Don't worry. Look at that snow coming down. Time's up."

"Beverly, listen—"

"You'll be fine, Derek. I don't think those bruises will come back. But if they do, you come back, too. I'm not going anywhere, okay? I'll be waiting right here."

Several months after her last encounter with Derek, the phone rings. It's Janet, and just like that they are on speaking terms again. Janet invites her out to Sulko, and one morning Beverly finds herself standing in front of her nieces' class as a special guest for Careers Day. Little girls in violet vests sit patiently on the carpet. Their drawings shimmer on a corkboard wall near the window, bright shingles fluttering under pins. Beverly demonstrates a massage on a child volunteer, and the other students gather in a circle and dutifully grasp one another's shoulders. She's amazed to see how fearlessly they touch each other, pure pleasure flowing from tiny hands to shoulders without any of the circuit breakers that are bound to come later. The class runs into the lunch hour, but during the Q&A even her nieces are too shy to ask a question. At last, at the teacher's violent, whispered encouragement, one loopy-looking kid with pigtails the bright orange of cooked carrots raises her hand.

"What do you like the most about your job?"

"Oh, that's an easy one!" Beverly summons a smile for the girl. "Helping."

Most days, she doubts she helped the sergeant at all. She thinks it's far more likely that she aggravated his condition, or postponed a breakdown. But a picture comes to her of Zeiger walking down the street into vivid light, the tattoo moving with his muscles. She wants to believe that this is possible—that he lifted the gauze to find the welts healed and the tattoo settling into a new shape. Not even in her fantasy can she guess what it might look like. In her wildest imaginings, Zeiger finds both things—a story he can carry, and a true one.

The Graveless Doll of Eric Mutis

The scarecrow that we found lashed to the pin oak in Friendship Park, New Jersey, was thousands of miles away from the yellow atolls of corn where you might expect to find a farmer's doll. Scarecrow country was the actual *country,* everybody knew that. Scarecrows belonged to country men and women. They lived in hick states, the *I* states, exotic to us: Iowa, Indiana. Scarecrows made fools of the birds and smiled with lifeless humor. Their smiles were fakes, threads. (This idea appealed to me—I was a quiet kid myself, branded "mean," and I liked the idea of a mouth that nobody expected anything from, a mouth that was just red sewing.) Scarecrows got planted into the same soil as their crops; they worked around the clock, like charms, to keep the hungry birds at bay. That was my impression from TV movies, at least: horror-struck, the birds turned shrieking circles around the far-below peak of the scarecrow's hat, afraid to land. They haloed him. Underneath a hundred starving crows, the TV scarecrow seemed pretty sanguine, grinning his tickled, brainwashed grin at the camera. He was a sort of pitiable character, I thought, a jester in the corn, imitating the farmer—the *real* king. All day and all night, the scarecrow had to stand watch over his quilty hills of wheat and flax, of rye and barley and three other brown grains that I could never remember (my picture of scarecrow country was ripped directly from the 7-Grain Quilty Hills Muffins bag—at school I cheated shamelessly, and I guess my imagination must have been a plagiarist, too, copying its homework).

A scarecrow did not belong in our city of Anthem, New Jersey. Anthem had no crops, no silos, no crows—it had turquoise Port-o-Pottys and neon alleys, construction pits, dogs in purses, homeless women with powerful smells and opinions, garbage dumps haunted by white pigeons; it had our school, the facade of which was covered by a glorious psychedelic phallus mosaic, a bunch of spray-painted dicks. Cops leaned against the cement walls, not straw guards.

We were city boys. We lived in these truly shitbox apartments. Our familiarity with the figure of the scarecrow came exclusively from watered-down L. Frank Baum cartoons, and from the corny yet frightening "Autumn's Bounty!" display in the Food Lion grocery store, where every year a scarecrow got propped a little awkwardly between a pilgrim, a cornucopia, and a scrotally wrinkled turkey. The Food Lion scarecrow looked like a broom in a Bermuda shirt, ogling the ladies' butts as they bent to buy their diet yogurts. What we found in Friendship Park in no way resembled that one. At first I was sure the thing tied to the oak was dead, or alive. Real, I mean.

"Hey, you guys." I swallowed. "Look—" And I pointed to the pin oak, where a boy our age was belted to the trunk. Somebody in blue jeans and a striped sweater that had faded to the same earthworm color as his hair, a white boy, doubled over the rope. Gus got to the kid first.

"You retards." His voice was high with relief. "It's just a doll. It's got straw inside it."

"It's a *scarecrow*!" shrieked Mondo. And he kicked at a glistening bulb of what did appear to be straw beneath the doll's slumping face. A little hill. The scarecrow regarded its innards expressionlessly, its glass eyes twinkling. Mondo shrieked again.

I followed the scarecrow's gaze down to its lost straw. Long strands were blowing loose, like cut hair on a barbershop floor. Chlorophyll greens and yellows. Some of the straw had a jellied black look. How long had this stuff been outside him, I wondered—how long had it been *inside* him? I scanned his sweater for a rip, a cold, eel-like feeling thrashing in my own belly. That same morning, while eating my Popple breakfast tart, I'd seen a news shot of a foreign soldier watching blood spill from his head with an expression of extraordinary tranquillity. Calm came pouring over him, at pace with the blood. In the next room, I could hear my ma getting ready for work, singing an old pop song, rattling hangers. On TV, one of the soldier's eyes fluttered and shut. Then, without warning, the story changed, and the footage sprang away to the trees of a new country under an ammonia-blue sky. I'd sat there with jam leaking into my mouth, feeling suddenly unable to swallow—where was the cameraman or the camerawoman? Who was letting the soldier's face dissolve into that calm?

"Let's cut it down!" screamed Mondo. I nodded.

"Nah, we better not," Juan Carlos said. He looked around the woods sharply, as if there might be a sniper hidden in the oaks. "What if this"—he pushed at the doll—"belongs to somebody? What if somebody is watching us, right now? *Laughing* at us . . ."

It was late September, a cool red season. I wondered who had chosen to bind the scarecrow to this particular tree—our tree, the one that belonged to our gang, Camp Dark. It was the tallest tree in Friendship Park, a sixty-foot oak overlooking a deep ravine, which we called "the Cone." Erosion had split the limestone bedrock, creating a fifteen-foot drop to an opening that looked like the sandy bottom of a well; it couldn't have been more than seven feet across at its widest point. The rock walls were smooth. It didn't seem like you could get to the bottom safely without a parachute. Mondo was always trying to persuade us to throw a mattress down there, and jump. The Cone had become an open casket of our trash. Way down at the bottom you could see wet blue dirt with radishy pink streaks along it, as exotic looking to us as a seafloor. Condoms and needles (not ours) and the silver shreds of Dodo Potato Chips bags and beer bottles (mostly ours) seemed to grow among the weeds. The great oak leaned its shadow into the Cone like a girl playing at suicide, quailing its many fiery leaves.

We'd been meeting under this oak for four years, ever since we were ten years old. Back then we played actual games. We hid and we sought. We did benign stuff in trees. We amassed a plastic weapons cache in the hollow of the oak that included the Sounds of Warfare Blazer, a toy gun that required sixteen triple-A batteries to make a noise like a tubercular guinea pig. Those were innocent times. Then we'd gotten shunted into Anthem's upper grades, and now as freshmen we came here to drink beers and antagonize one another. Biweekly we shoplifted liquor and snacks, in a surprisingly orderly way, rotating this duty. "We are Communists!" shrieked Mondo once, pumping a fistful of red-hot peanuts into the sky, and Juan Carlos, who did homework, snorted, "You are quite confused, my bro."

Friendship Park was Anthem's last green space, sixty acres of woods bordered by gas and fire stations and a condemned pizza buffet. THE PIZZA PARTY IS CANCELED read a sign above a bulldozer. The central acres of Friendship Park were filled with pines and spruce and squirrels that chittered some charming bullshit at you, up on their hind legs begging for a handout. They lived in the trash cans and had the wide-eyed, innocent look and threadbare fur of child junkies. Had they wised up, our squirrels might have mugged us and used our wallets to buy train tickets to the national park an hour north of Anthem's depressed downtown. Only Juan Carlos had seen those real woods. ("There was a river with a purple fish shitting in it" was all we got out of him.)

Behind our oak was a playground over which we also claimed dominion. Recently, the Anthem City Parks & Recreation had received a big grant, and now the playground looked like a madhouse. Padded swings, padded slides, padded gyms, padded seesaws and go-wheelies: all the once-fun equipment had gotten upholstered by the city in this red loony-bin foam. To absorb the risk of a lawsuit, said Juan Carlos; one night, at Juan Carlos's suggestion, we all took turns pissing hooch onto the harm-preventing pillows. Our park had a poop-strewn dog run and an orange baseball diamond; a creepy pond that, like certain towns in Florida, had at one time been a very popular vacation destination for waterfowl but was now abandoned; and a Conestoga-looking covered picnic area. Gus claimed to have had sex there last Valentine's Day, on the cement tables—"pussy sex," he said, authoritatively, "not just the mouth kind." Our feeling was, if Gus really did trick a girl into coming to our park in late February, they most likely had talked about noncontroversial subjects, like the coldness of snow and the excellence of Gus's weed, all the while wearing sex-thwarting parkas.

The oak was covered with markings from our delinquent forebears: V ♥ K; DEATH 2 ASSHOLE JIMMY DINGO; JESUS SAVES; I WUZ HERE!!! The scarecrow's head, I noticed, was lolling beneath our own inscription:

MONDO + GUS + LARRY + J.C. = CAMP DARK

A dorky name, Camp Dark, chosen when we were ten, but we wouldn't change it now. Membership capped at four: Juan Carlos Diaz, Gus Ainsworth, Mondo Chu, and me, Larry Rubio. Pronounced "Rubby-oh" by me, like a rubber ducky toy, my own surname. My dad left when I turned two, and I don't speak any Spanish unless you count the words that everybody knows, like "hablo" and "no." My ma came from a vast hick family in Pensacola, pontoon loads of uncle-brothers and red-haired aunts and firecrotch cousins from some nth degree of cousindom, hordes of blood kin whom she renounced, I guess, to marry and then divorce my dad. We never saw any of them. We were long alone, me and my ma.

Juan Carlos had tried to tutor me once: "*Rooo*-bio. Fucker, you have to coo the 'u'!"

My ma couldn't pronounce my last name either, making for some awkward times in Vice Principal Derry's office. She'd reverted to her maiden name, which sounded like an elf municipality: Dourif. "Why can't I be a Dourif, like you?" I asked her once when I was very small, and she poured her drink onto the carpet, shocking me. This was my own kindergarten move to express violent unhappiness. She left the room, and my shock deepened when she didn't come back to clean up the mess. I watched the stain set on the carpet, the sun cutting through the curtain blades. Later, I wrote LARRY RUBIO on all my folders. I answered to "Rubio," just like the stranger my father must be doing somewhere. What my ma seemed to want me to do—to hold on to the name without the man—felt very silly to me, like the cartoon where Wile E. Coyote holds on to the handle (just the handle) of an exploded suitcase.

The scarecrow boy was my same height, five foot five. He was a funny hybrid: he had a doll's wax head, with glass eyes and sculpted features, but a scarecrow's body—sackcloth under the jeans and the sweater. Pillowy, machine-sewn limbs stuffed with straw. I took a step forward and punched the torso, which was solid as a hay bale; I half expected a scream to roll out of his mouth. Now I understood Mondo's earlier wail—when the doll didn't make a sound, I wanted to scream for him.

"Who stuck those on its face?" Mondo asked. "Those eyes?"

"Whoever *put* him here in the first place, jackass."

"Well, what weirdo does that? Puts eyes and clothes on a giant doll of a kid and ropes him to a tree?"

"A German, probably," said Gus knowingly. "Or a Japanese. One of those sicko sex freaks."

Mondo rolled his eyes. "Maybe *you* tied it up, Ainsworth."

"Maybe he's a theater prop? Like, from our school?"

"He's wearing some *nasty* clothes."

"Hey! He's got a belt like yours, Rubby!"

"Fuck you."

"Wait—you're going to steal the scarecrow's *belt*? That ain't bad luck?"

"Oh my God! He's got on *underwear*!" Mondo snapped the elastic, giggling.

"He has a hole," Juan Carlos said quietly. He'd slid his hand between the doll's sagging shoulders and the tree. "Down here, in his back. Look. He's spilling straw."

Juan Carlos began jerking stuffing out of the scarecrow and then, in the same panicky motion, cramming it back inside the hole; all this he did with a sly, aghast look, as if he were a surgeon who had fatally bungled an operation and was now trying to disguise that fact from his staff. This straw, I recognized with a chill, was fresh and green.

"You got your 'oh shit!' face on, J.C.!" Gus laughed. I managed a laugh, too, but I was scared, scared. The crisp straw was scary to me. A terrible sweetness lifted out of the doll, that stench you are supposed to associate with innocent things—zoos and pet stores, pony rides. He was stuffed to the springs of his eyeballs.

Put it all back, Juan, and maybe we'll be okay—

"Uh. You dudes? Do scarecrows have fingers?" Mondo giggled again and held out the doll's white hand, very formally, as if he were suddenly in a cummerbund accompanying the scarecrow to the world's scariest prom. The hand dangled heavily from the doll's stapled sleeve. It looked like a plaster cast, with five slender fingers. The boy's face was molded out of this same white material. His features weren't generic, like a mall mannequin's head, but crooked, odd. Very skillfully misshapen. Based on somebody's real face, I thought, like the famous dummies in the wax museum. Somebody you were *supposed* to recognize.

The longer I stared at him, the less real I myself felt. Was I the only one who remembered his name?

"Weird. His face is *cold*." Juan Carlos slid a finger down the wax nose.

"What the fuck! He's wearing *Hoops*!" Gus knelt to show us the pair of black sneaker toes poking out from the scarecrow's cuffs. At school, we made a point of stealing Hoops from any kid stupid enough to wear them—Hoops were imitation Nikes, glittered with an insulting ersatz gold, and just the sight of a pair used to enrage me. The *H* logo was a flamboyant way to announce to your class: Hey, I'm poor!

"He's not wearing his glasses," I mumbled. Now I was afraid to touch him, as if the humid wand of my finger might bring him to life.

"Can it blink?" Mondo asked, grabbing at its eyes. "My sister has this doll that blinks . . . uh-oh. Oops."

Mondo turned to us, grinning. There were shallow indents in the wax where the doll's eyes had been.

"Oh shit!" Gus shook his head. "Put them back in."

"I *can't*. The little threads broke." He held them out to show us, the eyes: two grape-size balls of glass. "Any of you bitches know how to sew?"

Intense pinks were filtering through the autumn mesh of the oak. Sunset meant the park was officially closed.

"Seriously?" Mondo asked, sounding panicky. "Anybody got glue or something?"

A firefly was lighting up the airless caves of the doll's nostrils, undetected by the doll. *You're even blinder now,* I thought, and a heavy feeling draped over me.

Mondo seemed to be catching on: "Don't we know this kid?"

He stood on his toes and peered into the scarecrow's face with a shrewdness that you did not ordinarily expect from Mondo Chu—who was encased in baby fat that he couldn't age out of, with big, slabby cheeks that squeezed his eyes into a narcoleptic squint. There was some evidence that Mondo did not have the happiest home life. Mondo was half Chinese, half *something*. We'd all forgotten, assuming we'd ever known.

Don't say it.

"Oh!" Mondo fell back on his heels. "It's *Eric*."

"Oh." I took a backward step.

Juan Carlos paused with one hand inside the doll's back, still wearing a doctor's distant, guileful expression.

"Who the fuck is *Eric*?" Gus snarled.

"Don't you assholes remember him?" Mondo was grinning at us like a *Jeopardy!* champ. He waved the doll's wax hand at us. "Eric Mutis."

Now we all remembered him: Eric Mutis. Eric Mutant, Eric Mucus, Eric the Mute. Paler than a cauliflower, a friendless kid who had once or twice had seizures in our class. "Eric Mutis is an epileptic," our teacher had explained a little uncertainly, after Mutant got carried from the room by Coach Leyshon. Eric Mutis had joined our eighth-grade class in October the previous year, a transfer kid. The teacher never introduced him. Kids rarely moved to Anthem, New Jersey; generally the teachers made a New Boy or a New Girl parade their strangeness for us. Not Eric Mutis. Eric Mutis, who seemed genuinely otherworldly, even weirder than Tuku the Guatemalan New Boy, never had to stand and explain himself to us. He arrived in exile, sank like a stone to the bottom of our homeroom. One day, several weeks before the official end of our school term, he vanished, and I honestly had not spoken his name since. Nobody had.

In the school halls, Eric Mutis had been as familiar as air; at the same time we never thought about him. Not unless he was right in front of our noses. Then you couldn't ignore him—there was something provocative about Eric Mutis's ugliness, something about his wormy lips and lobes, his blond eyelashes and his worse-than-dumb expression, that filled your eyes and closed your throat. He could metamorphose Julie Lucio, the top of the cheer pyramid, a dog lover and the sweetest girl in our grade, into a true bitch. "What *smells*?" she'd whisper, little unicorn-pendant Julie, thrilling us with her acid tone, and the Mute would blink his large eyes at her behind his glasses and say, "I don't smell it, Julie," in that voice like thin blue milk. Congenitally, he really did seem like a mutant, sightless, incapable of shame. Mutant floated among us, hideous, yet blank as a balloon—his calm was unrelenting. He was ugly, most definitely, but we might have forgiven him for that. It was his serenity that made the kid monstrous to us. His baffling lack of contrition—all that oblivion rolling in his blue eyes. Personally, I felt allergic to the kid. Peace like his must be a bully allergen. A teacher's allergen, too—the poor get poorer, I guess, because many of our teachers were openly hostile to Eric Mutis; by December, Coach Leyshon was sneering, "Pick it up, Mutant!" on the courts.

At school, Camp Dark beat down kids as a foursome. We did this in an animal silence. We'd drag a hysterical kid behind the redbrick Science Building—usually a middle schooler, a sixth- or seventh-grader—and then we would hammer and piston our fists into his clawing, shrilling body until the kid went slack as rags. I heard those screams like they were coming out of my own throat and found I couldn't relax until the kid did. I sensed there was some deep assembly-line logic to what we did: once we got a kid screaming, we were obliged to shut him up again. I thought of the process as what they call "a necessary evil." We were like a team of factory guys, manufacturing a calm that was not available to us naturally anywhere in Anthem. We desperately needed this quiet that only our victims could produce for us, the silence that came after an attack; it was as essential to our friendship as breathing air. As blood is to a vampire. We'd kneel there, panting together, and let the good quiet bubble out of the snotty kid and into our lungs.

That year, Eric Mutis was one of our regulars. We stole the Mute's Hoops sneakers and hung them from the flagpole; we smashed his gray Medicaid glasses three times before Christmas; and then he'd come to school in a new pair of the same invalid's frames, the same nine-dollar Hoops. How many pairs of Hoops did we force him to buy that year—or, most likely, since Eric Mutis queued up with us for the free lunch program, to steal?

"Why are you so stubborn, Mutant?" I hissed at him once, when his face was inches away from mine, lying prone on the blacktop—closer to my face than any girl's had ever been. Closer than I'd let my ma's face get to me, now that I'd turned thirteen. I could smell his bubble gum and what we called the "Anthem cologne"—like my own clothes, Mutant's rags stank of diesel, fried doughnut grease from the cafeteria.

"Why don't you *learn*?" And I Goliath-crushed the Medicaid glasses in my hand, feeling sick.

"Your palms, Larry." Eric the Mute had shocked me that time, calling me by name. "They're bleeding."

"Are you retarded?" I marveled. "*You* are the one bleeding! This is *your* blood!" It was both our blood actually, but his eyes made me furious. That blind light, steady as a dial tone.

"WAKE UP!" I backed away graciously, to give Gus space to deliver the encore kick.

"Listen, Mutant: DO . . . NOT . . . WEAR THAT UGLY SHIT TO SCHOOL!"

And Monday came, and guess what Mutant wore?

Was he wearing this stuff out of rebellion? A kind of nerd insurrection? I didn't think so; that might have relieved us a little bit, if the kid had the spine and the mind to rebel. But Eric Mutis wore that stuff brainlessly, shamelessly. We couldn't teach him how to be ashamed of it. ("Who did this? Who did this?" our upstairs neighbor, Miss Zeke from 3C, used to holler, grinding her cross-eyed dachshund's nose into a lake of urine on the stairwell, while the dog, a true lost cause, jetted another weak stream onto the floor.) When we attacked him behind the redbrick Science Building, he never seemed to understand what his crime had been, or what was happening, or even—his blue eyes drifting, unplugged—that it was happening to *him*.

In fact, I think Eric Mutis would have been hard-pressed to identify himself in a police lineup. In the school bathroom he always avoided mirrors. Our bathroom floor had sloping blue tiles, which made the act of pissing into a bowl feel weirdly perilous, as if at any moment you might get plowed under by an Atlantic City wave. Teachers used a separate faculty john. I was famous for having nearly drowned a kid in the sink. Even the Mute knew this about me—that was the one lesson he took. "Well, hallo there, Mutant," I'd whistle at him. More than once I watched him drop his dick and zip up and sprint past the bank of sinks when I entered the bathroom, his homely face pursuing him blurrily and hopelessly in the mirrors. This used to make me happy, when kids like Eric Mucus were afraid of me. (Really, I don't know who I could have been then either.)

Now I wondered if the real Mutis would have recognized this doll. Would the Mute have known his own head on the scarecrow?

That night we spent another hour staring at the doll of Eric and debating what to do with him. The moon rose over Friendship Park. Everybody got jittery. Gus finished our beers. Mondo shot the glass eyes like marbles.

"Well," Gus sighed, dragging down his dark earlobes, his baseball signal to us that he had lost all patience. "We could do an experiment, like. Seems pretty simple. One way to find out what old Eric Mutant here—"

"The *scarecrow*," Mondo hissed, as if he regretted ever naming it.

Gus rolled his eyes. "What the *scarecrow* is doing in the park? What it's supposedly protecting us from? Would be to cut him down."

We had been riffing on this: What threat, exactly, was this scarecrow keeping away from Friendship Park? What could the doll of a child scare off, a freak like Mutant?

The oak shivered above us; it was almost nine o'clock. Police, if they came upon us now, would write us up for trespassing. *Come upon us, officers.* Maybe the police would know the protocol here, what you should do if you found a scarecrow of your classmate strung up in the woods.

"I don't think that's a good idea, Gus," said Juan Carlos slowly. "What if it's here for a good reason? What if something bad does come to Anthem? It would be our fault."

I nodded. "Look, whoever put this up is one sick fuck. I don't want to mess with the property of a lunatic . . ."

We kept on making a good case for leaving the doll and getting the hell out of Friendship Park when Gus, who had fallen quiet, stood up and walked toward the oak. A knife sprang out of Gus's pocket, a four-inch knife that nobody had known Gus carried with him, one of the kitchen tools we'd seen used by Gus's pretty mom, Mrs. Ainsworth, to butterfly and debone chickens.

"GUS!" we cried.

But nobody tried to stop him.

Gus sawed through the rope easily and gave the doll a lit-tle push—joylessly, dutifully, like a big brother behind a swing set—launching him headfirst over the roots of the oak. He tum-bled bonelessly into the Cone, which might have been funny if viewed on television; but the fall we watched beneath the orange eye of the forest moon, with that bland face flipping up at us, the taxidermy of Eric Mutis's head on the scarecrow's body, that was an awful sight. He landed on the rocks with a baseball crack. I don't know how to describe the optical weirdness of the pace of this event—because the doll fell *fast*—but the descent felt unnatu-rally long to me, as if the forest floor were, just as quickly, lunging away from Eric Mutis. Somebody almost laughed. Mondo was already on his knees, peering over the edge, and I joined him: The scarecrow looked like a broke-neck kid at the bottom of a well. Facedown on an oily soak of black and maroon leaves. His legs all corkscrewed. One of his white hands had gotten twisted all the way around. He waved at us, palm up, spearing the air with his long, unlikely fingers.

"Okay," Gus said, sitting back down next to where he'd dug his red beer can into the leaves, as if we were at the beach. "You're all welcome. Everybody needs to shut up now. Let's start the clock on this experiment."

We emerged from the park at Gowen Street and Forty-eighth Avenue. A doorman waved at us from a fancy apartment building, where awnings sprouted from eighty windows like golden claws. When the streetlights clicked on without warning, I think we all stifled a scream. We stood in a huddle, bathed in deep-sea light. Even on a nonscarecrow day I dreaded this, the summative pres-sure of the good-bye moment—but now it turned out there was nothing to say. We split off in a slow way, a slow ballet—a moth, touring the air above our heads, would have seen us as a knot dis-solving over many moth centuries. It occurred to me that, given the life span of a moth, one kid's twitch must take a year to complete. Eric's doll would have twirled down for decades.

That night marked a funny turning point for me; I started thinking about Time in a new way, Time with a capital *T,* this substance that underwent mysterious conversions. On the walk home I watched moths go flitting above the stalled lanes of cars. I called Mondo on the phone, something I never did—I was surprised I even had his number. We didn't talk about Eric Mutis, but the effort of not talking about him made our actual words feel like fizz, just a lot of speedy emptiness. You know, I never tried to force Eric Mutis from my mind—I never had to. Courteously, the kid had disappeared from my brain entirely, about the same time he vanished from our school rolls. Were it not for the return of his scarecrow in Friendship Park, I doubt I would have given him a second thought.

I am in the shower, Eric Mutis is where?

I got into the habit of juxtaposing my real activities to Mutant's imaginary ones: Was he blowing out twisty red-and-white birthday candles? Doing homework? What hour of what day was it, wherever Eric Mutis had moved? I pictured him in Cincinnati squiggling mustard on a soggy ballpark frank, in France with an arty beret (I pictured him dead, too, in a dreamy, compulsive way, the concrete result of which was that I no longer ate breakfast). "You don't want your *Popple,* Larry?" my ma screamed. "It's a Blamberry Popple!" The Blamberry Popple looked like a pastry nosebleed to me. What was Eric eating? How soundly was he sleeping? ("Did we break Mutant's nose?" I asked Gus in homeroom. "At least once," Gus confirmed.) Now each of my minutes cast an hourglass shadow, and I divided into two.

But inside the Cone, as it turned out, the scarecrow of Eric Mutis was subdividing even faster.

Every day for a week, we went back to stare at the facedown scarecrow in the ravine. Nothing much happened. There was a mugging at the Burger Burger; the robber got a debit card and a quart of milkshake. Citywide, bus fare went up five cents. A drunk driver in the Puerto Rican Day parade draped a Puerto Rican flag over his windshield like a patriotic blindfold and crashed through a beautiful float of the island of Puerto Rico. Nothing occurred on the crime blotter that seemed connected to Eric Mutis, or Eric Mutis's absence. No strange birds came to roost in the oaks of Friendship Park now that the scarecrow's guard was down. Downed by us. Drowned in air, for the world's stupidest experiment.

If I closed my eyes I could feel the slippery weeds crushed underneath his face.

"Did Eric have a dad? A mom?"

"Wasn't he a foster kid?"

"Where did he move to, again?"

"Old Mucusoid never said—did he? He just disappeared."

At school, the new guidance counselor could not help us find our "little pal"—the district computers, she said, had been wiped by a virus. Mutis, Eric: no record. No yearbook picture. ABSENT, read the empty blue oval between the school-mandated grimaces of Georgio Morales and Valerie Night.

We consulted with Coach Leyshon, whom we found face-deep in a vending-machine jelly roll behind the dugout.

"Mutant?" he barked. "That dipshit didn't come back?" We broke into Vice Principal Derry's file cabinet and made depressing, irrelevant discoveries about the psychology of Vice Principal Derry—a *Note to Moi!* memo, for example, that read, in harsh red pen, BUY PENCIL SHARPENER.

Next we consulted the yellow pages at the city library. Ma Bell's anthology of false alarms. We thought we found Mutant in Lebanon Valley, Pennsylvania. Voloun River, Tennessee. Jump City, Oregon. Jix, Alaska, a place that sounded like a breakfast cereal or an attack dog, had four Mutis families listed. We called.

Many dozens of Mutises across America hung up on us, after apologizing for their households' dearth of Erics. America felt vast and void of him. Gus whammed the phone into its receiver, disgusted. "It's like that kid hatched out of an egg. What I want to know is: Who made him into a scarecrow?"

This time we weren't even sure what sort of listing to scout for. Who made a doll of a boy? We scanned the book for ridiculous headings: SCARECROW REPAIR, WAX KIDS. I found an address for a puppeteer who had a workshop in Anthem's garment district. Gus biked out there and did reconnaissance, weaving around the bankers' spires of downtown Anthem and risking the shortcut under the overpass, where large, insane men brayed at you and haunted shopping carts rolled windlessly forward. He spent an hour circling the puppeteer's studio, trying to catch him in the act of Dark Arts—because what if he was making scarecrows of *us*? But the puppeteer turned out to be a small, bald man in a daffodil print shirt; the puppet on his table was a hippopotamus, or perhaps some kind of lion. On Gus's fifteenth revolution around his studio, the puppeteer lifted the window, gave a cheery wave, and informed Gus that he'd just telephoned the police.

"*Great*," sighed Juan Carlos. "So we still have no clue who made that doll."

"But how the fuck you going to confuse a hippo and a *lion*, bro!" Mondo screamed. Mondo's reactions often missed the mark. The anger of Mondo I pictured as this fierce and stupid bird that kept landing on the wrong tree, whole woods away from the rest of us.

"Chu, shut up. You got a brain defect."

"Maybe Mutant did it," I said, almost hopefully. I wanted Eric to be safe and alive. "Did he know that we hang out in the park? Maybe he roped the scarecrow there to screw with us."

"Maybe it was Vice Principal Derry," said Juan Carlos. "One time, I looked through Derry's office window and I see Mutant on his couch. And I sort of thought, 'Oh, good, he's getting some help.' But then Derry catches me looking, right? And he stands up, he's fucking *pissed,* he shuts the blinds. It was so weird. And I saw the Mute's mug—"

I could see it, too, Mutant's leech-white face behind the glass, I *had* seen it framed in Derry's office window, Eric Mutis swallowed by Derry's leather sofa, wearing his queer gray glasses. "And he looked . . . bad," he finished. "Like, scared? Worse than he did when we messed with him."

"Why was he in Derry's office?" I asked, but nobody knew.

"I saw him get picked up from school," Mondo volunteered. "After second period, you know, 'cause he had one of his twitch fests? The, uh, the seizures? And this dude in the car looked so old! I was like, Mutant, is Darth Vader there your dad?"

This, too, was something we all suddenly remembered seeing: a cadaverous man, a liver-spotted hand on the steering wheel of a snouty green Cadillac, tapping a cigar, and then Mutant climbing into the backseat, the rear window as foggy as aquarium glass and the Mute's head now etched dimly behind it. He always climbed into the backseat, never used the passenger door, we agreed on that. We all remembered the cigar.

Gus hadn't stopped frowning—it had been days since he'd told a truly funny joke. "Where did Mutis live in Anthem? Does anybody remember him saying?"

"East Olmsted," said Mondo. "Right? With a crazy aunt." Mondo's eyes widened, as if his memory were coming into focus. "I think the aunt was black!"

"Chu," Juan Carlos sighed. "That is not your memory. You are thinking of a Whoopi Goldberg movie. Nah, Mutant's parents were rich."

"Oh my God!" Mondo clapped a hand to his face. "You're *right*! That was a *great movie*!"

Juan Carlos directed his appeal to Gus and me. "Kid was

loaded. I just remembered. I'm, like, ninety percent sure. That's why the Mute pissed us off so bad . . . wasn't it? Pretending he didn't have shit. I think they lived in the Pagoda. Serious."

I almost laughed at that—the Pagoda was an antislum, a castle of light. Eric Mutis had never lived in the Pagoda's zip code. In fact, I had visited the house where Eric lived. Just one time. This knowledge was like a wild thumper of a rabbit inside me. I was amazed that no one else could hear it.

Wednesday morning, I went to Friendship Park on an empty stomach, alone. The sun came with me; I was already twenty minutes late for Music II, a class that I was certainly failing, since I stood in the back with Gus and made a Clint Eastwood seam with my lips and sang only in my mind. It was the class I loved. Mrs. Verazain put on old records where the dead violinists seemed to saw through Time, to let a soft green light flood out of the past and into the voices of my friends—back then I would have said that Music calmed me down better than pot and I didn't like to miss it.

But I had my own business with the scarecrow of Eric Mutis. I'd been having dreams about both Erics, the real one and the doll. I slept with a pillow under my stomach and imagined it loaded with straw. In one dream, I got Coach Leyshon's permission to sub myself in for Mutis, lashing my body to the oak tree and eating horsey fistfuls of bloodred straw; in another, I watched the doll of Eric Mutis go plunging into the Cone again, only this time when his scarecrow hit the rocks, a thousand rabbits came bursting out of it. Baby rabbits: furless thumbs of pink in the night, racing under the oaks of Friendship Park.

"Eh-ric?" I called softly, well in advance of the oak. And then, almost inaudibly: "Honey?" in a voice that was not unlike my ma's when she opened my bedroom door at three a.m. and called my name but clearly didn't want to wake me, wanted instead who-knows-what? I got on my knees and peered into the ravine.

"Oh my God."

The scarecrow was missing its left arm. Whatever had attacked it in the night had been big enough to tear the arm off at the root. Gray straw spewed out of the hole. *You're next, you're next, you're next,* my heart screamed. I ran and I didn't slow down until I reached the glass umbrella of the number 22 bus stop. I did not stop until I burst into Music II, where all my friends were doing their *do re mi* work. I pushed in next to Gus and collapsed against our wall.

"You're very late, Señor Rubio," said Mrs. Verazain disgustedly, and I nodded hard, my eyes still stinging from the cold. "You're too late to be assigned a role."

"I am," I agreed with her, hugging my arm.

There was one day last December, right before the Christmas break, where we got him behind the Science Building for a game that Mondo had named Freeze Tag. The game was pretty short and unsophisticated—we made a kid "It," the way you'd identify an animal as a trophy kill, if you were a hunter, or declare a red spot the bull's-eye, so that you could shoot it:

"Not it!"

"Not it!"

"Not it!"

"Not it!"

We'd grinned, our four bodies in our white gym shirts advancing through the cattails. Nobody ever mowed the grass behind the Science Building. Mutant would stand there with weeds up to his waist, waiting for us. He never ran, not the second time we played Freeze Tag with him, and not the hundredth. The rules were simple and yet Eric Mutis stared at us with his opaque blue eyes, staked to the ground, and gave no sign of understanding the game.

"You're *it,*" I'd explained to Eric.

After school, everybody followed me toward Camp Dark in a line.

"Here comes the army!" cackled a bum with whom we sometimes shared beers, one of a rotating cast of lost men whom Gus called the Bench Goblins. He was sprawled across his bench on a bed of newspapers like Cleopatra. He had a long, stirrup-shaped face that grinned and grinned at us when we told him about the scarecrow of Eric Mutis.

"No," he said, "I don't see nobody come this way with no *doll*."

"Last week," I prodded, but I didn't think that unit of time meant anything to this man. He batted his eyelashes at me, smoothing the oatmeal of wet newspapers beneath his cheek.

We trudged forward. All last night it had rained; the leaves were shining, and the foam-padded playground equipment gleamed like some giant's dental kit.

"So what do you think did it, Rubby?" Gus asked.

"Yeah. An animal, like?" Mondo's eyes were gleeful. "Is it all clawed up?"

"You'll see. I dunno, guys," I mumbled. "I dunno. I dunno."

In fact, I knew a little more about the real Eric Mutis than I was letting on.

We traded theories:

Hypothesis 1: A human took the arm.

Hypothesis 2: An animal, or several animals, did the
    butchering. Smart animals. Surgical animals. Animals
    with claws. Scavengers—opossums, raccoons. Carrion
    birds.

Hypothesis 3: This is being done by . . . Something Else.

I spent the march preparing for my friends to lose their shit when they saw the mauled doll of Eric. To scream, take off running. But when they peered into the Cone, they responded in a way I could never have predicted. They started to laugh. Hysterically, like three hyenas, Gus first and then the other two.

"Good one, Rubby!" they called.

I was too shocked to speak.

"Oh, shit, that is fantastic, Rubby-oh. This is a classic."

"This is your best yet," Juan Carlos confirmed with gloomy jealousy.

"Dang! *Larry.* You're like a goddamn acrobat! How did you get *down* there?"

Eyes rolled at me from every direction. It occurred to me suddenly that this was how Camp Dark must look to kids like Mutis.

"Wait—" My laugh sank into a growl. "You think *I* did that?"

Everybody nodded at me with strange solemnity, so that for a disorienting second I wondered if they might be right. How did they think I had managed the amputation? I tried to see myself as they must be imagining me: swinging down the ravine on a rope, a knife in my back jeans pocket, the orange moon washing over the Cone's rock walls and making the place feel even more like an unlidded casket, the doll waiting for my attack with a patience rivaled only by that of the real Eric Mutis . . . and then what? Did my friends think I'd swung the arm back to the surface, à la Tarzan? Carried Mutant's arm home to mount on my bedroom wall?

"I didn't do it!" I gasped. "This is not a joke, you assholes . . ."

I got up and vomited orange Gatorade into the bushes. It was all liquid—I hadn't been eating. Days of emptiness rose in me and I dry-retched again, listening to my friends' peals echo around the black park. Then I surprised myself by laughing with them, so uncontrollably and with such relief that it felt like a continuation of the retching. (In fact I think this is exactly what I must have been doing—disgorging my claims. Purging myself of any attachment to my innocence, and crawling on my hands and knees back inside our "we.")

After a while the laughter didn't sound connected to any of us. We blinked at one another under the downpour, our mouths open.

"And the Oscar for puking goes to . . . Larry Rubio!" said Juan Carlos, still doubled over.

A bird floated softly over the park. Somewhere just beyond the tree line, buses were carrying cargoloads of sleepy adults home to Anthem from jobs in more affluent cities. Some of these commuters were our parents. I felt a little stab, picturing my ma eating her yellow apple on the train and reading some self-improvement book, on a two-hour return trip from her job at a day nursery for rich infants in Anthem's far richer sister county. I realized that I had zero clue what my ma did there; I pictured her rolling a big striped ball, at extremely slow speeds, toward babies in little sultan hats and fat, bejeweled diapers.

"My ma's name is Jessica," I heard myself say. Suddenly I could not stop talking, it was like chattering teeth. "Jessica Dourif. Gus, you met her once, you remember." I glared at Gus and dared him to say he'd forgotten her.

"What the hell are you talking about, Rubby?"

Below us, several pigeons had landed on the scarecrow's shredded body. They attacked him with impersonal savagery. Tore at his threads. A gash down the doll's back was hemorrhaging dirty-looking straw, and one pigeon dug its entire flashing head into the hole. *Now YOU need a scarecrow,* I thought.

"I've never met my father," I blurted. "I can't even say my own fucking last name."

"Larry," Juan Carlos said sternly, standing over me. "Nobody cares. Now you pull yourself together."

What followed over the course of the next eight days progressed with the logic of a frightening nursery rhyme:

On Tuesday morning, the scarecrow's second hand was gone. I joked that the white fingers were crawling through the park, hailing a cab, starting a new life somewhere, incognito, maybe with a family of gullible tarantulas in New Mexico.

"Shut up, Larry." J.C. grinned. "We know that hand is in your locker."

On Wednesday, the scarecrow was missing both Hoops sneakers and both feet. Everybody but me snickered about that one. Once Gus and I had gotten a three-day suspension for yanking off the Mute's Hoops sneakers and his crusty socks and holding an "America the Great" sparkler to his bare feet—just to mess with him.

"Larry!" Gus said, clapping my back. "That wall is steep as hell! How did you climb up the rocks with two *shoes* in your hands?"

"I am not doing this," I said quietly.

"Maybe," I added in a whisper, "we can fish him up? Hook him out? Please . . . ?"

"Ha! Are you *crying,* bro?"

Everybody complimented me on my "acting." Yet they were the real actors, my best friends—pretending to believe the impossible, that I was the guy to blame for the attacks, that the nightmare in progress below us was a prank. Only Mondo would let me see his smile tremble.

On Thursday, the remaining arm was gone. Torn cleanly from the torso, so that you got an unsettling glimpse of the gray straw coiled inside the scarecrow's chest. I pled my case with my eyes now: *Not-it, not-it, not-it!*

"What's next, Rubby? You going to carry a guillotine down there?"

"You bet," I snarled. "How well you all know me. Next up, I'm going to climb down there and behead Eric Mutis with an ax."

"Right." Gus grinned. "We should follow you home. We're gonna find Mutant's arm under your pillow. The fake one, and probably the real one, too, you psycho."

And they did. Follow me home. On the same Saturday afternoon that we discovered that Eric's legs were missing. "Come over," I said in a high voice, "check my whole house. Motherfuckers, this has got to end." The doll we left in the Cone was a torso and a head. Pulpy, crushed. It had started to resemble a disintegrating jack-o'-lantern. I was "It." I was the only suspect. Under a dreary sky we exited the park, everybody but me laughing about how they'd been fucked with, faked out, punked, and gotten.

"You rotten, Rubby-Oh," grinned Gus.

"*Something's* rotten," agreed Mondo, catching my eye.

My ma and I lived on Gray's Ferry, in ear-splitting proximity to the hospital; from my bedroom window I could see the red and white carnival lights of the ambulances. Awake, I was totally inured to the sirens, a whine that we'd been hearing throughout Anthem since birth—that urgent song drilled into us so frequently that our own heartbeats must have synced with it, which made it an easy howl to ignore; but I had dreams where the vehicular screams in the urgent care parking lot became the cries of a gigantic, abandoned baby behind my apartment. All I wanted to do in these dreams was *sleep* but this baby wouldn't shut up! Now I think this must be a special kind of poverty, low-rent city sleep, where even in your dreams you are an insomniac and your unconscious is shrill and starless.

When we got to my place, the apartment was dark and there was no obvious sustenance waiting for us—my ma was not one to prepare a meal. Some deep-fridge spelunking produced a pack of spicy jerky and Velveeta slices. This was beau food, a souvenir from her last live-in boyfriend, Manny Somebody. As the son, I got to be on a first-name basis with all these adult men, all her boyfriends, but I never knew them well enough to hate them in a personal way. We folded thirty-two cheese slices into cold taco shells and ate them in front of the TV. Later I'd remember this event as a sort of wake for the scarecrow of Eric Mutis, although I had never in my life been to a funeral.

They searched my apartment, found nothing. No white hands clapping in my closet or anything. No stuffed legs propped next to the brooms in the kitchen.

"He's clean," shrugged Gus, talking over me. "He probably buried the evidence."

"I *do* think we need to bury him," I started babbling. "We could go down there, dig the doll a deeper hole." I swallowed, thinking about his face in the mud. "Please, guys—"

"No way. We are *not falling for that,*" said Juan Carlos quickly, as if wary of falling into the Cone himself.

Accusing me, I saw, served a real utility for the group—suddenly nobody was interested in researching scarecrows at the library with me, or trying to figure out where the real Eric Mutis had gone, or deciphering who was behind his doppelgänger doll. They had their answer: I was behind it. This satisfied some scarecrow logic for my friends. They slept, they didn't wonder anymore. That's where my friends had staked me: behind the doll.

"Let's go there one night, and just see who comes to shred and tear at him like that. Whatever comes for Mutant, we'll scare it off." I swallowed hard, staring at them. "And then we'll know *exactly . . .*"

Mondo snapped the TV on.

It felt like we sat in the dark for hours, the silence growing and leafing into suffocating densities above us, sinking around the sofas like tree roots. Nobody but me seemed to notice when the television station switched to pure static. My ma had an ancient RCA TV, with oven dials for controls and rabbit ears; I always thought it looked more authentically futuristic than my friends' modern Toshiba sets. Spazzy rainbows moved up and down, imbuing the screen with an insectoid life of its own. Here was the secret mind of the machine, I thought with a sudden ache, what you couldn't see when the news anchors were staring soulfully at their teleprompters and the sitcom families were making eggs and jokes in their fake houses.

Eric's face—the face of scarecrow Eric—swam up in my mind. I realized that the random, relentless lightning inside the TV screen was how I pictured the interior of the doll—void, yet also, in a way that I did not understand and found I could not even think about head-on, much less explain to my friends, *alive*. Rainbows furrowed the glass. With the TV on mute you could hear a hard clock tick.

"Hey! Rubio!" Gus finally asked. "What the *fuck* we watching?"

"Nothing," I snapped back; a wise lie, I thought. "Obviously."

Over the next three days, the doll continued to disappear. Once the major appendages were gone, the increments of Eric that went missing became more difficult to track. Patches of hair vanished. Bites and chews of his shoulders. Morsels. By Monday, two weeks after we'd found it, over half the scarecrow was gone.

"Well, that's that," said Juan Carlos in a funny voice. In the Cone, green straw was blowing everywhere now. All that bodiless straw gave me a nervous feeling, like watching a thought that I couldn't collect. Eric's head was still attached to the sack of his torso.

"That's all, folks," echoed Gus. "Going once, going twice! Nice work, Rubby."

I leaned against the oak, feeling nauseated. With a sickening lurch, I understood that we were never going to tell anyone about Eric. Nobody who saw the wreck in the Cone would believe our story. Why hadn't we gotten the police when we first found the scarecrow, or even Vice Principal Derry? Even yesterday that had still been an option, but today it wasn't; we all felt it; we hadn't acted, and now the secret was returning to the ground. Eric Mutis was escaping us again in this terrible, original way.

That Friday, the scarecrow's head was gone. Now I thought I detected a ripple of open fear in the others' eyes. All the laughter about my "prank" died out.

"Where did you put it?" Mondo whispered.

"When are you going to stop?" said Juan Carlos.

"Larry," Gus said sincerely, "that is really sick."

Hypothesis 4.

"I think we made him," I told Chu on the phone. "Eric's scarecrow. I don't know how, exactly. I mean I know we didn't stitch him up or anything, but I think that we must be the reason . . ."

"Quit acting nuts. I know you're faking, Larry. Gus says *you* probably made him. My dinner's ready—" Mondo hung up.

ABOUT THAT STATIC—sometimes that was all I saw in the real Mute's eyes. Just a random light tracking your fists back and forth. Two blue-alive-voids. When we laid him flat in the weeds behind the Science Building, it was that emptiness that made us wild. I hit Mutant so hard that I could feel myself split—it was the strangest feeling, as if I was inside two bodies at once, my own and the Mute's lying prone beneath me. Cringing under the blows of my own knuckles. I couldn't stop hitting him, though—I was afraid to. I'd wake up, or he would, and then the pain would really begin. Somehow I swear it really did feel like I had to keep hitting him, to protect the both of us from what was happening. Out of the red corner of one eye I could see my wet fist flying. The slickness on it was our snot and our blood.

Only one time did anybody succeed at stopping us.

"Leave him alone," called a voice that we immediately recognized. We all turned. Eric Mutant breathed quietly through his mouth in the weeds below us.

"You heard me." This was Mrs. Kauder, our school librarian. She walked briskly toward us across the never-mowed grass. A woman well past middle age, whose red-lipped face and white hair made her shockingly attractive to us. Here she came like a leopardess, flaunting all her bones.

J.C. surreptitiously wiped Eric's blood onto his own sleeve. Now we could credibly asseverate, to the librarian or to Coach Leyshon or to Vice Principal Derry, that our assault on Eric Mutis had been a fight. But the school librarian saw right through him. The school librarian fixed her green eyes on each one of us—except for Eric, she had known every one of us since elementary school. I felt a sudden, thrilling shame as her gaze covered me.

"Larry Rubio," she said, in a neutral voice, as if she were remarking on the weather. "You are better than this.

"Now you go back to your classrooms," she said, in this funny rehearsed way, as if she were reading our lives to us from one of her books.

"Now *you* go to Geometry, Gus Ainsworth—" She pronounced our real names so gently, as if she were breaking a spell.

"Now *you* go to Spanish, Juan Carlos Diaz and Mondo Chu—

"Now *you* go to Computers, Larry Rubio . . ." Her voice was as nasal as Eric's but with an old person's polished tremble. It was a terribly embarrassing voice—a weak white grasshopper species that we would have tried to kill, had it belonged to a fellow child.

"Remember, boys," the librarian called after us. "I know you, and you know better. You are good boys," she insisted. "You have good hearts.

"Now *you*, Eric Mutis," I heard her saying softly. "You come with me."

I remember feeling jealous—I wanted to go with Mrs. Kauder, too. I wanted to sit in the dark library and hear my name roll out of her red mouth again, like it was the Spanish word for something good. I think we needed that librarian to follow us around the hallways for every minute of every school day, reading us her story of our lives, her fine script of who we were and our activities—but of course she couldn't do this, and we did get lost.

ON SATURDAY, I convinced Mondo to meet me in Friendship Park. We were alone—Juan Carlos was working as a Food Lion bag boy, and Gus was out with some chick.

"Do you think Eric Mutis is still alive, Chu?" I asked him.

He looked up from his Choco-Slurpo, shocked.

"*Alive?* Of course he is! He changed schools, Rubby—he's not *dead*." He sucked furiously at chocolate sludge, his eyes goggling out.

"Well, what if he was sick? What if he was dying all last year? What if he got kidnapped, or ran away? How would we know?"

"Jesus, Larry. We don't know shit about shit. Maybe Mutant still lives right around the corner. Maybe he helped you to put the scarecrow up. Is that it, Larry?" he asked, and offered me the fudgy backwaters of the Slurpo even as he accused me of diabolical collusion. When Gus wasn't around, Mondo became smarter, kinder, and more afraid.

"Are you guys doing this together? You and Eric?"

"No," I said sadly. "Mutant, he moved. I checked his old house."

"Huh? You what?" Out of habit, Mondo heaved up to chuck the Slurpo cup into the Cone, momentarily forgetting that it was now a sort of open grave for Eric Mutis; with the freakishness of blind coincidence, Mondo happened to look up and notice an inscription on the sunless side of the oak:

ERIC MUTIS
♥ SATURDAY

"Larry!" he screamed. Someone had cut this into the bark very recently. The letters leaked an apple-green sap. They were childishly shaped. Their carver had split the heart with a little arrow. When I saw this epitaph—because that is how they always read to me, this type of love graffiti on trees and urinals, as epitaphs for ancient couples—my throat tightened and my heart beat so fast that my own death seemed a likely possibility.

"Mutant was *here*!" Mondo cried. For a moment he'd forgotten that I was supposed to be the culprit, the engineer of this psychotic joke. "Mutant had a *girlfriend*!"

So then I filled in some blanks for Mondo. I offered Mondo the parts of Eric Mutis that I had indeed been hoarding.

On a Wednesday afternoon last spring, I was riding my bicycle through a gray suburb of Anthem, on my way to see a West Olmsted kid who owed me money, when a car came roaring around the corner and clipped me, sent me flying over the handlebars. Pain exploded on my left side, and I lay sprawled in a heap in the street, watching the driver roll obliviously down the block. I realized I knew the car. I'd last seen it in our school parking lot. A long green Cadillac. That gargoyle with the cigar, the Mute's caretaker, had nearly killed me. I crawled to the side of the road, and I was still sitting there ten minutes later, hypnotized by the light rolling around my bike spokes, when I saw the Mute jogging up the asphalt. Glare came off his large square glasses, which made him look like a strange cartoon character.

"Hi, Larry," he'd said. "You all right? Sorry. He didn't see you there."

I gaped up at him. I had plenty to say: *Is that maniac your dad? Mr. Hit and Run? Your caretaker or whatever? Because I could sue, you know.*

Instead I watched my hand slide into the Mutant's hand and form a sticky mitt. I let the Mutant help me up. I waited for him to say something about the time I'd smashed his specs but the Mute, true to form, said nothing. I was so dazed that I kept my own mouth shut and followed him down the street, using my bike as a rolling crutch. We stopped at an evil-looking house, a yellow split-level, number 52; the door knocker was a filth-encrusted brass pineapple. More tackiness and incoherence awaited me within Casa Mutis. In what I presumed was the living room, all the blinds were drawn. No pictures on the walls (my ma had wallpapered our place with framed photos of my dumb face). It smelled like roach spray. The single couch was loaded with dirty clothes and magazines, a Styrofoam container of stringy gray meat and rice. I had time to notice whiskey bottles, ashtrays. Mutant made no apologies but hustled me into a bedroom.

Something was alive in the corner. That was the first thing I noticed when I entered the Mute's room: a stripe of motion in the brown shadows near the shuttered window. It was a rabbit. A pet, you could tell from the water bottle wired to its cage bars. A pet was not just some animal, it was yours, it was loved and fed by you. Everybody knows this, of course, but for some reason the plastic water bottle looked shockingly bright to me; the clean, good smell of the straw was an exotic perfume in the Mute's bedroom.

Mutant, meanwhile, was fishing around in a drawer.

"You think this will fit you, Larry?"

Eric held out a shrunken, wrinkled sweater that I recognized.

"Uh-huh."

"You better now, Larry?"

"Terrific. Extra super."

Had I gone home in my blood-soaked shirt, my ma would have freaked. She'd have been so aghast at my brush with Death that she'd try to kill me herself. Ma punished me any time I flaunted my mortality, reminded her that her son was also a bag of red fluid. Eric Mutis seemed to know this instinctively. He handed me a shirt, white socks, and I wondered why he had to be such a retard in school.

I pulled Mutis's sweater on. I knew I should thank him.

"That's a rabbit?" I asked like some idiot.

"Yeah." Now Eric Mutis smiled with a brilliance that I had never seen before. "That's my rabbit."

I crossed the room, in Eric Mutis's boat-striped sweater, to acquaint myself with Eric Mutis's caged pet, feeling my afternoon curve weirdly. The rabbit's tall ears were pushed flat against its skull, which I thought made it look like a European swimmer.

"I think you are spoiling that rabbit, dude."

Mutis had stocked this place for the apocalypse, turned his room into a bunny stronghold. Big fifty-pound bags of straw and food pellets slouched in every corner, under the Mute's bed. Pine straw. Timothy, orchard, meadow. ORGANIC ALFALFA—PLUS CALCIUM! said one bag. *Jesus, where does Mutant get the money for organic alfalfa?* I wondered. There was almost nothing else in the room: a purple cassette deck, some schoolbooks, a twin bed with the Goodwill label still on the headboard.

"My Christ, do they put steroids in that alfalfa?" I peeled off the price sticker, feeling like a city bumpkin. "Twenty bucks! You got ripped off!" I grinned. "You need to buy your grass from *Jamaica,* dude."

But he had turned away from me, bending to whisper something to the quivering rabbit. Seeing this made me uncomfortable; his whisper was already a million times too loud. I felt a flare-up of my school-day rage—for a second I hated Eric Mutant again, and I hated the oblivious rabbit even more, so smugly itself inside the cage, sucking like an infant at its water nozzle. Did Mutant know what kind of ammo he was giving me? Did he honestly believe that I was going to keep his love nest a secret from my friends? I strummed my fingernails along the tiny cage bars. They felt like petrified guitar strings.

"What's his name?"

"Her name is Saturday," said Eric happily, and suddenly I wanted to cry. Who knows why? Because Eric Mutis had a girl's pet; because Eric Mutis had named his dingy rabbit after the best day of the week? I'd never seen Eric Mutis say one word to a human girl, I'd never thought of Eric Mutis as a lover before. But he was kicking game to this rabbit like an old pro. Just whispering love music to her, calling down to her, "Saturday, Saturday." Behind the cage bars his whole face was changing. Softening, like. This continued until he wasn't ugly anymore. What had we found so repulsive about him in the first place? His finger was making the gentlest circle between the rabbit's crushed ears, a spot that looked really delicate to me, like a baby's head. The rabbit's irises were fiery and dust dry, I noted, swiping hard at my own snotty face with Eric's sleeve.

"Want to pet her?" Mutant asked, not looking at me.

"*Hell* no."

But then I realized that I *could* do this; I could do anything in the Twilight Zone of the Mute's closet-size room—nobody was watching me but the Mute and the voiceless thing in the cage. Some hard pressure flew out of my chest then and launched me forward, like air out of a zigzagging balloon. I let Mutant guide my fingers through the cage door. I followed his lead, brushing the green straw off Saturday's fur. Still I thought this was pretty stupid behavior, until I petted her hide in the same direction that Mutant was going and felt actually electrified—under my palm, a cache of white life hummed.

"Can I tell you a secret?"

"Whatever. Sure."

At that moment, it was my belief that he safely could.

Mutis smiled shyly at me, opened a drawer. There was so much dust on the bureau that the clean gleam of Saturday's cage made it look like Incan treasure.

"Here." The poster he thrust at me read LOST: MY PET BUNNY, MISS MOLLY MOUSE. PLEASE CALL ###-####! The albino rabbit in the photograph was unmistakably Saturday, wearing a sparkly Barbie top hat someone had balanced on her ears, the owner's joking reference, I guessed, to that old magician's trick of pulling rabbits out of hats—a joke that was apparently lost on Saturday, whose red eyes bored into the camera with all the warmth and personality of the planet Mars. The owner's name, according to this poster, was Sara Jo. "I am nine," the poster declared in plaintive hand-lettering. The date on the poster said "Lost on August 22." The address listed was 49 Delmar, just around the corner.

"I never returned her." His voice seemed to tremble in tempo with the rabbit's shuddering haunches. "I saw these posters everywhere." He paused. "I pulled them all down." He stepped aside to show me the bureau drawer, which was filled with multiples of the Miss Molly poster. "I saw the girl who put them up. She has red hair. Two of those, what are they called . . ." He frowned. "Pigtails!"

"Okay." I grinned. "That's bad."

Suddenly we were laughing, *hard;* even Saturday, with her rump-shaking tremors, appeared to be laughing along with us.

Eric stopped first. Before I heard the hinge squeak, Eric was on his feet, hustling across the room on ballerina toes to shut the bedroom door. Just before it closed I watched a hunched shape flow past and enter a maple cavity that I assumed was their bathroom. It was the same old guy who had almost mowed me down in the snouty green Cadillac on Delmar Street not thirty minutes ago. Relationship to Eric: unclear.

"Is that your father?"

Eric's face was bright red.

"Your, ah, your grandfather? Your uncle? Your mom's boyfriend?"

Eric Mutis, whom we could not embarrass at school, who would return your gaze without shame no matter what names you called him, did not answer me now or meet my eyes.

"That's fine, whatever," I said. "You don't have to tell me shit about your situation. Honey, I can't even say my own last name."

I barked with laughter, because what the hell? Where the hell had that come from, my calling him "honey"?

Eric smiled. "Peaches," he said, "that's just fine."

For a second we stared at each other. Then we roared. It was the first and last joke I ever heard him try to make. We clutched our stomachs and stumbled around, knocking into one another.

"Shh!" Eric said between gasps, pointing wildly at the bedroom door. "Shhh, Larry!"

And then we got quiet, me and Eric Mutis. The rabbit stood on her haunches and drank water, making a white comma between us; the whole world got quieter and quieter, until that kissy sound of a mouth getting water was all you could hear. For a minute or two, catching our breath, we got to be humans together.

I never returned Mutant's sweater, and the following Monday I did not speak to him. I hid the cuts on my palms in two fists. It took me another week to find a poster for Saturday. I figured they'd be long gone—Eric said he'd torn them all down—but I found one on the Food Lion message board, buried under a thousand kitty calendars and yoga and LEARN TO BONGO! flyers: a very poorly reproduced Saturday glaring out at me under the Barbie hat and the words LOST: MY PET BUNNY. I dialed the number. Sure enough, a girl's voice answered, all pipsqueaky and polite.

"I have news that might be of some interest to you," I said, in the old-man-with-a-flu voice that I used to excuse my own school absences.

She knew right away.

"Molly Mouse! You found her!" Which, what an identity crisis for a rabbit. What kind of name is that? Worse than Rubby-oh. Kids should be stopped from naming anything, I thought angrily, they are too dumb to guess the true and correct names for things. Parents, too.

"Yes. That is exactly right. Something has come to light, ma'am."

I swayed a little with the phone in my hand, feeling powerful and evil. "I know where you can find your rabbit." Then I heard myself reciting, in this false, ancient voice, the address of Eric Mutis.

At school, I breathed easier—I had extricated myself from a tight spot. I had been in real danger, but the moment had passed. Eric Mutis was not ever going to be my friend. Twice I called Sara Jo to ask how Molly Mouse was doing; her dad had gone to the Mutis house and via some exchange of threats or dollars gotten her back.

"Oh," the girl squealed, "she's doing *beautiful,* she loves being *home!*"

At school, I may have been the only one to note the change in Mutant. Whenever anybody called him Mucus or Mutant, and also when our teacher called him, simply, "Eric M.," his whole face puckered with strain—as if he were too weak to hoist up his own name off the mat. When we hit him behind the Science Building, his eyes were true blanks, emptied of even one flickering thought—just like a doll's eyes, in fact. Two telescopes fixed on a lifeless blue planet. Nobody had understood Eric Mutis when he arrived late in October, and then by springtime my friends and I had made him much less scrutable.

"Larry—" he started to say to me once in the bathroom, several weeks after they'd come for Saturday, but I wrung my hands in the sink disgustedly and walked out, following Mutant's example and avoiding our faces in the mirror. We never looked at each other again, and then one day he was gone.

On Sunday night, Mondo and I crossed the playground in a slow processional.

"Jesus H., are we graduating from something? Mondo, are we getting married? Dude, let's pick up the pace. Mondo?"

"This is stupid," he mumbled, staring down the grass alley toward the deeper shadows. "This is crazy. No way did we make the scarecrow."

"Let's just get this done."

I was glad he was afraid—I hadn't known that you could feel so grateful to a friend, for living in fear with you. Fear was otherwise a very lonely place. We kept walking toward the scarecrow.

An idea had come to me last night, after telling Mondo the story of Saturday. An offering to make, a way to appease whatever forces I had unleashed a year ago, when we'd made the real Eric into a doll.

"Get *what* done?" Mondo was muttering. "You won't even tell me why you're going down there. Who gives a fuck what happens to the scarecrow? Why save a doll?"

But I knew what I had to do now. I wouldn't let the Attacker, whoever or whatever it was, dismantle the doll of Eric Mutis completely, carry him out of our memories a second time.

"Do you want to go home? Do you want to wait until he's totally gone?"

Mondo shook his head. His cheeks were as swollen and red as the playground foam.

Somewhere far above the park, a plane roared over Anthem, dismissing our whole city in twenty seconds.

Nobody was around, not even the regular bums, but the traffic on I-12 roared reassuringly just behind the tree line, a constant reminder of the asphalt rivers and the lattice of lights and signs that led to our homes. Friendship Park looked one hundred percent different than it did in daylight. Now the clouds were blue and silver, and where the full moon shone, new colors seemed to float up around us everywhere—the rusty weeds on the duck pond looked tangerine, the pin oak bulged with purple veins.

At the bottom of the ravine, all that was left of Eric's scarecrow was the torso. Something had drawn its delicate claws down the scarecrow's back, and now there was no mistaking what the straw inside it actually was, where it had come from—it was rabbit bedding, I thought. Timothy, meadow, orchard. Pine straw. I took a big breath; I was going to need Mondo's help to get down there. He'd have to belay me with the rope I'd brought, while I crawled down the rock face like a bug.

"It's moving!" Mondo screamed behind me. "It's getting away."

I almost screamed, too, thinking he meant the doll. But he was pointing at my black knapsack, which I'd slouched against the oak: a little tumor bubble was percolating inside the canvas, pushing outward at the fabric. As we watched, the bag fell onto its side and began to slide away.

"Oh, shit!" I grabbed the bag and slung it over my shoulders. "Don't worry about that. I'll explain later. You just hold the rope, bro. Please, Mondo?"

So Mondo, still gaping at my knapsack, helped me to tie the eighteen-meter phys-ed rope to the oak and loop one end around my waist. It was almost forty minutes before my feet scraped the floor of the Cone. At one point I stumbled and let go of the rock wall, swinging out, but Mondo called down that it was okay, I was okay (and I don't think it's possible to overstate the love I felt in that moment for Mondo Chu)—and then I was crouching, miraculously, on the mineral-blue bottom of the Cone. The view above me I will never forget: the great oak sprawling over the ravine, fireflies dotting the lagoons of air between its humped roots like tiny underworld lights. Much higher up, in the real sky, snakes of clouds wound ball-round and came loose.

The scarecrow's torso was featureless and beige, like a long sofa cushion. This doll was almost gone, the boy original, Eric Mutis, was nowhere we could discover, and somehow this made me feel as if I had broken a mirror, missed my one chance to really know myself. I tried to resurrect Eric Mutis in my mind's eye—the first Eric, the kid we'd almost killed—and failed.

"You made it, Rubby!" Mondo called. But I hadn't, yet. I unzipped my backpack. A little nose peeked out, a starburst of whiskers, followed by a white face, a white body. I dumped it somewhat less ceremoniously than I had intended onto the scarecrow's chest, where she landed and bounced with her front legs out. It wasn't the real Saturday—but then this doll wasn't the real Eric Mutis either. I figured I couldn't in good conscience steal the real Saturday back from Sara Jo—I was no expert in atonement but that seemed like a shitty way to go about it. Instead I'd bought this nameless dwarf rabbit for nineteen bucks at the mall pet store, where the Dijon-vested clerk had ogled me with true horror ("You do not want to buy a *hutch* for the animal, sir?"). Many of the products that this pet-store clerk sold seemed pretty antiliberation, cages and syringes, so I did not mention to him that I was going to free the rabbit.

Mondo was screaming something at me from the ledge above, but I did not turn—I didn't want to let my guard down now. I kept my feet planted but I let my own torso sway, as if in imitation of the huge oak dancing its branches far above me. "Get away!"

I hollered at the sky above the substitute rabbit, wheeling my arms to scare off any unseen predators. If I'd lost the real Eric and Saturday, I could protect this memorial I'd made. Large shapes caught at the corner of my eye. Would the thing that had carried off the doll of Eric Mutis come for me now? I wondered. But I wasn't afraid. I felt ready, strangely, for whatever was coming. The substitute rabbit, I saw with wonderment, was rooting its little head into the pale fibers sprouting out of the scarecrow; it went swimming into the straw, a backward reenactment of its birth from my black book bag—first went its furry ears, its bunching back, the big velour skis of its feet. I spread my arms above the rabbit, so no birds dove for it. I had a knife in my back pocket. The thought occurred to me that I was the scarecrow's guardian now, and the symmetry of this reversal both pleased and terrified me. Yes: now I would stand watch over what remained of Eric Mutis. It was only fair, after what I'd done to Mutant. I would be the scarecrow's scarecrow. My shadow draped over the remains of the doll. The torso looked weirdly reanimated now with the tiny rabbit digging sideways into its soft green interior, palpitating like a transplant heart. I stood with my arms stretched wide and trembling, and I felt as if the black sky was my body and I felt as if the white moon, far above me, unwrinkled and shining, was my mind.

"La-arry!" I was aware of Mondo calling to me from the twinkling roots of the oak, lit up all wild by the underworld flies, but I knew I couldn't turn or climb out yet. Owls might come for Eric's new rabbit in a rain of talons. City hawks. Something Worse. How long would I have to stand watch down here, I wondered, fighting off the birds, to make up for what I'd done to Eric Mutis? The rabbit bubbled serenely through the straw at my feet. Somewhere I think I must still be standing, just like that.

ACKNOWLEDGMENTS

I am enormously grateful to the following people and institutions for their generous support: the Guggenheim Foundation; the American Academy of Arts and Letters; the New York Public Library Young Lions; the Bard Fiction Prize and the terrific Bard College crew; Daniel Torday, Robin Black, and the excellent students and faculty at Bryn Mawr; Mary Ellen von der Heyden; and The American Academy in Berlin and its extraordinary staff and Fellows.

Thank you to the editors and staffs of the following magazines and journals: Cheston Knapp and Michelle Wildgren at *Tin House;* John Freeman, Ellah Allfrey, and Fatema Ahmed at *Granta;* Michael Ray at *Zoetrope;* Willing Davidson at *The New Yorker;* Bradford Morrow at *Conjunctions.* I feel so lucky to have gotten to work with you, and these stories benefited tremendously from your keen reading and suggestions. I am indebted to Carin Besser for her enthusiasm and insight.

Thanks to Caroline Bleeke, Leslie Levine, Sara Eagle, Kate Runde, Kathleen Fridella, and the amazing teams at Knopf and Vintage. To Jordan Pavlin, my phenomenal and inspiring editor, and Denise Shannon, the world's best agent. And a final thank-you, and big love, to the people who stuck it out with me once again:

To my family

&

To my friends